Paradox of The Thief

A gripping archaeological thriller

Nigel Plant

Unearthed Quill

*A*CKNOWLEDGEMENTS

Thank you to my wife Lynn for her constant inspiration, help, and support in completing my first book.

Also, thanks to Simon as my editor-in-chief for all the constructive ideas and painstaking editing, resulting in a finely tuned novel.

Chapter 1

BASLOW, PEAK DISTRICT

SATURDAY

T HE FIRST SLIVER OF sunshine stretched its fingers through the window at the rear of Reed's red VW campervan, stirring him from his slumber. Reed came to the Peak District yesterday evening, as his girlfriend was away on a friend's weekend in Devon. He couldn't help but smile as the warmth of the day washed over him, making him eager for his favourite activity. He had arranged to meet his friend Euan at lunchtime to try the renowned Profit of Doom rock climb at Curbar Edge. Reed intended to do a warm-up climb on Froggatt Edge beforehand and slipped out of bed, putting on his running gear, ready for a quick run around Chatsworth Estate to get the day started.

Reed Hascombe was an all-action type of guy, proficient at rock climbing, good at Jeet Kune Do, and also a decent runner. He hailed from Sheffield, so the Peak District became his go-to place for rock climbing. Along with his mate Euan, they would get in several weekend climbs during the summer months.

Euan epitomised bromance to him. Their close-knit bond developed from being the best of pals since the age of twelve. They grew close when Reed's father became imprisoned for burglary, an outcome because of debts from gambling. As a result, his mother raised him and his younger sister all by herself. The family became homeless for some time as his mother couldn't keep up the

1

mortgage payments, forcing them to lodge with his grandparents. It didn't work well as all three shared a bedroom, so Reed lived with Euan and his parents for several weeks while his mother organised a new home for the family. The situation forced Reed to mature quicker than necessary. He felt a need to be protective towards his family, so embarked on training to become proficient at Jeet Kune Do. He vowed not to end up like his father. Later in his teenage years, he became obsessed with video games, which led him to work as a graphic designer for Screwed Software in Sheffield.

Reed placed the kettle on the two-ring stove so he could brew his first cup of coffee of the day before heading out on the run, enjoying the bitter taste of his preferred Columbian coffee. His campervan was his pride and joy, having fitted it out himself with plenty of storage under the bed and fitted cupboards. He finished stretching and tied his long black hair up into a bun, leaving the car park where he'd spent the night.

Reed jogged along the lane heading into the Chatsworth estate, passing through the gate, and continued on the trail leading across the grounds, with the grand old house in the distance. He turned towards Edensor, running through the quaint village built in the 19th century, marvelling at the chocolate-box design of the houses. Reed climbed the slope to the ridge, then swooped back towards Chatsworth House. He stretched his legs to awaken his body, ready for the challenges ahead that day. He returned to the campervan, grabbed a cereal bar from a cupboard and set off in the van to Curbar Gap car park. Getting an early start before the crowds would gather later in the day.

—◆○◆—

Reed changed his clothes into a Nirvana t-shirt, camo shorts and sunglasses, then grabbed his climbing gear from the campervan,

2

striding off along the trail towards Froggatt Edge. It'd been his twenty-seventh birthday two months ago and Emily had presented him with new climbing shoes. He wanted to try them out. A multitude of cliff face rocks swamped the area, their jagged edges sculpted into distinct segments by the relentless forces of rain, wind, and sun. The sight of their rugged formations inspired grand thoughts, as a wind whispered secrets of days past. When Reed reached his desired spot, he put on his helmet, climbing shoes and harness, ensuring he had sufficient chalk in his bag and some climbing cams. He secured the rope to a tether point, attaching it to his harness using a belay device and a carabiner, ready to descend.

Double checking everything looked secure, he shimmied down, reaching the base of the gritstone rock. He took his time ascending, cautious of slippery handholds as the sun shining over the ridge hadn't warmed up the rocks. He felt the rough texture of the weathered rocks beneath his chalky fingertips, a testament to the enduring power of nature. Near the top of the climb, Reed squinted at the sun through cracks in the rock. As he approached the top, he faced a challenging section. Which way around the outcrop? He opted for the right, but his hand slipped as he lifted his foot. With his left hand still hanging on, he sought a foothold.

He breathed a sigh of relief and thanked his lucky stars for the protective helmet. After bumping his head, he took some time to relax his muscles and plan the final ascent. As he gazed upwards, a glint of something metallic caught his eye in the fissure just above his right hand. Reed shifted right to improve his view, using a cam from the harness to lock in another holding point. He spotted a small metal container in the fissure.

Reed couldn't reach the container, but an idea came to mind. He ascended the remaining short section to the top and manoeuvred over the final ledge. Releasing the rope, he grabbed his phone from his harness pocket. After several rings, Euan's phone went to voicemail, so Reed ended the call and dropped Euan a message on

WhatsApp.

Reed: *'Aye up, mate, I've found something interesting. Call me!'*

Euan called back within seconds.

"Reed, how's it going?" said Euan in his distinct northern accent.

"Brilliant, mate, but I need your help."

"What've you forgotten?"

"I've just climbed up a new section on Froggart Edge and lost my grip. I ended up taking a different route and spotted a metal container in a fissure. It's out of my reach. Can you bring a metal pole or something similar with a hook on? It needs to be three feet long."

Euan enthused, "Interesting. What does it look like?"

"It's only small and looks old."

"It might be a box for someone's cigarette roll-ups."

"Nah mate, it's more than that. I can sense it. It's unusual."

Euan paused before replying, "I'll find some tools, and be there as quick as possible."

"That's excellent, thanks mate, see you soon," Reed said.

Reed edged towards the fissure, searching for the container from above, spotting the top corner. He perched on a nearby rock, considering how to reach the container without it slipping further away. He checked his bag for any food whilst he waited for Euan to arrive. Nothing there. He sat back and just relaxed in the morning sunshine instead.

Reed watched a group of climbers indulging in bouldering on the rocky section several yards away. Their constant chatter floated across on the breeze. His thoughts drifted off to his family and wondered what his mum was doing today. He gave her a quick call to catch up whilst he waited for Euan. A further hour passed before he heard the enthusiastic tones of his mate jogging towards him with various implements in his arms. He noticed Euan's signature green beanie on top of his ginger hair, which he'd matched with a pair of green shorts and an orange Stone Roses t-shirt. Reed laughed to himself. No matter what Euan tried, he never quite got his colour co-ordination on point with the t-shirt clashing with his hair. No matter how many times Reed told him not to wear orange, he took no notice, but it made Euan the person he was. Funny, interesting and full of character with a heart of gold. Reed loved him like a brother, no matter what.

"I've got two canoe paddles and a clothes prop," Euan said as he smiled at Reed, who laughed at his choices. "It's all I could find."

"Nice t-shirt mate, let's try your tools."

Reed and Euan had been friends since their days at high school, sharing a love of rock climbing. They both still lived in Sheffield so they could spend time together on their favourite hobby. Euan, a self-employed electrician, builds drones for a hobby and loves experimenting by adding new modifications to them.

Reed showed Euan the container stuck in the fissure, passing him the clothes prop to move the container. He wasn't having much luck. Nothing appeared to be happening. The container seemed quite stuck. Euan used more force, and the container moved a few inches, but caused the clothes prop to catch. The hollow aluminum clothes prop bent. It wasn't strong enough. They paused for a breather.

"Do you remember the day at Kinder Downfall when you found a silver ring?" asked Euan.

"How could I forget that day when I met Emily!" Reed replied, grabbing the canoe paddles and lifted the container only for it to slip off and fall. It dropped nearer the fissure entrance, yet remained out of reach.

"Perhaps we should push it out, Reed?"

"Brilliant idea, try that."

Euan started pushing the container towards the opening in the fissure, which brought it closer again. Reed took over, exerting more effort, but it caught on a small protrusion. With a big effort, he pushed it beyond the protrusion. The momentum carried it over the edge, down the rock face.

"Oh, shite, let's get down there quick before someone grabs it."

The lads snatched up everything, rushed along the ridge path, sprinting down the sloping path to the bottom of the rocky cliff face. It wasn't on the dirt section. They searched the undergrowth for the container. The overgrown ferns coupled with the prickly gorse bushes made it difficult to locate the container. Several minutes later Reed shouted, "got it, mate" and brandished the container in the air with a whoop.

"Let's have a look at it," Euan asked as Reed passed him the container, running his fingers over the surface with a feather symbol on one side. The rough curved rectangular container was around the size of a large pencil case with hinges at one end. A wax-like substance sealed the container where it closed. Its appearance resembled silver.

"I've got some tools at the campervan. Let's see if we can open it there," Reed said. Picking up their gear, they headed back to the campervan, both wondering what could be inside this interesting item.

Back at the campervan, Reed passed Euan a stanley knife to prise open the container. Whilst Euan did this, Reed knocked together a couple of tuna sandwiches and cups of coffee for a late lunch. Euan struggled to open it, so Reed grabbed a small hammer and screwdriver to prise the container open. With some effort, he broke the seal and opened the container.

Inside was a piece of parchment, scroll-like, about nine inches long, wrapped in a piece of twine. Reed untied it, admiring the parchment, he realised it must be ancient. He opened the scroll out so Euan could see. They both gazed at it with interest. It looked like a map. Drawn on it was a large rock, trees to the right, with a tiny arch amidst them. It showed a rocky edge on its left side. The parchment didn't contain any words, just a wavy line beneath the arch.

"What do you think, Euan?" asked Reed, his voice tinged with growing excitement.

"Could it be a treasure map?" said Euan.

"Let's give Emily a call. She might have some ideas. You know she loves anything historical."

The phone rang twice before Emily picked up. Reed explained to his girlfriend what had happened, and the items discovered.

"Wow, that sounds interesting. I'd love to see it. What're your thoughts on the scroll?" asked Emily.

"I might be over-reacting but it resembles a treasure map, pinpointing something," Reed said.

"If it's old, we should get it carbon-dated. I'm still in touch with my year group from the university on Facebook. I'm sure one of them will know the next step to take. Shall I contact them?" she asked.

"Yes, please. Let me know if you hear anything useful. I'll see you tomorrow evening at home."

"Okay Reed, enjoy the rest of your climbing."

"Enjoy the rest of your weekend, Em."

Reed turned to Euan and explained Emily's plan. He suggested they should stay overnight in the campervan and get a climb in tomorrow morning after sampling the local beer during the evening, to which Euan agreed. They packed up the gear, locked the campervan and wandered into Baslow to check out the local pubs. They enjoyed an evening of food, beer, and some live music in the Devonshire Arms.

After a night of rest, they woke up early on Sunday to attempt the Profit of Doom climb on Curbar Edge, ensuring they were the first ones there to avoid the crowds. After a successful morning climbing and speculating about their find and its contents, they headed back to Sheffield, wondering what the map was.

Chapter 2

CENTRAL NOTTINGHAM

SUNDAY

PEARSON TOOK A GULP of his third cup of coffee when his alert system pinged. He checked the alert and noticed the keywords ancient, treasure and carbon-dating flashing up. He traced the posts, finding a Facebook group discussing an old container someone had discovered in the Peak District. It contained a piece of parchment that may be a treasure map. Someone in the group suggested a contact in archaeology could carbon-date the item next week. This would interest his boss, setting to work digging deeper into the information available.

MI5 and other government bodies used software to track internet activity. But they weren't alone. Pearson had built a monitoring system himself. Two years ago, he persuaded Eric Coulson to give him a job. Whilst it meant unsocial hours, Coulson paid well and Pearson enjoyed the work. The software he developed scanned social media apps for relevant keywords. Eric Coulson's business focused on trading artefacts, which he bought cheap, then selling them for huge profits. Coulson had gained an excellent reputation because of the high demand for artefacts. Last month, he sold a dagger belonging to Julius Caesar for a seven-figure sum.

Because of a potential bonus he could earn, Pearson had an incentive to help find suitable items. He worked on checking through the online conversations. He traced each person within

9

the chat group by their phone numbers using his database. Pearson pored over their social media activity. He decided he had enough concrete information to share. He grabbed his phone and called Coulson.

"I've some interesting news, Mr Coulson."

"Yes, what is it Pearson?" came the terse response.

"Some information's come up on our alert system. Someone has discovered what they say is an ancient container with a feather symbol. Inside was a piece of parchment that resembles a treasure map. They found it in the Peak District yesterday and are planning on carbon-dating the items."

"That sounds interesting, Pearson. Who has the items?"

"I'm not sure, but a girl called Lynsey Dewhurst is getting them carbon-dated with a colleague on Monday or Tuesday. It might be nothing, but I thought it seemed worth investigating."

"Any photos of the items?" Coulson asked.

"No one's posted anything online yet. They're just chatting about it in a Facebook group."

"Have you got the names and addresses of the individuals involved?"

"I have Lynsey's and the girl who started the conservation, Emily Barrington," responded Pearson. "I wanted to flag it up today so we can make plans for tomorrow."

"In that case, what are you waiting for?" came the forthright response from Coulson.

"It's a Sunday morning," Pearson replied timidly.

"I don't care if it's Christmas Day, Pearson. Get Ambrose and Bentley on it now," concluded Coulson, putting the phone down.

Pearson calmed himself and thought through his next steps before phoning the other two members of the team. Mr Coulson's reaction hinted at something significant. He knew his boss had a lot of experience in artefacts, having spent time in his younger years on archaeological digs and working in museums across the globe.

Pearson picked up the phone and rang Ambrose first. She would be more vocal than Bentley about working on a Sunday.

"What do you want on a Sunday, Pearson?" came the curt answer from Ambrose.

"We have a job to get started on today."

"I'm enjoying a family barbeque at the moment, so call me tomorrow, Pearson."

"I'm afraid I can't, as the boss wants us to start now."

"You could have waited until tomorrow to phone him! I'm not happy Pearson."

"And get sacked, Ambrose."

"Okay, where're we meeting?"

"I'll text you the address on the secure message system. It's in Nottingham."

"Are you phoning Bentley?" asked Ambrose.

"Yes, I'll do it now."

"Give me an hour, though," she concluded, finishing the conversation. Pearson then phoned Bentley and explained what was happening. He seemed more amenable to it and then sent them an encrypted message for the location.

'Perky Coffee Shop, Parliament Street, Nottingham.'

Maria Ambrose was Mr Coulson's senior operative. She enjoyed working for him and loved the variety of the job. She could use her Muay Thai skills learned over many years whilst in the military. Once she left the forces, she honed her skill for lock-picking. Whilst working, she liked to be professional, wearing practical business suits in case she had to indulge in a spot of action. The colour of her suits needed to complement her blonde hair. The job didn't allow for a normal life, but her partner always understood about her working hours. They had been a couple for several years, living in Nottingham's suburbs. They enjoyed the best of both worlds: city liveliness and suburban privacy. When not working, she loved nothing better than reading a crime thriller novel.

An hour and a half later, Ambrose stepped into the busy coffee shop in central Nottingham, greeted by the aroma of brewed coffee and the buzz of conversation. The cafe displayed a modern look with its minimal design. The space contained a dozen booths of similar size around the edges. Practical tables filled the room's centre. All of them were busy with customers.

Bentley and Pearson sat in a booth on the far side when she arrived. Ambrose listened to what Pearson had discovered. He suggested visiting Lynsey Dewhurst's address first. She appeared to be the one responsible for carbon-dating the container.

If they found nothing, they would go to Emily Barrington's place as she started the Facebook conversations. Pearson shared the first address with Ambrose after leaving the coffee shop. The walk to the flat took five minutes. Pearson handed Ambrose a small electronic device.

"What's this Pearson?" she asked.

"It's a chip that records sounds for thirty minutes. It aligns with a Wi-Fi Hotspot connector, allowing me to piggyback onto it from my phone or laptop and download the data files. Then I have to decrypt the files."

Ambrose snorted, "Enough tech stuff. What do we do with it?"

Pearson showed Ambrose the top side of the device, pointing out the small magnets present. "If you can't find what we're looking for, conceal it somewhere by attaching it to something metal."

"Right, let's go Bentley," she instructed, walking up the outside stairs to the first-floor flat and putting her long blonde hair into a ponytail.

Ambrose knocked on the front door, still no answer after

the second knock. She peered in the window and, with no signs of activity or lighting, concluded no-one was home. They double-checked no-one appeared to be watching their impending illegal entry. Ambrose pulled out her lock-picking set and unlocked the door whilst Bentley kept watch. They were inside within a minute. The flat looked cosy, with an open plan lounge kitchen area, including a bedroom and bathroom. It had plain decorations, hinting it was a rental property. The flat smelt of a floral perfume, wafting from a plug-in freshener near the front door, permeating around the whole room.

"You know the drill Bentley. Leave everything as we found it. Let's hope we get lucky the first time."

"I'll search the two rooms on the left," Bentley confirmed.

Ambrose checked a letter on the table and confirmed the address as Lynsey Dewhurst's. They searched the rooms of the one-bedroom flat. Checking inside the wardrobe and in the kitchen cupboards. Despite their thorough search, the ancient container wasn't there.

"There's nothing here Bentley. Put Pearson's listening device somewhere out of sight and let's get back to him."

Ambrose checked the flat was tidy before they departed. As they approached Pearson, Ambrose shook her head.

"No joy on this one. Let's head off to Sheffield."

"Did you leave the device?" asked Pearson.

"Yes, of course we did."

"Okay, thanks. Let's grab something to eat before we go, I'm hungry. We should get to Sheffield around five. Let's hope Emily Barrington is there," suggested Pearson.

"Good idea. I missed my burger because of you, Pearson."

"Yeah, yeah, whatever Ambrose."

"Shall we try here before we hit the motorway?" Bentley said as he pointed to a crowded cafe across the road.

"Sounds good to me," said Ambrose.

They trooped into the cafe, found a table at the back, placed their order and planned the next step of their mission. After finishing their food, they returned to Ambrose's car to head up the motorway to Sheffield, hoping to catch Emily Barrington at home to bring this mission to a swift conclusion.

Chapter 3

FULWOOD, SHEFFIELD

SUNDAY

REED AND EUAN WERE relaxing in Reed's dining room, chatting and drinking beer at the six-seater table. Pictures of Reed's favourite climbs in the Peak District adorned the walls of the dining room. Reed's phone pinged with a message from Emily.

Emily: *'Hi Reed, Lynsey has a friend at The Peaks Uni who could help on Tuesday. Any good? xx'*
Reed: *'I can't do Tuesday, but Euan can. He knows Lynsey, that should be okay? x x x'*
Emily: *'Yes, I'm sure she wouldn't mind xx'*
Reed: *'Great, thanks Em x x x'*

Reed finished the message and turned to Euan, saying,
"Emily's setting up a meeting for you at The Peaks University on Tuesday so we can get the container carbon-dated. We should find out soon afterwards if the container is valuable or worthless. I'd go mate, but have a big presentation to prepare for this week. I'm just too busy to take half a day's holiday."

"Who am I meeting mate, one of Emily's friends?"

"Yes, Lynsey, do you remember her from our party earlier this year?"

"Oh yes, she's a researcher, isn't she?" Euan said, smiling.

"Something like that. Can you meet her on Tuesday morning?"

"Yes, of course. I've got a job this week in Rotherham, but that's flexible. Where do I meet her?"

"Not sure mate, but I'll let you know and provide Lynsey's number for you just in case," said Reed.

"Brilliant stuff. I'll be off now. Thanks for an interesting weekend!"

"It was different. Look, you take the container with you and I'll keep the map as I want to show Emily and get her thoughts. I've taken a picture of the container."

"Great, I'll pop round Tuesday evening, Reed."

"See ya, mate."

Downing the last of his beer Reed had given him, Euan picked up his bag as Reed waved his friend off. Reed finished his beer, checked the time, and knew he had a couple of hours before Emily returned from her weekend away. He utilised his time by washing and tidying up the campervan.

Reed parked the campervan in the driveway of his and Emily's two-bedroom semi-detached house. Emily's car sat alongside the campervan. It made it easier to plug in the cable to recharge the battery for the campervan through the lounge window. It took him the best part of an hour to clean the van. Reed considered what to prepare for their tea as he finished wiping the hob down when he heard someone speak to him outside.

"Excuse me, sir, we're looking for Emily Barrington and believe she lives here?"

Reed turned towards the voice and observed two individuals present. A young, fit lad in black attire, standing behind the speaker, a woman who seemed in charge, wearing a smart blouse and trousers set, flashing ID at him.

"Who wants to know?"

"We're private investigators hired by a solicitor to assist a family member in contacting Emily."

"Can I see your badge again?" asked Reed.

The woman flashed her badge. Reed thought it looked okay. Maybe private investigators required a badge to work?

"So does Emily live here?"

"She does, but she's out."

"And who are you? When will she be back?"

"I'm her partner Reed Hascombe. Emily won't be back until later on, so I think it's best if you call again tomorrow. Have you got a number or card? I'll get Emily to call you and arrange a time?"

"Sorry, we can't leave a contact number, but will call back again tomorrow. What time's best?"

"She should be back by six."

"Okay, thank you. We'll call back at six o'clock tomorrow."

"Can you tell me what family member it is? Why do they want to contact her?" asked Reed.

"Sorry, sir, I'm not at liberty to divulge anything, only to Emily. We'll go through everything with her once we meet."

"Oh, okay."

Reed felt unsettled as he reflected on their departure. He wondered why a private investigator would come round at Sunday tea-time. Why did it need two people? Something didn't quite sit right, but he resolved to discuss it with Emily when she arrived home. Reed popped into the house and prepared spaghetti bolognese for their tea when his phone pinged with a notification.

Emily: *'I'll be home around seven-thirty xx'*
Reed: *'Okay Em x x x'*

———◄O►———

Pearson sat in Ambrose's car a hundred yards down the road from Emily Barrington's house. He watched Ambrose and Bentley approach the vehicle. His laptop laid open on his knees and he sneezed again. He wasn't good at sitting in other people's spaces. As the pair entered the car, he said,

"We need to make sure Emily lives here by identifying her when she arrives home."

Pearson plucked up a picture of Emily from one of her social media accounts and showed his colleagues.

"Let's wait until it's dark and they've gone to bed, then you can check inside the campervan Ambrose. Any feedback on your conversation?"

"He said she'd be back later, so we committed to a six o'clock revisit tomorrow. He's busy tidying up the campervan and recharging it, so may have used it over the weekend. It's possible the container's in the house or campervan. We'll search the vehicle tonight, coming back tomorrow if we need to check through the house."

"Sounds like a plan. Did you get the campervan's reg number?" asked Pearson.

Bentley shared the registration number with Pearson, enabling him to access the ANPR data for the vehicle. He traced the car. It departed Sheffield on Friday evening, went towards the Peak District, and returned on Sunday afternoon. He told his colleagues about it.

Pearson spent some time scanning the social media of Emily Barrington whilst the other two relaxed. The suburb road fell silent as the setting sun illuminated the car with a soft, warm glow. He wasn't very good at tuning out, but after waiting for some time, he spotted a girl in the distance walking towards them, nudging Bentley.

"Bentley, that's her, I think. Get out there and verify it for me, please."

Bentley jumped out and walked towards the girl, careful not to make it obvious. After he'd passed her, he crossed the road before circling back to the car and jumping in.

"Yes, that's her alright. That's our target."

"Let's wait till dark to start on the campervan."

Pearson sat there, hoping they would find the container in the campervan.

Chapter 4

FULWOOD, SHEFFIELD

SUNDAY

E MILY MET REED AT a pub in Edale a few years ago and felt attracted to him straightaway. He had a kind soul, although behaved like a typical lad occasionally. Despite them not being married, she felt very much in love with him. The house represented their genuine commitment to each other. Her parents approved of Reed, as he was very protective of her. While Reed was athletic, Emily was more sedentary, preferring a shopping trip to walking in the Peak District. But their personalities complimented each other. Whilst Reed took a zealous approach to situations, Emily took a down-to-earth, kind approach to life. She wasn't super-fit like Reed, but her curvy body shape was enough to manage a day's walking. Reed's detailed account of the weekend's events fascinated Emily as he showed her a photo of the metal container.

"That looks like a fereter Reed. It's a portable reliquary, a small container used to transport items of importance. People would use it for transporting jewels, ashes, and scrolls. I've never seen one, but covered it in my history degree course. The church and wealthy individuals used them."

"They've used wax to seal it and hidden inside was this scroll."

Emily looked at the scroll with its symbols and agreed it could be a treasure map. She brought up Lynsey's friend working in archaeology, who would carry out carbon-dating on the fereter.

"I'm planning on showing the map piece to Phil at work, see what his thoughts are. He likes random old stuff and may have an idea," said Reed.

He slipped the parchment into a zipped pocket in his work backpack. Reed remembered the visit from the private investigators earlier and explained what they said.

"Any ideas on which relative it could be, Em?"

"No idea, but I'll call Mum and ask her. She must have heard something. Seems absurd, as Mum and Dad haven't moved in thirty years, so it'd be easy to find their address and get my details from them."

Emily picked up her phone to give her mum a quick call. She was close to her parents as she was an only child, but they didn't spoil her. They taught her to value money, to be polite and kind to others. Emily's mother couldn't shed any light on why a distant relative's solicitor would need to get in contact with her.

"They were quite cagey, but their identification looked okay. I don't know their names or who they work for," said Reed.

"Well, I guess we will find out more tomorrow."

Emily rose to close the lounge curtains, gazing at the moon and reflecting on Reed's news. She turned on the television after relaxing on the corner sofa. Her thoughts drifted off to what the private investigators would tell her tomorrow.

A hundred yards down the road from Reed & Emily's house sat Ambrose and the other two employees of Coulson. They waited for lights to go out at houses close to the target property before making a move. The streetlights went out an hour ago. Ambrose assumed the local council wanted to save money. Perfect conditions for their mission. She had checked in with her boss earlier, explaining what they had found out and their next steps.

"Have you got any recordings from the flat we visited earlier?" Ambrose enquired of Pearson.

"Only TV programmes, she hasn't spoken to anyone as far as I can hear."

"So, it's likely the container is still in the campervan or the house."

Bentley put on the radio for some background noise. They all whiled away another couple of hours until after one in the morning. Ambrose pointed to Bentley. They should go check out the campervan, leaving Pearson in the car.

Ambrose exited the car, hustling along the street under cover of darkness before hiding in the shadows of the campervan. They listened for several minutes, hearing nothing but the rustle of leaves and the screech of a cat in the distance. Ambrose retrieved her lock-picking kit, opening the door. Bentley stood outside to check for anyone coming towards the house.

She opened cupboards, lifted the mattress, and rummaged through storage boxes that held some climbing gear, but found nothing resembling an old metal container. The moonlight coming in through the rear window allowed Ambrose to survey the inside of the campervan. Where else would someone hide a container? She lowered herself to the floor, delving under the front seats, running her hands along the edges of the van, searching for hidden spaces. After hunting for fifty minutes, she accepted the item wasn't inside the campervan. She placed one of Pearson's sound recording devices on the underside of the metal wash basin. They both hurried back to Pearson, waiting in the car.

"Nothing, Pearson. I searched every cupboard, box and cubby hole. You better let Mr Coulson know by sending him a secure message. We need to search the house tomorrow morning after they've gone to work. It's too late to go home; we'll have to return here in four hours. Let's grab some kip and hope they both go to work early."

Settling into the car seat, Ambrose took a moment to survey their surroundings. Relieved to see no one was watching, she closed her eyes and relaxed.

———◇———

As the sun streamed in through the front windscreen, Bentley's watch alarm buzzed nonstop, filling the confined space of the vehicle and waking all three occupants.

"Bloody hell, Bentley. Does it have to be that loud?" Ambrose said as she rubbed her eyes, prompting Bentley to shut it off straightaway.

"Yes, we need to be alert and ready for action this morning."

Bentley announced his plan to find coffee and breakfast nearby as he stretched his muscles. He picked up his phone using Google Maps, searching for fast-food chains near their location, but only discovering a Tesco Express two streets away.

"I'll pop round to Tesco's, get coffees and food to eat, then come back past the house to see what's happening."

As he opened the door, Bentley wasted no time in putting distance between himself and the car, avoiding the house and turning left onto the next street. His early morning stroll led to daydreams of his potential fighting career. He trained hard and was desperate to win the upcoming fight in several weeks' time. It would give him a chance at a higher level. His mum had worked hard to give him this opportunity and he would be always grateful for her sacrifices.

After getting to the Tesco Express, purchasing coffees and sausage rolls, he headed back a different way, which would take him past the house. Getting back in the car, he said, "The curtains are open. Hopefully, they'll leave soon so we can finish this mission."

He gave out the coffees and sausage rolls, which they all

devoured, and Pearson opened up his laptop to find a secure message from Mr Coulson.

Mr Coulson: *'Once you have searched their place, come to my house, either with or without the container. I've cleared my diary for this morning.'*

Pearson shared this with his colleagues as they finished their coffee and breakfast. Bentley played some music through the car speakers from his phone. Ambrose rebuked him. He knew they were tolerant of him being Mr Coulson's nephew. Their wariness stemmed from uncertainty about his feedback to the boss, which he liked to play on. Coupled with his boxing skills and large muscles from hours in the gym, Bentley had a quick temper getting him into trouble. Because of this, his mother persuaded her brother to give him a chance where he could use his obvious skills.

They waited for another hour, watching Reed and Emily emerge from the house and enter her car before driving away. Bentley heard Ambrose whisper in his ear, "Let's give it fifteen minutes, then we'll move Bentley."

Bentley slipped on his gloves, passing Ambrose her gloves and together they headed towards the house. The neighbourhood seemed pleasant, with well-maintained semi-detached houses from the fifties. Bentley slipped around to the rear and stood watching whilst Ambrose opened the back door with her lock-picking kit. Tall fruit trees at the bottom of the garden shielded them from prying neighbour's eyes as they entered the house.

They stepped into the dim kitchen fitted with grey units and multiple electrical appliances on the worktop. Ambrose disappeared up the creaky staircase to check the rooms upstairs, leaving Bentley to search downstairs. He looked around each room, leaving nothing unturned or unopened, returning everything the way he found it. An hour later he stood in the dining room, admiring the pictures on the wall of various rocks, when Ambrose appeared, explaining she had found nothing either. Bentley pulled out one of Pearson's recording listening devices. He placed it on the inside of a metal table lamp in the lounge before they left the house.

Bentley knew his uncle's strictness all too well, and he felt certain when they reached the house near the village of Cotgrave, without the container, they would face some harsh criticism. He wondered if their efforts were a wild goose chase and maybe Pearson had it wrong.

Chapter 5

CENTRAL SHEFFIELD

MONDAY

REED WALKED TO SCREWED Software from the bus stop in the centre of Sheffield. Emily gave him a lift to her workplace, Sheffield Secondary School, earlier. He reflected on the fereter, map and his deadline of Thursday to complete a presentation for a new client. Inside the office, Reed spotted his mate Phil Blackett at the coffee machine and walked over to get himself a cappuccino.

"Aye up, Phil mate," he said as his friend's head turned and cracked into a smile beneath his beard.

"Reed, how's it going? Did you enjoy your weekend climbing?"

"Excellent, I've got something to show you. How's your weekend?"

"The weather looked nice, so I went for a bike ride. What have you got?"

"Come over to my desk in a minute and I'll show you," Reed said as he punched the buttons on the coffee machine to get himself a hefty dose of caffeine.

Reed ambled to his work cubicle, one of a cluster of eight identical workspaces, connected to the manager's office at the end. The gentle hum of computers filled the air, mingling with the chatter of colleagues. Earlier that year, Screwed Software became part of a bigger group with its own set of clients. Reed was the lead graphic designer, so often had to deal with the clients himself.

When Phil popped over, Reed retrieved the map piece from the zipped pocket of his laptop backpack, unfolding it on the desk as Phil bent over to get a better look, pulling his glasses from his pocket.

"Interesting mate, where'd you get this?" asked Phil.

"I found a metal container called a fereter, according to Emily. It's a portable container used for transporting jewels and scrolls. I found it in a fissure in the rocks at Froggatt Edge where I was climbing. I messed up some handholds and ended up off the route. Then I spotted it. It's got a feather-like symbol on it and I found this scroll inside. What do you think?"

"Looks like it's showing something in a cave. What does this big rock mean?" he asked.

"I'm not sure. I've been too busy to do any research."

"Could it be a landmark? I'm not busy today. Let me take a photo and do some research online for you."

"Okay mate, I appreciate it. I'm flat out on this presentation, which has to be ready for Thursday. I've also got a photo of the fereter, if that helps?"

"Print it off and I'll have a look this morning."

Later on, Phil popped his head around Reed's desk screen and beckoned him to come to his desk. Reed gestured with a single finger, one minute, before making his way over.

"Any joy mate?"

"There are hundreds of large rocks across England and plenty in the Peak District. There are also lots of rocky outcrops and rock edges around. You know more about them than me. I can't find any reference to a feather symbol. Perhaps there's a hidden secret within the Peak District."

"Let me get this right, Phil. You think the map is a clue to a hidden secret somewhere in the Peak District near a large boulder?"

"Yeah, that's all I've got right now," he answered, his tone reflecting a sense of disappointment.

"Mmmm, interesting. The container looks old. I guess a few hundred years ago, things like rock edges and large, distinctive rocks would be key landmarks. Thanks for looking. My climbing mate, Euan, is getting the fereter carbon-dated tomorrow. Let's see if it all fits together."

"Glad to be of help. Could be an exciting adventure," finished Phil, stroking his beard.

Reed popped out for his lunch early, stopping by his favourite sandwich shop to grab a ploughman's, then settled on a bench in the Winter Garden. The array of greenery and soft patter of waterfalls in this oasis in the city allowed his thoughts to wander.

As he munched on his lunch, Reed reflected on Phil's conversation earlier and wondered if his mate had a point. Reed's knowledge of the Peak District was excellent because of his climbing and running activities. He thought about places the map could refer to, hoping the container emerged to be a genuine artefact.

Chapter 6

COTGRAVE, NEAR NOTTINGHAM

MONDAY

N ESTLED IN THE NOTTINGHAM countryside was a vast country manor house owned by Eric Coulson. The sprawling grounds had picturesque views and a sweeping driveway. It has a distinct profile near the village of Cotgrave with its pillared entrance, ivy-covered walls and six bedrooms.

Coulson continued his discussions with the team in the house's grand library with its high ceilings. Soft light filtered through the large sash windows, casting a warm glow on the mahogany bookshelves. The faint aroma of a delectable lunch prepared by his skilled chef wafted through the air, teasing their taste buds. Coulson resolved to be more involved, feeling disappointed with what had happened thus far.

"Right, enough chatter. We need action. I've no intention of letting this opportunity go to waste because you lot can't organise a piss-up in a brewery! Pearson, I want a summary of anything relevant from all three recording devices. Got that?"

"Yes boss," came Pearson's immediate answer.

"Bentley, go back to Sheffield, attach a tracking device to the campervan without drawing attention. And for fuck's sake, change your clothes. Add a hat or something. Use some initiative, lad. Ambrose, ring Alejandro Garcia, the manager at The Peak University's archaeology department. See what he knows about tomorrow's tests. If you have to twist his arm with money, normal limits apply. Use the office for the phone call."

"Should we meet Emily Barrington at six o'clock, boss?" Ambrose asked.

"No, that doesn't gain us an advantage at this point. Meanwhile, I'll contact our connections in the artefact world. Hopefully, I'll get some information. Is everyone clear ?"

"Yes, boss," came the answer in unison.

"Let me know as soon as possible if you find anything useful. We'll meet again at eight o'clock tomorrow morning to give us the opportunity to plan properly. Let's get on with it."

After their departure, Coulson reverts to his phone, making some calls in search of answers, but he gained nothing new from the conversations. He concluded the individuals who had the container were unaware of its possible significance. He poured himself a rum and coke and sat contemplating what the container may be. Then it was time to visit his basement.

———◄O►———

When Coulson realised he could make serious money from the illegal selling of relics and artefacts, he purchased the country manor. Instead of using bank safe deposit boxes for his stock, he built *The Safe*.

To access it, he would visit a cloakroom off the hallway, look into the mirror and a hidden retina scanner triggered a sliding panel by his side. A tight lobby became accessible, with stairs descending into another lobby. Access to *The Safe* was via a hand scanner outside the steel-clad door.

This room served as his safe for relics and artefacts available to sell, along with some of his own collection. The room measured forty feet by fifteen feet and doubled as his clean-up area. Once he owned an item, he didn't allow it to leave his safe until sold. Coulson did the restoration and cleaning of items himself, skills learnt after spending many years on archaeology digs in his youth. A partition divided the room, separating the *'dirty'* items from those prepared ready for sale.

Coulson installed a hidden exit door at the rear of *The Safe*, providing him with an escape route. Another retina scanner inside a mirror opened a steel sliding door which led into a tunnel. This emerged in a wooded area on the grounds' north side. His routine involved checking the tunnel and its electronics every month. This ensured they wouldn't let him down if ever needed. The walls, ceiling, and floor had six-inch steel plates as part of the design, for maximum security. By installing multiple CCTV cameras throughout the property and gardens, he could maintain constant surveillance.

Pearson had devised a secure system on the dark web, enabling him to list Coulson's items for sale. Each item had multiple photos and provenance, if he had any. Clients became part of an exclusive club, each given a login to access the items for sale. If interested, the clients would call Coulson or drop a message on the secure system.

Coulson received a message from a client earlier today inquiring about an item for sale. A silver goblet rumoured to have been in Queen Victoria's cherished possession, dating back to the 19th century. He donned his white gloves and picked up the goblet, admiring its ornate stem he had restored back to its former glory. The goblet was available for £300,000 and the client had offered £250,000. He considered this a fair offer, decent enough to get him interested.

Along with his wife, they enjoyed a luxurious lifestyle and needed regular large sales to maintain this, along with the extortionate costs of running the large house. He sat in his chair mulling over the offer whilst checking the goblet, ensuring it looked in pristine condition. He would counteroffer the client's suggestion, hoping to squeeze more out of him. After all, he had golf club membership to pay for, too. With his decision made, he returned the prized goblet to the velour-covered shelf and left *The Room*, returning to the library to phone the client.

After agreeing a price with the client, he sauntered to the window and surveyed his gardens, another part of his country manor house his business had afforded him. He left the extensive book collection in his library, heading into the large open hallway. He reached the door that led to his gym. Determined to have a hard workout, he entered and prepared himself for an intense session. Coulson was approaching his late fifties and wanted to keep fit.

What had piqued his interest was the feather like symbol. It niggled at him like a broken dream, a finger-touch away from the answer. He mulled over the most effective approach to secure the container.

Chapter 7

FULWOOD, SHEFFIELD

MONDAY

E MILY ARRIVED HOME EARLY, as she expected the private investigators to visit. She placed her handbag in the dining room and headed upstairs, jumping in the shower, still with no idea what a family relative wanted with her. She dressed in jeans and a t-shirt, brushed her wavy brown hair and left it to dry as she busied herself with putting an oven tray bake together for tea.

Emily enjoyed cooking, and her home life with Reed was everything she wanted. Between them, they had made their home comfortable and a haven from the outside world. After completing her degree course at The Peaks University, it became a natural progression for her to start teacher training. Something she had wanted to do since her teenage years after her enjoyable work experience in a primary school for a week. She enjoyed being a teacher and hoped to have children with Reed. With an hour to spare, she picked up the year ten homework assignment on Henry the Eighth to mark.

Before long, the clock showed five to six. She popped upstairs, peered out of the front bedroom window, expecting the private investigators to arrive. Thirty minutes passed, and no one had come to the house. She had concerns why someone in the family was attempting to trace her? It wasn't anyone she had regular contact with. Could it be some distant cousin? Emily wondered if she had the wrong time. Reed was working late because he needed to complete his presentation by Wednesday evening. She picked up her phone and called him.

"Hi Em, what happened with the private investigators?" he asked.

"They haven't turned up Reed. You told them about six, didn't you?"

"Yes, I said you'd be home by six. Maybe they played it safe and intend coming round later?"

"Yes, I guess so, anyway I've put a tray bake in the oven. What time will you be back?"

"I'm just finishing. I'll be back in forty minutes, assuming the bus is on time."

"Okay, see you soon Reed."

Emily continued marking the history homework at the table in the dining room and concluded the private investigators weren't coming at all. She finished the pile of essays, cleared the table and set it for their tea, using the bamboo place mats she had purchased on a shopping trip to the Meadowhall shopping centre. As she waited for Reed to come home, her thoughts turned to the metal fereter and map. She realised she hadn't arranged a place or time for Lynsey to meet Euan. She picked up her phone to call Lynsey at home.

"Emily, how're you?"

"Fine thanks Lyns, did you have a chat with your friend today?" she asked.

"Yes, I did. He said to meet at ten o'clock. Apparently, there are various processes involved, including the carbon-dating, which could take several days. He needs to compare the carbon element to those artefacts already dated to offer a reasonable idea of age. If the container proves to be ancient, he's asked if he could use it as part of his research program?"

"I'll have to ask Reed, see what he says first. I think the container's a fereter. It's a small reliquary used to transport valuable items like jewels and scrolls. It's his mate Euan who's bringing the fereter to you. Where should he meet you tomorrow?" asked Emily.

"Is that the ginger-haired guy Reed goes rock climbing with I met at your party earlier this year?"

"Yes, that's the one."

"Tell him to meet me at nine-thirty at the Sheriff's Cafe, then we'll go together to meet my friend. Give him my number in case anything crops up. If you could get an answer from Reed on using the container before we meet, please, Emily."

"That's brilliant Lyns, thanks for your help."

"No problem, Em. Do you have any thoughts about who the fereter belonged to?"

"I don't know. Reed's been pretty busy today, but I'll catch up with him. He gets home soon. I owe you lunch sometime. Catch you later, Lyns."

"Yes please, see you, Em."

Soon after her phone call, Reed arrived home. They chatted about work whilst eating their Mexican tray bake with black beans. The topic of conversation shifted towards the fereter and map as Emily explained the plan she agreed with Lynsey. Reed messaged Euan.

Reed: *'Aye up, mate, can you meet Lynsey tomorrow at 9.30 am at the Sheriff's Cafe on The Peaks Uni campus? thanks.'*
Euan: *'Of course, I'll call you afterwards.'*

"Aren't you going to your Jeet Kune Do class tonight, Reed?" asked Emily.

"It's too late. I've missed the start. Plus, this fereter is exciting and I'm wondering what the map is about."

"Once we get a date for the fereter, we can speculate with more certainty. You should have included the map. The parchment could help determine the age." Emily replied.

"I'd prefer to hold on to the map for now. That's the crucial part and if the container's old, I'm thinking we should head out to the Peak District next weekend with Euan and his drone. We shouldn't waste any time. If there's something interesting to explore, let's start right away. We shouldn't miss out on any discoveries."

"You can't just go digging stuff up in the Peak District Reed. It's crucial to handle anything you find that may have scientific or historical importance in the proper manner. We should speak to Lynsey about it before we do anything."

"Get her to come as well?" Reed asked.

"Okay, yes, let's see where we are tomorrow evening, also I doubt you can use drones in the Peak District either," Emily concluded.

Chapter 8

COTGRAVE, NEAR NOTTINGHAM

TUESDAY

C OULSON ROSE EARLY, EAGER for the day ahead, grabbing thirty minutes in the gym before breakfast and prepared his thoughts for the day's plan of action. The main gate intercom buzzer went forty-five minutes before expected. Pearson's face appeared on the gate camera. He buzzed him in. Coulson waited with the front door open as Pearson pulled up in his battered old mini that had seen better days.

"You're early Pearson? I appreciate such dedication. I asked you to update me last night with any information discovered, didn't I?"

"Tiredness overcame me, so I had an early night. I got up early to prepare everything for the meeting today. There are several important things to update you on. I drove over as soon as I was ready."

"Okay, let's grab a coffee and review it," Coulson said, heading off to the kitchen. Pearson slipped into the library, removed his laptop laying a summary of his notes on the table. They explained the WhatsApp message from Reed to Euan and the recorded conversation between Lynsey and Emily. Coulson appeared with the coffees, grabbed the notes, read them, then stared at Pearson with a face of thunder.

"So, if you hadn't gone to bed early and prepared at midnight, we had a chance of getting the fereter yesterday evening? Instead, you had a pleasant sleep! You test my patience, Pearson. Another fuck up! You know any fereter is likely to have particular importance?"

"Yes, boss, that's why I've headed over early so we can track ANPR data for Euan Spencer as he leaves Sheffield. That way, we can get Ambrose and Bentley in action sooner," replied Pearson.

"Let me summarise. Reed Hascombe and his friend Euan Spencer found the fereter. Euan will be at the cafe in The Peaks University to meet Lynsey Dewhurst at nine-thirty today. The archaeology department is evaluating the fereter. With an unknown person. Is that correct?"

"Yes, let me investigate if there's any ANPR data for his vehicle yet." With a sense of determination, Pearson hustled over to his laptop, his fingers flying over the keys as he revealed no information for the day. "It'll take him an hour in the rush-hour traffic, so he wouldn't leave until around eight," Pearson said.

"Okay, let's reroute Ambrose and Bentley now. By heading straight to the University, they can scope out the cafe ready to intercept this person."

Coulson grabbed his mobile from the table, dialling Ambrose. She answered within two rings.

"Ambrose, Pearson has fucked up. Drive to The Peaks University now. I'll call Bentley, you pick him up. Pearson will drop a photo in the secure messaging system of the guy bringing the fereter and the girl he's meeting at nine-thirty at the cafe. Also, give Alejandro Garcia a call and tell him to find out who's doing the carbon-dating for them. He needs to confiscate the fereter if you can't intercept the guy. Don't cause a scene or draw attention."

"Okay, got it. What's a fereter?" asked Ambrose, somewhat puzzled by this new term.

"It's a container used to transport valuable items by wealthy individuals or the church."

"Can Pearson send me the car reg, too?"

"I'll get Pearson to put everything in the system and don't forget to give me updates."

"Yes boss," she acknowledged.

"You heard everything, Pearson, get it done. I want this fereter. You're working here today, Get comfortable."

"I'm on it."

Coulson couldn't shake off a persistent feeling about the feather symbol that was mentioned. However, he couldn't quite grasp why. He recognised an artefact like this was significant, especially with the added intrigue of an ancient map.

Coulson incurred excessive costs the previous month. Mrs Coulson insisted on purchasing a holiday villa in Marbella. He bought the villa for a staggering seven-figure sum. More reason to push his team to find some artefacts, boosting his bank balance. This could be an excellent opportunity to gain additional funds.

Chapter 9

THE PEAKS UNIVERSITY

TUESDAY

E UAN DROVE INTO THE car park at The Peaks University, finding a parking spot. He checked Google Maps to locate the Sheriff's Cafe. The car park looked crowded with limited space. He searched for a sign-post and noticed students walking towards the cafe. Heavy backpacks and books weighed their shoulders down.

Euan had been friends with Reed since school. He started as an apprentice electrician with his previous employer, but after several years, he became self-employed, building a profitable business, enabling him to make a decent living. Euan enjoyed the time he spent with Reed as they attempted rock climbs in the Peak District during the warmer months. His floppy ginger hair was his main distinguishing feature and often wore green beanies to contrast the colour of his hair. He lived a bachelor life in his terrace house, but wasn't one for heavy drinking sessions with groups of lads. He valued his family and felt close to his parents and younger sister. His bond with Reed was strong, like that of a brother. They had supported each other in difficulties during the past fourteen years, even sharing a rented house for a period. His passion for electronics led him to drones, and he enjoyed flying them during the winter. He found the sight of one soaring in the sky exhilarating.

He was running later than he planned because of heavy traffic on the M1 and would be late meeting Lynsey. Upon arriving on campus, Euan grabbed his backpack from the front seat, hauled it onto his back and walked towards the cafe. He had the metal fereter packaged in bubble wrap in the main part of his backpack, wedged in with a t-shirt, to stop it from moving around. As he approached the entrance to the cafe, he noticed two people standing at the door close to some bushes, but couldn't see Lynsey, so he picked up his mobile and called her.

"Hi Lynsey, sorry I'm a bit late. Where are you?"

"Oh, hi Euan, I'm inside the cafe."

"Great, I'll come straight in."

As he stepped forward to open the door, the blonde woman standing nearby approached Euan.

"Excuse me, sir, I wondered if you could help me. My car won't start and I need someone strong to help my friend push start it. Would you be able to help, please?"

"Oh sorry, I'm late for a meeting, but if you're still having trouble, I can help afterwards. Where's your car parked?" asked Euan.

The woman pointed towards the car park. "Over there. That would be awesome, thanks! Where's your meeting?"

"I'm not sure, in the university somewhere, I'll come to the car park when I've finished and help if you haven't got it started by then."

Euan couldn't wait to get inside the cafe as he opened the door.

"Thank you," the woman concluded.

Euan hurried inside to avoid any further delays, taking in the cafe decor. The spacious room boasted lofty ceilings adorned with a fresh coat of white paint which illuminated the space. As he stepped inside, he looked towards the serving counter on his left, where a small queue waited. A pleasant coffee aroma wafted through the air, mingling with the sound of friendly chatter amongst the customers. The cafe housed around thirty tables and chairs, each adorned with a delightful colour scheme of light green and white. As he looked around the room, he spotted Lynsey, thinking she looked fabulous in her summer dress, with her dark hair tied back into a ponytail. As he approached her table, he tripped over a sausage dog laying on the floor and smashed into Lynsey's table. The dog yelped and Euan had to apologise to the elderly owner, feeling embarrassed. Fortunately, the owner of the sausage dog saw the funny side of his mishap and waved Euan away. He had been focusing his attention on Lynsey and spotted her smile at his mishap.

"You look amazing as always, Lynsey. Can I get you a coffee?" he asked.

"We're short on time. Maybe we can get a coffee afterwards? I'd love to have a quick look at the fereter before we meet my friend, though."

Euan reached for his backpack, opening the zip and pulling out the wrapped-up fereter. He unrolled the bubble wrap, leaving the fereter standing on it. He watched as Lynsey pulled some white gloves out of her pocket, slipping her fingers inside. Lynsey spotted his quizzical look.

"You're supposed to wear gloves to stop fingerprints and oils getting on to artefacts. That looks old and interesting. The feather design is quite faint and crude. Is the map inside?"

"No, Reed kept the map himself, as he wanted to show his friend at work," said Euan.

As Lynsey examined the container, out of the corner of his eye, Euan noticed someone sitting down on the table next to them. He turned and spotted the young lad with the needy blonde woman outside. When he turned his gaze towards the door, he caught sight of the blonde woman watching him. When their eyes locked, she averted her gaze. As Euan turned his attention back to the lad, he prepared to acknowledge him, but the lad's eyes darted away as soon as they made contact. It seemed like they were watching him. Lynsey removed her gloves and stood up.

"Let's go to meet Onni. He's Finnish. I've just said it's a metal container you found, but no other detail. He's eager to help. Let's see what he thinks."

"Let's take the rear door Lynsey."

Euan guided her towards the rear door and as they left the cafe, he glanced back, noticing the lad coming towards the same door. He shut the door and whispered to Lynsey, "Before I came inside the cafe, a blonde woman and a young lad asked me to help them bump-start their car and they've both been staring at me in here. The young lad is coming towards this door. Let's get a move on. Their behaviour's strange, almost like they're following me."

"Oh, perhaps they spotted the fereter?"

Lynsey grabbed Euan by the arm, dragging him around the corner of the building. She broke into a run as the young lad turned the corner behind them. Euan followed her inside another building. They crashed through a series of sharp turns in the corridors before Euan ran straight into a cleaners bucket. It toppled over, spilling dirty water everywhere. Euan splashed through it and spotted Lynsey waving to him to leave the building through another door, the sounds of the angry cleaner chasing him down the corridor. He struggled to keep up with her as she ran across an open grass area. He limped into the archaeology department behind her, his leg aching from the mishap. Euan felt out of breath, but relieved they had evaded the young lad.

———◆O◆———

As they entered the building, Lynsey dialled her friend's number and sat down in the reception area. Euan noticed plenty of information about archaeology on the walls. He read a poster looking for volunteers for a summer journey to Egypt. The trip focused on exploring a lost valley. They waited awhile before a tall blonde guy came into the reception room. Lynsey rose to greet her friend.

"Onni, how are you? This is my friend Euan."

"Hiya mate," Euan responded, extending his hand to shake Onni's.

"Hello Euan, pleased to meet you. I'm okay Lynsey, hope you're well too?"

"Yes, thanks Onni. Where are we gonna check out the container?"

"We can use this room," he said, pointing to a nearby door. He guided them both into a small room with four simple chairs and a tiny desk. Switching the light on as they entered, the room flooded with bright light from the overhead daylight bulbs. Sitting down, Euan pulled out the bubble wrapped object and unfolded it again. He felt unnerved as both Lynsey and Onni pulled on their white gloves whilst Onni placed an eyepiece to his eye, picking up the fereter with his other hand. After spending several minutes looking at the artefact in the hushed environment, Onni explained his thoughts in his clipped Scandinavian accent.

"This is interesting. It appears to be a fereter, which is a portable reliquary used to transport items of high value. Religious people, royalty and people with plenty of money used them. These markings on the top resemble a feather symbol. It appears to be silver, but I need to carry out some tests to verify it. My guess would be between the twelfth and fifteenth century. What's fascinating is this symbol." Onni paused for breath before continuing. "You'll notice some wax around the edges. I can carry out carbon-dating on that to improve the age assessment. Where did you find it, Euan?"

Onni's information surprised Euan, his thoughts scrambling to catch up. He held back the fact about a map. Reed appeared to be being careful with that part of the discovery, so followed his friend's wishes and didn't mention it.

"Oh, my friend found it in the park where he lives in Sheffield."

He glanced at Lynsey to ensure she didn't contradict him, which she didn't after seeing his look.

"We're supposed to log everything that comes into the department with a full record of the place found and finders' details. You said it was to be unofficial, didn't you Lynsey?"

Lynsey squirmed in her seat, feeling a little uncomfortable having to dupe her friend, but she went along with Euan's explanation.

"Yes, if you can just keep it to yourself for now Onni please, I promise to buy you lunch tomorrow,"

Lynsey smiled at Onni. He nodded to both of them, showing he understood they weren't being straight with him, putting his eyepiece back in his pocket. "I understand. You want to keep it a secret for personal reasons. Anything inside the container?" Onni asked Euan.

"Nah mate, it was empty," Euan lied.

"I can get the carbon-dating carried out this afternoon. Tallow, made from animal fats, is the probable source of the wax. Can I take photos and use them in my research paper?"

"Reed said that's fine, so yes," Euan said, trying to keep his excitement in check for now.

"Thank you. Shall I return the container to Lynsey when I've finished?"

"Yes, that would be awesome. Appreciate your help, Onni."

"Thanks. If the fereter is significant, I'd like some recognition for my part in the discovery."

"Yes, of course, thanks so much, Onni," Lynsey said.

Lynsey got to her feet and clapped Onni on the shoulder. Euan picked up his backpack, leaving Onni to wrap the container and take it with him. They all left the room. Euan shook Onni's hand before he and Lynsey left the building, walking back to the cafe.

"Bloody hell Lynsey, that's exciting. I need to ring Reed and tell him the news."

"You shouldn't have lied about where you found it, Euan. It could be of huge historical importance."

"I'm sorry for making you feel uncomfortable. Reed and I want to use the map for an adventure. I can always come clean about the location at a later date."

"I guess. He won't log the fereter. You could decide to tell him later. He can choose to pretend he hadn't seen it."

"Thanks, Lynsey. Can I get you a coffee now?"

"Yes, okay, just a quick one. I need to shoot as I've some work to do today, cappuccino please."

Euan stood in line to order the coffees at the cafe, scanning the room for the suspicious-looking lad and blonde woman he had seen earlier. He couldn't see them, so he forgot about it for now. He would discuss it with Reed later when they spoke. They chatted in the cafe for around ten minutes before Lynsey bid him farewell to head back to work and Euan strode back to his car. Once there, he called Reed and updated him on Onni's thoughts and the wax carbon-date timescales. Whilst chatting, Euan thought he noticed the young lad again, sitting in a black Audi car in the same car park, but couldn't be sure.

"Oh, and mate, a strange blonde woman and young lad seemed to watch me once I got to the cafe. Then the lad followed us, but we lost him. I swear he's sitting in a car about fifty yards from me."

"On Sunday, after you left, a blonde woman and young lad arrived at the house searching for Emily. They were supposed to return yesterday evening around six, but never showed up. What do they look like?"

"The woman is medium height, blonde hair, dressed in a smart trouser suit, and the young lad looks like he works out with dark hair, I'd say, early twenties."

"It's the same people! I wonder what's going on. Maybe it's related to the fereter, but how the hell would anyone know about it unless we've told them? Our friends are the only ones who are aware. See if they follow you when you leave, but be careful, mate. I've got to crack on with this bloody presentation. I appreciate your help. How about coming over tonight for a beer and continuing our conversation?"

"Okay. I'll be around about seven-ish."

Euan finished up and glanced over to the car with the young

lad in. He reminded him of his younger sister, who always banged on about MMA fights, an aggressive nature, ready for a fight. He started the engine of his blue Ford Focus Estate, exited the car park and stopped up the road a hundred yards on to see if he was being followed. Glancing at his mirror, he watched the black car emerging from the car park as he waited on the side of the road. They had no option but to overtake him. He glanced over and noticed the blonde woman sitting in the passenger seat. She was trying to act nonchalant, but he couldn't help but wonder why they were following him.

Chapter 10

THE PEAKS UNIVERSITY

TUESDAY

A MBROSE CALLED MR COULSON after they had passed Euan Spencer sitting in his car. He picked up straight away,

"Ambrose, what's happening? Have you got the fereter?"

"Not yet. He met the girl, then disappeared into the university somewhere we couldn't get to. We found his car and waited until he returned, planning on tracking him. He made a phone call, then drove off. We followed, but he stopped and parked on the side of the road. We had no choice but to go past him."

"Ambrose, you drive me to despair. Have you seen or spoken to Garcia?"

"I wanted to touch base with you beforehand."

"Right, get yourselves back to the university, meet Garcia, and get him to find which one of his staff met them and retrieve the fereter. If you have to persuade him with some cash, then do it. Call me back once it's done."

The call ended, causing Ambrose to release a muted sigh. She indicated to Bentley to turn the car around, realising they had to return to the university. She looked through her contacts and found Alejandro Garcia's number. After hitting the dial button, she waited. After six rings, it went to voicemail.

"Alejandro, it's Ambrose. I need to see you straightaway. Meet me at the Sheriff's Cafe as soon as possible. If you aren't there in an hour, I'll come looking for you," Ambrose dictated after the beep.

Bentley drove into the university car park, reversing into a space. Ambrose jumped out of the car, beckoning Bentley to follow her as they made their way back to the cafe for the second time. After ordering at the serving counter, they sat in a prominent position near the door, consuming their cake and coffee. Bentley decided on a double fudge brownie whilst Ambrose stuck to her favourite carrot cake. She contemplated what to say to Garcia when he arrived; the solution shaped by her phone call with Mr Coulson earlier. She would often practise being tough with her partner, not something she found natural. Thirty-five minutes had passed when an angry-looking Alejandro Garcia burst through the door of the cafe.

"Why are you bothering me at work? I'm unhappy with your behaviour and will speak to Mr Coulson about it."

Garcia drummed his agitated fingers on the table in front of Ambrose. Ambrose just stared at him for a few seconds before responding.

"He asked us to see you this morning."

"Oh, I see. I'm still not happy about it. You know we always do our business at his house."

"Well, this time we are doing our business at the university Alejandro, because it involves one of your staff."

"What do you mean?"

"We believe there's an artefact of extreme importance to Mr Coulson in your department, brought in earlier by two people. They arrived around ten and met one of your employees. Based on information Pearson supplied, it's called a fereter. Find out who it is, retrieve the fereter and meet us at Mr Coulson's house this evening. Is that clear?" Ambrose outlined, showing him the pictures of Euan Spencer and Lynsey Dewhurst on her phone.

"Yes. I need further information about the fereter. What metal it's crafted from? What size is it?"

"Based on Pearson's information, it's about the size of a pencil case with a feather design on the lid. There's also a map inside."

"Okay, I'll check with my staff, but it won't be today. I've thirty employees to speak to. How much do I get paid?"

"I don't care, Garcia, just sort it. Be there at seven this evening. Of course, there'll be the normal monetary compensation for a job well done, plus a bonus if you get the fereter to Mr Coulson this evening."

"Leave it with me Ambrose, I'll be in touch."

Ambrose fired at Garcia as he departed the cafe. "Don't be late Garcia, you know Mr Coulson is a stickler for time."

Garcia entered his office all agitated and pondered on the best course of action to find the fereter. Sitting there running his fingers through his short dark hair, he gazed at the family photo on his desk. The humble office, lined with oak effect filing cabinets, where Garcia kept all his records, had white painted walls, like most university offices.

Garcia reflected on what working for Mr Coulson meant. He enjoyed the extra money, which enabled him to purchase a property on the outskirts of Seville. In the future, he planned to return to his hometown in Spain when he had enough available funds, but he was taking a risk of getting caught and losing his job every time he helped Mr Coulson. When they had started the arrangement, he had insisted everything he did was to be conducted at Mr Coulson's house. If he needed to use any equipment at work, he would bring items in concealed and organise to work late so no one could question him on items not recorded in the departments system.

What Ambrose said meant someone else in his department appeared to be performing an undercover test. It felt hypocritical of him to question his staff, but he knew Mr Coulson wasn't about to accept he couldn't help. Mr Coulson recruited him two years ago. He considered it shrewd to agree, but once he entered the arrangement, it felt there was no route out. His only option was to continue until he could gather sufficient funds to return to Spain.

He needed to speak to his three team leaders, but before that, he planned to review the daily log to see the latest entries. He tapped away on his computer, finding the daily log, and reviewed the list. The log was slim, several coins and pottery, but no metal fereter. He called his team leaders to the modest office. They stood squeezed into the space as he spoke to them.

"It's come to my notice someone has brought an item into the department without recording it on the daily log, a fereter. Please speak to each of your staff and bring the culprit, with the fereter, to me as soon as possible. Thank you."

One of the team leaders jumped in with a question. "So we don't know who?"

"No, someone informed me two people entered the building carrying a fereter. I need an answer as soon as possible today from each of you."

The team leaders left the room and busied themselves approaching their staff to discover who held the fereter. After a couple of hours, they had all returned to Garcia's office, advising him none of the staff were aware of the fereter. Garcia called Ambrose and informed her of the outcome.

"You need to carry out a detailed search of your department, Alejandro. Check every desk, every cupboard!"

"It'll take me hours, Ambrose. How am I expected to accomplish that and make it to Mr Coulson's by seven?"

"Fine, I'll tell him, but you stay late until it's found."

Ambrose ended the call, leaving Garcia feeling anxious. Aware some staff locked their desk drawers, he considered how to achieve this. He remembered he had some master keys and dug them out of his locked drawer. He started checking in the storage cupboards and equipment rooms to get ahead of time, resigning himself to staying late tonight.

———————◄O►———————

Onni sat at his desk, thinking as he considered what had just happened with his team leader. He had denied having the fereter against his better judgment, as Lynsey had requested of him. Being honest with himself, he liked her and felt a little miffed at meeting Euan this afternoon. He sensed a connection between them.

Anyway, he rebuked himself and took some action, as he didn't want to get into trouble with his team leader for lying and flaunting the rules. He picked up the silver fereter from his work bag, transferred it to a plastic sample bag, and went to the toilet cubicle. Once there, he scraped some wax off the fereter into the sample bag, then hurried outside to his car and deposited the fereter in his glove box to keep it safe.

When Onni returned to his workstation, he grabbed the bag containing the wax and took it to the carbon-dating machine to get this completed as soon as possible. Waiting for the machine to finish its assessment seemed to take ages. He glanced over his shoulder many times, making sure no one watched his activity.

After forty minutes, the machine completed its assessment. As he reviewed the results, it became clear the fereter dated back to the late medieval times. Onni returned to his desk, picked up his phone and placed a call to Lynsey, informing her his team leader was on to him. He also told her the resulting carbon-dating test had confirmed the fereter to be genuine and several centuries old. He also asked if he could be involved with anything further.

Chapter 11

SHEFFIELD HIGH SCHOOL

TUESDAY

E MILY FINISHED HER CLASSES for the day, unwinding in the simple staff room at the high school. Warm sunlight streamed through the window, casting a gentle glow into the room. The aroma of coffee filled the air, mingling with the hint of ink from the textbooks scattered on the table. Since completing her training three years ago, Emily had been a dedicated teacher, passionate about sharing the intricacies of history with curious teenagers. Emily sat in a tired but comfy armchair, enjoying the relaxing ambiance as her thoughts drifted off to the fereter and map. A puzzle, something she felt comfortable with. At home she loved nothing better than watching a thriller box-set. She enjoyed the challenge of working out the killer before the finale. She pondered when to head home, then her phone pinged with a message from Lynsey.

Lynsey: *'Hi Em, I've had a call from my friend saying there have been some questions about the fereter. The carbon-dating of the wax shows it's genuine, and he wants to explain his findings to the team. What should I tell him?'*
Emily: *'I don't know Lyns, I'll give Reed a call and let you know.'*

Emily phoned Reed.
"Hi Em, how's it going?"

"Fine, thanks Reed. We've a problem. I've had a message from Lynsey, saying her friend's manager was asking questions about the fereter. The carbon-dating has proved it's genuine, and he'd like to explain his findings to everyone. What do you think?"

"Oh, something strange is going on. Euan mentioned he spotted the same people who came to our house on Sunday afternoon at the university today. This suggests they know we have the fereter and believe it's valuable. Tell Lynsey to come to ours tonight with her friend and bring the fereter. Euan's coming over. We can go through everything then. I'll decide after meeting Lynsey's friend how much to share with him," Reed responded.

"Okay, I'll order pizzas for everyone. What time shall I say? Seven ish?"

"That sounds spot on Em, see you later."

After a moment of contemplation, Emily picked up her phone and dialled Lynsey's number, knowing she was still at work.

"Hi Em, that's quick."

"Hi Lyns, I've spoken to Reed. We're having a get-together with Euan this evening at our place. Would you and Onni like to join us? Get him to bring the fereter, please. He can share his thoughts with the group. Reed will show his map, but please refrain from mentioning it to Onni for now. Reed wants to decide how much to share with him. The events of today have changed the situation."

"Okay, I'll ask him. He seems quite keen. I'll give him a ring and explain. What time?"

"Around seven, I'll get pizzas for everyone."

"Excellent. I need to go as I've got to complete this research paper I'm working on. I'll knock off at six latest. See ya later, Em." said Lynsey.

"Yes, bye Lyns."

———◄O►———

Emily finished her coffee and marked some homework in the staff room, knowing she wouldn't have time to complete it later. She struggled to stay focused on the task at hand, her thoughts drifting off to the map and fereter. Her watch showed close to five o'clock, but her ten-minute journey home still gave plenty of time to prepare for the evening. Emily picked up her phone and pencil case, dropping them into her handbag before she waved goodbye to the remaining colleagues in the staff room, heading to the staff car park for the drive home.

Prior to starting the engine, Emily considered Reed's view of the whole situation. With Euan encouraging him, she felt he regarded this as a thrilling adventure. She felt inclined to follow the rules by giving the fereter and map to the authorities. Then she remembered what Lynsey had said about the manager of the archaeology department questioning his staff about the fereter. How did he know it was inside the archaeology building? The more she thought, the more concerned she became. Putting all thoughts to one side, she started her engine and headed off home.

Chapter 12

COTGRAVE, NEAR NOTTINGHAM

TUESDAY

T HE GRANDFATHER CLOCK CHIMED five o'clock in the hallway of Coulson's country manor house, but he didn't hear it. He sat in the office with his team. Earlier, he had taken a phone call from Ambrose, telling him Garcia hadn't found the fereter yet. All the staff had denied any knowledge of seeing it. He felt irritated as they seemed to keep missing opportunities to get hold of the fereter and instructed Ambrose and Bentley to return to the house to discuss the next steps.

"Are you suggesting someone at the university has conducted carbon-dating of the wax from the fereter?" Coulson asked as he eyed his team.

"Yes, according to the message," Pearson replied.

"And do we know when?"

"No sorry, no details."

"Ambrose, call Garcia now. Tell him to have everyone's bags searched before they leave. We must get ahead of this. Fereters always carry something precious," said Coulson.

Ambrose picked up her phone, finding Garcia's number, and dialled him.

"Garcia, it's Ambrose. We've had confirmation someone has carbon-dated the wax from the fereter today. You need to get all the staff bags searched before they leave."

"That's crazy, Ambrose. I can't do that. Some staff will have left already," Alejandro replied.

"Stand by the exit and insist on it. Mr Coulson will need to think hard about making the university aware of your off-campus activities!"

"Okay, I'll try, but I won't be able to meet at the house unless I find it soon. Please tell Mr Coulson I'm doing my best."

"Make sure you are, Alejandro. We need you on board with this. Let me know when it's done."

Coulson waited for Ambrose to finish the conversation. "Pearson, what're we doing next?" he asked.

"I've no new information, but I think they'll meet to discuss the carbon-dating results. I'm guessing this from the message between Lynsey Dewhurst and Emily Barrington. It sounds like the person in the archaeology department will provide an update on their findings. I'm hoping this happens at Emily Barrington's house. We can capture the meeting on the sound recorder in their lounge. Once we hear the conversation, we should gain some information on the whereabouts of the fereter and map."

"We also have the tracker on the campervan. Is it working?" Coulson probed further.

"Yes, it's showing as stationary at the house in Fulwood."

Coulson looked over at Ambrose. "Keep on top of Garcia."

"I'll chase him up in thirty minutes."

"I wonder if his heart is in it. He just doesn't like the dark side of our business. Have a chat with him tomorrow, Ambrose, apply some pressure, and consider alternatives. It might be time to change our expert."

"Yes, boss, I'll look into our options."

"That's all for now. Ambrose, update me later on Garcia. Pearson, make sure you get any information from the listening gadgets to me tomorrow morning," Coulson said, giving them a wave of his hand to show the meeting was over.

Chapter 13

FULWOOD, SHEFFIELD

TUESDAY

REED SAT IN THE lounge relaxing with his first beer of the evening, looking forward to the discussions later. Especially Onni's thoughts regarding the fereter. He felt in two minds about whether to mention the map to him. He would gauge his thoughts on the Finnish archaeologist before deciding.

After chatting with Euan earlier on the phone, they preferred an adventure using the map. Just up their street. He thought Euan appeared keen because he could use his drone for something useful for a change, instead of just admiring the view. Thinking further ahead, he wondered if they would find some hidden treasures. What if they were deep underground? How would they find them? Maybe Onni had some ideas? He would need to share the map with him. A knock at the door interrupted his thoughts, but Emily answered it before he could move.

Euan walked into the lounge with a beer in his hand. They discussed the couple who appeared at their house on Sunday and at the university earlier. The discovery of the fereter suggested a strong connection.

"How'd they discover we have the fereter?" asked Emily.

"Phil and I discussed that at work. He thinks the government monitors messages and social media for terrorist information. So it's possible for criminals to use the same sort of software," said Reed.

"Well, that'd explain it," Euan said.

"Just what I was thinking, mate, in which case it makes you think the fereter is valuable."

"Perhaps we should turn it over to the proper authorities," Emily interjected.

"We think we should use the map first. See if it leads to any treasure."

"It'd be fun, Em. When's Lynsey getting here?" Euan said, diverting the course of the conversation.

"She said about seven-ish but it's already twenty minutes past that," Emily replied.

"I'm just hungry," he said, rubbing his stomach.

Soon after that, the doorbell rang again. Reed jumped up and collected the pizzas from the delivery man, who arrived early. Emily had ordered delivery for seven thirty, assuming everyone would arrive by then. The selection included ham and pineapple, meat feast, and pepperoni. He carried them through to the kitchen, placing in the oven on a low heat to keep them warm.

Emily entered the dining room with her phone ready to call Lynsey, when the doorbell rang for the third time that evening. Reed let Lynsey and Onni in their front door, guiding them into the dining room. After introductions, he brought out plates and the pizzas from the oven. The conversation drifted around to the fereter and Onni took his opportunity to provide an update on events since he met Euan and Lynsey earlier. He retrieved the fereter from his bag and placed it on the table in its sample bag.

"Thank you for inviting me. I believe the fereter originates from the late medieval period. The item's silver and may interest the British Museum. Only a handful of similar examples exist. The results of the wax carbon-dating confirmed the age to be between six hundred and eight hundred years old," Onni said, pausing for a bite of pizza and a swig of beer.

"The situation then became difficult as in the afternoon, my team leader asked if I brought a fereter into the department without registering it. The manager, Mr Garcia, said someone received the item today, wanting to know what staff member it was. I denied it. I had scraped some wax off into a sample bag while hiding in a toilet cubicle in order to test it without divulging I had the fereter. Before I carried out the operation, I moved the fereter to the glove-box in my car. Just before I left work, Mr Garcia stood at the exit asking to search everyone's bags. I felt relieved I'd moved it earlier and the wax sample bag sat in my drawer," Onni said in his clipped Scandinavian accent. Onni paused, took another bite of his pizza, and continued.

"I've carried out some research on the feather symbol, and believe the fereter may have connections with Robin Hood. I found reference to the feather symbol in some old archeological papers written by a professor from thirty years ago. He claimed to have seen a feather symbol in a cave in the Peak District, but it went unverified. Back in Finland, I played a lot of archery, our club was called 'Hood', started in 1946. In the world of archaeology, when Robin Hood and his merry men are associated with ancient objects, it creates a buzz. There's a firm belief he existed, with plenty of rumours about hidden treasures he may have left. I'm fascinated to find out more, so if you'd allow me, I'd like to be part of the team searching into this, please," Onni finished, smiling.

"That's intriguing. You took a risk today. I'm guessing you'd be in trouble if they discovered you with the fereter?" asked Reed.

"The university doesn't allow private tests, so getting caught could lead to disciplinary action. I know some staff members conduct tests for friends, but only on insignificant items like coins. I kept it a secret for now because I felt motivated by my own self-interest. If I registered the fereter, other staff would get involved. I wanted the opportunity of being included in your team."

"Okay. Are you thinking there's money involved?" asked Reed, attempting to understand the guy.

"Maybe, but that's not my main reason. I could write a research paper on the fereter and receive an accreditation. This would be an amazing opportunity for my career, especially if the fereter leads to a treasured item of Robin Hood. Once the fereter is registered, it's likely I won't be involved. So you see, I'm keen to progress with this. My career depends on it."

"I understand Onni. You appear a decent enough person and, in all truth, we'll need someone like yourself to help. So, here's the thing. The fereter had a scroll inside. Sorry for not mentioning it earlier. I was being cautious. I don't know you and couldn't take the chance you'd pass over the scroll to the authorities. It appears to be a map showing the whereabouts of something," said Reed.

Euan chimed in. "Another thing, Onni, we didn't find it in the park. We found it three feet down in a fissure on Froggart Edge in the Peak District. Sorry about lying to you."

Reed retrieved the map from his pocket and laid it on the table so everyone could examine it. He watched Onni's eyes widen. Now, he felt comfortable with the guy as he appeared sincere and interested in both items, like everyone else.

"Wow, that's amazing. May I look at it?" Onni exclaimed, reaching for his white gloves in his backpack.

"Of course."

"I understand why you didn't tell me everything. I never expected it would be this exciting."

A hushed silence descended over the group as Onni peered at the map, broken by Emily's warning, "I've some concerns about digging in the Peak District and using the drone. What do you think, Onni?"

"You can't do either, according to the law. We'd need to get permission from the landowner to dig on their land and fly drones over it."

"I understand, but they could refuse, so we should try ourselves first. If they agree, and we find an artefact, they'd have a claim on ownership of it. If we need to dig deep, then yes, we should follow the law." Reed said.

"I agree Reed, that's my thoughts. This could be the greatest adventure of our lives," said Euan, backing up his mate with gusto whilst finishing his last piece of pizza.

"I shouldn't agree with that, but I do. It's a unique opportunity that may never occur again. We could stumble upon a groundbreaking discovery. If we do, then we can pass it over to the authorities. The downside is we could get fined or arrested if we declare it later than required by the rules," said Onni.

"That's what I'm worried about," Emily said, looking at Reed.

"Yes, I know. Before we dismiss it, let's give it a shot and see how it goes."

With Euan and Onni in agreement, he just needed Emily to agree, as Lynsey would go along with her.

"Come on, Em! Let's have an adventure this weekend and see what happens. One weekend can't hurt?" Reed cajoled her.

"Okay, let's do this. Are you in Lynsey?"

"Yes, I agree for now," Lynsey said.

"Brilliant, I've a plan for the weekend, lets go into the lounge. Everyone get a drink," Reed said. He selected another beer from the fridge before ambling into the lounge and settling in the chair, enabling the others to use the corner sofa. He waited for them to settle and outlined his plan.

"First, I'm worried about these two people who keep cropping up. They know we have something of interest. They'll use software to monitor our phones, messages and social media, so I suggest we try to keep them to a minimum and talk through anything face-to-face. Let's meet again on Thursday evening. We'll come to Nottingham. Can you suggest anywhere suitable, Lynsey or Onni?"

"My flat's tiny. What about the pub '*Ye Olde Trip To Jerusalem*' in the centre? It's got lots of nooks and crannies. We can discuss the next steps without being disturbed?" Lynsey suggested.

"Sounds perfect. Shall we say seven thirty? Once my

presentation's over on Thursday, I can relax. I'm planning to get a safe deposit box tomorrow to store the fereter and map. There's a public vault near my office. I think it's safest with those two goons continuing to snoop around. On Friday, I'll return and collect the map ready for the weekend. We should do some research on Robin Hood's known locations and large boulders in the Peak District. Can you girls do that, please?" Reed said.

"Yes, sure, we'll do the research," Emily said as Lynsey nodded her agreement.

"Considering the type of terrain we'll investigate, we should consider what equipment required. We've got climbing gear in case it leads to anything in remote spots. I'm not sure how we go about finding hidden artefacts, though. Can you help with this, Onni?"

"We'll need some digging tools and a handheld metal detector. When we're on archaeological digs, we use GPR devices which we have at work, but it's not possible to borrow one. Questions would be asked, plus they're six feet long and very conspicuous."

"Can you sort those tools, please Onni? Euan, you sort out the drone ensuring it's fully charged, and bring your climbing gear?"

"Will do. I've been doing some updates on the drone but haven't finished them yet. I'll get that done tomorrow evening."

"Okay, I'm thinking we'll go to the Peak District on Friday evening in the campervan Em?"

"Yes, that's fine, Reed."

"Then it's up to you guys if you want to join us. Let me know on Thursday your plans," Reed said.

They chatted more about the discovery, the suspicious people, and their plans for the weekend. They enjoyed another drink each before Lynsey headed back to Nottingham, feeling drained after a stressful day. Euan stayed longer to finish his beer.

"Is Onni her boyfriend?" Euan asked Emily.

"Not sure, Euan. Why's that? Do you have a soft spot for her?"

"Maybe Em, we'll see."

Downing the last drop of his beer, Euan got to his feet, checked his watch, and announced, "Time for me to leave. It's almost ten. Thanks for the pizzas, and I'll see you Thursday."

"Sure thing mate, see you later."

"Yes, bye Euan," Emily said.

Reed waved him out the front door. Returning to the lounge, he reclaimed his seat on the teal corner sofa and, putting his arm around Emily, he said, "It's all quite exciting. Don't you agree, Em?"

"I've some reservations about your plan, and I'm concerned about those two people. What if they become violent?"

"I'm sure it'll be fine Em, you know I can look after myself. I've honed my Jeet Kune Do skills over the past fourteen years and feel confident I'd defend us on a one-to-one basis."

"I understand, but have you considered what might happen if they appear at our house if you aren't here?" Emily said with concern in her voice.

"You shouldn't be at home on your own if you feel uncomfortable. Can you finish your marking at school?"

"Okay, yes. I'm tired. Let's get some sleep after this program finishes, Reed. We've some busy days ahead of us."

Chapter 14

CENTRAL NOTTINGHAM

WEDNESDAY

P EARSON HAD BEEN AWAKE for an hour before his alarm went off at eight o'clock and sat at his desk, busy on his laptop. He had lived in his one-bedroom flat in central Nottingham for eighteen months, having purchased it after securing a permanent job with Mr Coulson. His flat was on the fourth floor of a modern city centre building. He enjoyed a view over the city which encompassed the castle, quite enjoyable at night when everything became lit up. The flat included a simple balcony but enough space to have a chair and a metal round table outside, enabling him to work there in the warmer months. He wasn't the tidiest of individuals and had to rely on his mum coming over once a week to clean the flat, although his work filing was immaculate. The silvery grey painted lounge overlooked the city. Pearson positioned the sofa to offer him the chance to indulge in both TV entertainment and admire the city skyline visible through the balcony doors.

He hadn't slept well. He knew the listening device recordings required checking, hoping to find something worth his effort. At eight o'clock last night, he had fallen asleep. He roused from his evening slumber about two hours later. He connected to all three devices to download the recordings from them. The only one that had anything available was Emily and Reed's lounge one, having a full thirty minutes on it. He reset it and recovered the next block of data later on. This also had a full thirty minutes of data, which gave him some optimism.

He rebuked himself again for falling asleep in the evening. There was an hour's worth of conversations to listen to, taking notes to brief Mr Coulson. He completed his task and listed down the key points he gleaned from the conversations. Pearson tapped out a secure message to Mr Coulson and Ambrose, asking for a three-way Zoom meeting that morning to discuss his findings.

Soon after Pearson sent the message, Mr Coulson set a time to join the meeting. Pearson pulled together his notes and grabbed another cup of caffeine-filled coffee. Pearson waited until the others joined the meeting and then explained the information on the listening devices.

"It didn't surprise me when I learned Reed and Emily held a meeting at their house last night. As I expected. I have sixty minutes of conversation. There were five people there: Reed, Emily, Lynsey, Euan, and an unknown person who sounded like the missing link from the archaeology department. They've worked out Ambrose and Bentley have been following them. They think you're private investigators trying to steal the fereter. There were several comments about the map, implying it's still in their possession at their house. Then they appeared to move out of the lounge as pizzas got delivered. There's nothing else until later on when one of the group expressed concerns you guys might turn aggressive. Then general chatting whilst they watched a television programme."

"Why didn't you get more of the conversation, Pearson?" Coulson asked.

"The device can only record thirty minutes. Then it requires downloading to clear the buffer."

"So why didn't you do that?"

"Hmmm, I wasn't sure if they were meeting and I was busy during the evening."

"Sometimes Pearson, you drive me crazy."

"Yes, boss, I'm making plans to increase the recording time on the devices."

"You better bloody hurry with the plan, then!"

"It's possible they went into the dining room, and we only had one device. Bentley placed it in the lounge," interjected Ambrose.

"I despair, no forethought, no planning, which leads to no action. We need to make progress. They know who you are, Ambrose. Go there and offer to buy the fereter and map from them. As before, play the part of the private investigators, taking Bentley along with you. A maximum budget of ten thousand pounds. Pearson, find who the mysterious person from the archaeology department is. We can put some pressure on them through Garcia. Is that all clear?" Coulson said.

Yes, they both answered.

"Right, get on with it."

Pearson relaxed a bit after finishing the Zoom meeting. Picking up a cheese sandwich from the fridge, he hoped Ambrose could persuade them ten grand was a fair price for finding an old metal fereter and map.

Chapter 15

CENTRAL SHEFFIELD

WEDNESDAY

REED SAT AT HIS desk working on finalising his presentation for tomorrow, trying to complete it this morning. He intended to have a longer lunch break today, to organise a safe deposit box for the fereter and map. As Reed took a sip of his coffee, he added his last design to the presentation as Phil popped his head around.

"Aye up, mate, no lively chatter this morning. Is everything alright?"

"Almost done with this presentation. A couple more slides to add."

"Oh good. How did last night go?" Phil asked.

"Incredible, lots to tell you. I'm going to the safe deposit box at lunchtime. Fancy coming? I can update you then."

"Sounds good. What time?"

"When I've completed this, around one?" Reed suggested.

"Okay mate, catch up then."

Reed worked away on his presentation, adding more words to flesh out the proposal and ensuring he added his four separate suggestions. After running the spellcheck on the complete document, he made the corrections, generated the slides and read through it. The remaining tasks were his notes and any last-minute changes this afternoon. He felt the visual aspect looked superb, with an overall red and white theme in line with the client's branding and logo. Saving his work and locking his computer, he grabbed his backpack and walked by Phil's desk to collect him on the way out. They set off at a brisk pace, passing the sandwich shop and the Winter Gardens, as Reed relayed the plan from last night's meeting.

"That sounds incredible," Phil exclaimed.

"It's going to be an adventure. We may even find some treasure."

"So this guy from the archaeology department, he knows his stuff?" Phil asked.

"He seems to. He's keen to become involved and brought the fereter back, so I feel like I can trust him. Do you fancy joining us?" Reed said.

"Not for me, mate, climbing hills and trekking miles. I'm happy to do some online investigation for you?"

"Emily and Lynsey are doing research, but the more information we have, the better. We've planned another meeting on Thursday in Nottingham. If you discover any useful information before then it'd be a fantastic help. Here's the safe deposit box building. Let's get this sorted. I want to grab a bacon sandwich on our way back."

<hr />

The building in front of them was of red brick construction with a bright gold shop front showing they were at Sheffield Vaults. A single glass door with one of those long vertical metal handles created the entry point. A security guard prowled the building inside and out. He held the door open for them as they entered. The reception area had a minimalist design, just a comfortable blue sofa for customers to relax on. A sleek low-level glass coffee table adorned the space, accompanied by several magazines for visitors to peruse. Reception sat close to the front door, with another exit door having a keypad on it, which Reed assumed led to the vault area.

The receptionist greeted them as they entered. Reed explained he was looking for a short-term option for a storage box. He agreed to the three-month term costing eighty pounds, which he paid with his card and filled in the paperwork. After providing his identification, the security guard appeared to escort them through to the main room to allocate access codes and keys.

"Do you have anything to put in your box today, sir?" the guard asked.

"Yes please. Is it okay for my friend to come into the vault area?" asked Reed.

Reed knew Phil would love to check out the fereter and vault.

"Of course, sir, that's up to you."

He led them into the vault, passing Reed the key to box number seventeen.

Reed inserted the key into the lock, feeling a satisfying click as the mechanism released. He pulled his safe deposit box out from the wall of pristine units, their shiny surfaces reflecting the bright light of the room. As he surveyed the space, the metallic glint of the floor and ceiling caught his eye, adding a sense of security to his mission. Reed couldn't help but feel a wave of relief as he realised this hidden sanctuary would safeguard the fereter and map. He placed the safe deposit box on the table in the middle of the room and pulled out the wrapped fereter from his backpack. As he unwrapped the fereter, he said to Phil, "This is it, mate. What do you think?"

"Oh wow, it looks old," Phil said.

Phil looked over the metal fereter, inspecting the feather symbol on the lid. Reed pulled out the map from his zip pocket in his backpack, placing it alongside the fereter in the safe deposit box. Happy with that, he replaced the box into its position in the wall, locking it and replaced the map with the key in the zip pocket. Together, they exited the vault, with the guard locking the access door behind them.

"I'll need to return on Friday. What's the procedure for gaining access to my box, please?" Reed said to the receptionist.

"We've scanned your photo ID. You provide your access code. We

PARADOX OF THE THIEF

check against our records and if they match, we open the vault door for you. You must bring your box key with you, as we don't provide copies. If you lose your key, it means having to follow the security process to get a new one. It takes several days. That's all in your welcome email. Any problems, please let us know," responded the receptionist.

"Okay, thanks. Sounds straightforward and very secure. Thanks for your help today."

They left the building, strolling back to the office, stopping by the sandwich shop to grab lunch. Reed chose a brie and bacon sandwich, whilst Phil went for his standard ham and cheese roll.

"That's secure now and I don't have to worry about those goons bothering us at the house or anywhere else trying to steal the fereter and map. Thanks for coming, Phil."

"No problem mate, adds a bit of excitement to the day."

Chapter 16

FULWOOD, SHEFFIELD

WEDNESDAY

AMBROSE PARKED THE CAR a couple of houses away from Reed's property and sat briefing Bentley on her plan. As the sun set, they exited the vehicle, striding to the house in question, making sure the tracker on the campervan in the driveway wasn't visible. Ambrose knocked on the front door. She felt comfortable carrying out this part of the job; she found it easy to offer people money for items they had no real understanding of its value. Ambrose intended to talk to Reed and appeal to the greedy side of his nature. Everyone had one.

The door opened and Reed Hascombe stood in front of Ambrose, his mouth ajar and somewhat surprised at seeing her on his doorstep again.

"Hello again sir, we wondered if we may come inside and discuss something with you, please?" asked Ambrose.

"I'm happy to talk on the doorstep," responded Reed.

"I'd like to apologise for being dishonest with you during our previous conversation. We weren't here on behalf of a distant relative. We know you have possession of a silver artefact and wish to discuss an offer with you."

"So, you're not private investigators, right?"

"We are sir, and work on behalf of many individuals and corporations," Ambrose said, flashing her badge.

"Okay, come inside, but I want the truth this time, otherwise you can leave."

"Thank you, sir."

Ambrose followed Reed into the house, with Bentley close behind. As they entered the lounge, Emily Barrington offered them a seat on the corner sofa as she greeted them. As they sat down, Ambrose pulled out a piece of paper, a list of prompts for the conversation, in order to glean information before making an offer. Ambrose began with her questions.

"We're working with a person interested in artefacts found in the Peak District. We believe you've discovered a silver fereter. Is that correct?"

"Before I answer that, who are you working for?" Reed asked.

"I'm not at liberty to discuss that, as our clients insist on remaining anonymous."

"If you aren't able to be transparent with me, then I don't feel inclined to discuss anything further," Reed said.

"Let's not make it difficult sir, we've evidence you found it at the weekend. You also took it to the archaeology department at The Peaks University yesterday. I was there with my colleague and we observed the artefact for ourselves."

"Okay, let's say I have the artefact. What do you want with it? I found it."

"You're aware of the law regarding finding artefacts that could be of historical importance?" Ambrose suggested.

"Yes, we're well aware of the laws, thank you," Emily interjected.

"You've reported the artefact to the local Finds Liaison Officer for Derbyshire?" asked Ambrose.

"That's not your concern," Reed said.

"It's possible you could face legal consequences, if it were to come to light, that you possess an artefact which isn't declared." Ambrose said.

Emily gave Reed a concerned look which Ambrose spotted and

realised she was onto something, pushing on with her questions.

"Where's the fereter now? Can we have a look at it?"

"No way," Reed said.

"In which case, I can't make you an offer for it, sir," Ambrose said.

"It's not here, so I can't show you. I'm interested to know why you wish to make me an offer for the item, considering it needs reporting to the Finds Liaison Officer," Reed responded.

"We work with individuals looking for sought-after artefacts. There's a large black market we operate in to provide this service. Our client wants to buy the fereter from you."

"So you're trying to blackmail me into selling it to you? And if I decide not to sell it to you, then you'll report me to the authorities?"

"Yes, something like that, sir. My client has suggested we offer you five thousand pounds for the fereter, subject to viewing it," Ambrose said.

Ambrose watched Reed's body language for any changes. Having spent several years in the military, she learned observation skills. He shifted in his seat with a hint of a smile appearing across his lips before he returning to his previous poker face. Ambrose realised he was aware of the potential value of the fereter.

"The fereter's silver, so I assume its value would exceed your offer. I think the museum would pay a lot more," Reed said.

"Maybe sir. I can increase the offer to eight thousand if that will seal the deal?" Ambrose proposed.

"Still not interested!"

"My last offer would be ten thousand. My instructions are quite clear. I can't go beyond that level."

"That's interesting, but I think it's worth more than your offer. Let me consider it. Perhaps I'll discuss it with the Finds Liaison Officer first," said Reed, trying to put some pressure back on to Ambrose, sensing she was very keen to get the fereter.

"I have to warn you, any conversations with the authorities will void my offer. It's common for people to sell items like these on the black market. If the authorities get suspicious about a specific item, it puts our clients at risk," responded Ambrose.

"Okay, I understand. Let me consider your offer. How'd I get in touch with you if I wish to accept the offer?" asked Reed.

"We'll come back tomorrow evening for your answer. What time's convenient for you, sir?"

"Sorry, I'm busy tomorrow evening. Shall we say Monday evening?"

"We don't like to wait that long after making an offer. How about Friday evening instead?" Ambrose asked.

"I'm busy Friday and all weekend. It'll have to be Monday evening," Reed insisted.

"Okay, Monday evening it is. We'll bid you folks goodnight and thank you for your time this evening." Ambrose got up to leave, turning on the doorstep to remind Reed that refusing their offer may lead to them reporting him to the Finds Liaison Officer.

Ambrose and Bentley walked back to the car. "They won't accept the offer, Bentley. He's intending to use the map this weekend. It's quite clear," Ambrose said.

"I had the same thought. He moved the return date to Monday, allowing them plenty of time to follow the map and search for treasure," responded Bentley.

"Better report back to Mr Coulson and update him on what happened."

———— ◆○◆ ————

Reed returned to the lounge, letting out a sigh, sitting down on the sofa.

"I told you this could be risky, Reed," Emily said.

"She's bluffing, Em. If they do these underhand deals, she won't be getting involved with the authorities."

"Yes, I suppose. That's a decent offer, isn't it?"

"I don't think so. It's worth way more than that. They know what fereter's are worth to collectors and are speculating on what the map may contain. You mentioned before the church and wealthy individuals use them to transport treasures. That'd be worth lots of money to private collectors," he said.

"Yes, very true. What are you thinking?" enquired Emily.

"We carry on with our plan. They won't come back until Monday. If we find nothing following the map, then we assess whether it's worth taking the ten grand. I still think it's worth more than that," finished Reed.

Chapter 17

THE PEAKS UNIVERSITY

THURSDAY

Lynsey sat at her desk in the Lightning Technology Research Centre, fiddling with loose strands of her dark hair tied up. Like most university departments, the decorations were sparse and full of expensive equipment. Her desk was a mere hub for engrossing research. Since a child, thunderstorms have captivated her senses. The rumbling sounds and brilliant flashes of lightning would ignite her imagination, as storm's raw power sent shivers down her spine. She imagined a god-like presence sitting in the clouds with a large fork directing lightning down to earth. Lynsey developed a stronger passion for the subject as a teenager. This led to her taking a science degree at The Peaks University, with the goal of joining the research centre. Having spent the initial eighteen years of her life in Cornwall, she now enjoys living in the midlands because her job is important to her. Her mum would come and stay with her on the odd weekend, but Cornwall remained her home. She made regular trips to see her parents and younger brother.

She continued to work on the research for the weekend adventure whilst she ate her cheese and salad sandwich for lunch. Lynsey had been friends with Emily since they met on campus at a student party while in the first year of their degree courses. The friendship continued even though they lived an hour apart, both passionate about their respective careers. They split the research between them, with Emily investigating places and locations linked to Robin of Loxley. They considered this to be a better option than researching Robin Hood, which would involve navigating through folklore and tales. Lynsey would research large rocks and known caves in the Peak District, as well as Sherwood Forest. With the three completed lists, they could cross reference them searching for a match.

She came across many caves in both areas, including two known as Robin Hood's cave. This seemed too obvious. The Peak District was renowned for caves ranging from those on the tourist trail like Peveril Cavern to little-visited caves like Reynard's Cave. The latter was a steep walk uphill to the entrance, which offered a better solution for hiding an item. She doubted any treasures connected to Robin Hood in the well-known caves would remain. After some thought, she created two categories and ranked each cave as either a tourist or lesser known one. Among the places she listed, Cresswell Crags was one example of multiple caves. Since this became a popular tourist destination, Lynsey doubted there was anything left to be discovered.

She allowed her thoughts to meander. Could someone have already discovered the treasure mentioned on the map? They would waste their time if it had. She ignored that thought, carrying on with her research into caves until she had her list. It occurred to her there could be a multitude of undiscovered caves across the Peak District that eluded any acknowledgments. Her thoughts drifted off to a trail race booked for a month's time, aware she needed to increase her training. Her phone pinged with a WhatsApp message.

Emily: *'I'll be there in an hour Lyns, I'll meet you at the cafe xx.'*
Lynsey: *'Okay, just finishing up my research x x.'*

Emily was coming down to Nottingham early so they could compare notes. They could cross reference their lists and see if anything popped out. Lynsey moved on to looking at large rocks in the area. It soon became obvious this was a smaller list. There were three distinct categories, those containing a cluster like Ramshaw Rocks or Robin Hood's Stride, stone circles like Nine Ladies on Stanton Moor, and then massive individual rocks. She recalled the map and remembered it was an individual rock leading her to prioritise this list ahead of the other two options. She couldn't find any rocks of significance in the Sherwood Forest area to add to that list. Concluding her research, she had reduced it down to: The Salt Cellar on Derwent Edge, Cork Stone on Stanton Moor, Eagle Stone on Baslow Edge, Mother Cap near Millstone Edge and Alport Stone near Wirksworth. The last location on the list didn't seem to fit with the others. The rock appeared to be quarried instead of being natural, leading her to discount it.

<hr />

Lynsey sat sipping on her latte in the Sheriff's Cafe, watching the door, when Emily arrived. She waved at her friend, getting up and beckoning her to join the queue to get a drink. They sat down at a table and pulled out their research notes.

"Before we start on our lists, I need to update you on what happened last night. Those two people came round the house and offered Reed ten grand for the fereter and map," Emily said to her friend.

"They must know we have it. What did Reed say?" Lynsey asked.

"He declined it, saying he'll think about it until Monday. If we find nothing at the weekend, he may decide to take the offer, but I doubt it."

"How are they aware he has the fereter?"

"The woman said they spotted it in the cafe when you and Euan met," Emily explained.

"That's possible. Euan noticed the young lad in the cafe watching us."

"Anyway, how'd you get on with your research?" Emily asked.

"I started looking at caves and there are hundreds in the Peak District, Sherwood Forest, and surrounding areas. It felt easier to divide them into two lists. I'm thinking we should explore the lesser-known caves first. I think treasures buried in the popular caves would have been discovered already," Lynsey said.

"That makes sense. I found the same problem with locations. There are all the known ones, through historical facts or those created in the folklore of Robin Hood," responded Emily.

"Reed has given us the hard part! I had more joy looking at large stones and rocks. There are three distinct types. I focussed on the massive individual rocks but discounted any rocks in clusters. Just one rock I wasn't sure about, the Coach and Horses rock formation on Derwent Edge. It seems individual but also a small cluster."

Lynsey shared her list with Emily and they agreed to remove Alport Stone. They then tried matching the other four within the list of cave locations. They also considered the map had a rocky outcrop near the large rock. Emily opened Google maps to review each location. This led them to remove Cork Stone from the list, leaving three massive rocks that appeared to fit with the positioning on the map, but couldn't link any known caves to any of them.

"We'll need Euan and his drone to help," Emily said.

"Agreed. It would be sensible to view the locations from an aerial perspective and correlate them with the map."

"What do you think of Euan?" Emily asked her friend.

"He seems like a decent bloke, enthusiastic about this adventure."

"We're wondering if Onni is your boyfriend?"

"Uh no, Em, I think he likes me, but he's just someone I got chatting to one lunch break. He seemed fascinated by my work on lightning. We meet up twice a week just for lunch. Why do you ask?" asked Lynsey.

"Euan is interested. I think he has a soft spot for you."

"Oh, has he now? I don't mind him, he makes me laugh. If he asked, I'd go on some dates to see how it goes."

"I'll let him know. A bit of matchmaking for a friend," Emily said, grinning.

"Why not? What time is Reed getting here?"

"Euan's picking Reed up from work at five thirty, so I guess they'll get to Nottingham about seven, especially with it being rush hour. I think they're getting something to eat on the way, pizzas knowing Euan!"

"Shall we see if Onni wants to grab something to eat before we meet later on?" asked Lynsey.

"That sounds like a plan. Call him."

While Lynsey spoke to Onni, Emily reviewed the lists again and decided she agreed with Lynsey's thoughts about it being more likely a lesser-known cave.

Chapter 18

COTGRAVE, NEAR NOTTINGHAM

THURSDAY

C OULSON HAD TAKEN TIME to reflect on their next course of action after Ambrose's briefing on the events of the previous evening. As the afternoon drew to a close, he had assembled the team in the office, ready to give them further instructions.

"Ambrose, do you think they would accept an increased offer for the fereter?" he asked.

"I guess if you offered a hundred thousand, they'd jump at it," she replied.

"I'm not spending that amount of money without knowing the significance of the map. The fereter on its own is worth thirty to forty grand, but no more. I'm not inclined to make a higher offer unless I see it. Sounds like twenty grand wouldn't cut it."

Coulson sipped his coffee, contemplating an increased offer, whilst his team waited. Something caught his eye outside, so swivelling round in his luxury office chair, he glanced out of the window. The gardener was going about his work, cutting the lawn each Thursday. An all-day job. He returned to the task at hand; having decided on his next course of action.

"Pearson, gather in-depth profiles of each of the four individuals. Let's identify any weaknesses. Maybe one of them will break ranks for twenty grand if they could get hold of the fereter," he said.

"I'll pull those together. What are your thoughts on the fereter?"

asked Pearson.

"I've been thinking it over and the feather-like symbol's been niggling me. It came to me this morning in the gym. I remember an elderly professor at a dig in Egypt many years ago who found Robin Hood fascinating. He rambled about it, believing one day some hidden treasures would come to light. He didn't specify what treasures, but several times he mentioned a feather-like symbol seen in a cave in the Peak District," Coulson outlined.

"That sounds incredible. I thought Robin Hood was a myth," said Pearson.

"Some historical evidence implies the myth may have some truth to it."

"I didn't realise that. I assumed it was a story."

Coulson reflected, "I've come across several rumours over the years, and should have considered the professor's suggestion sooner."

"I suppose there are lots of rumours that aren't true," said Pearson.

"Yes. If the fereter is a genuine artefact associated with Robin Hood, it would be the first discovery of its kind."

"If that's true, it would be an incredible result."

"Yes, it'd be worth one hundred grand, but without seeing it, it's too big a risk to take. Ambrose, anything from Garcia yet on the fifth member of the group?" Coulson said, turning his attention to Ambrose.

"He doesn't know."

"Mmmm, he might be a reasonable archaeologist, but when things move outside of his comfort zone, he isn't very effective. I think we need to operate assuming the fereter is Robin Hood related. We need to take a stealthy approach and observe their activities instead. Based on what you two have said, I'm going to assume they'll attempt to use the map for treasure hunting at the weekend. Remind me, Pearson, what gadgets do we have in play?" enquired Coulson.

"We have listening devices in their house, the campervan and also Lynsey Dewhurst's flat. We attached a vehicle tracker to the campervan. I'm checking their messages and social media," detailed Pearson.

"Check the vehicles every hour, Pearson. We need to be getting closer to understanding their plans."

"Hold on, I'll do that now," Pearson said, tapping away on his laptop. "Lynsey's car is in central Nottingham and has been since early this morning. I assume she's at work. The ANPR data on Emily's vehicle shows it in Nottingham. She could be at the university where Lynsey works. Euan's car was last recorded in north Sheffield, most likely at work. The campervan is still in the driveway," he outlined.

"If we assume they're planning to go into the Peak District at the weekend, we need to be ready to move," Coulson said. "I think you should be here, Pearson, because of signal and network issues. Ambrose, it's important you and Bentley are prepared to leave early on Saturday morning. Ensure you take the satellite phone with you."

"I'm hoping they'll go in the campervan so I can track them," said Pearson, "but bearing in mind Reed went there on Friday evening last weekend, should we plan to start then?"

"Well, unless they go early afternoon, they won't get much done on a Friday evening. It gets dark around eight o'clock," interjected Ambrose.

"Let's remain fluid on that one. Should Pearson detect any activity on the campervan tracker, it's essential you're prepared to leave when I say. Observe their activities and report back every hour. Take binoculars, hats, sunglasses, a change of clothes and anything else you think will be useful. No earphones or music Bentley. This is a covert operation. You aren't to be seen until I say so," Coulson instructed.

"Then what boss?" asked Ambrose

"If they find something interesting, take it with force. You have my permission to get stuck in if required, Bentley," he said with a laugh, knowing full well his nephew enjoyed a bit of action. "Ambrose, take the morning off tomorrow. Bentley, come over here by nine. I've a sale to close and require the usual level of security."

Chapter 19

CENTRAL NOTTINGHAM

THURSDAY

REED ENTERED THE PUB, *Ye Olde Trip to Jerusalem*, with Euan. Looking around, he could see the part of the building incorporating the caves that stood beneath Nottingham Castle. The pub exuded an old world ambiance, with its low ceilings adorned with aged dark wood beams. The soft lighting showcased a dark wood counter accentuated by the glow of beer taps, creating an authentic experience. A couple of people waited for their drinks, with groups around the pub sitting in booths. The seating was a burgundy velour design on benches and the atmosphere seemed relaxed with a younger crowd, more than likely students. They waited their turn at the bar while looking for the girls. Emily had sent a message earlier, letting them know they had arrived and discovered a cosy corner upstairs where they could talk without being overheard.

The barmaid asked Reed what they wanted. He went for the Dark Peak stout and Euan a pint of Stella Artois. They grabbed their drinks and looked for the stairs. Finding their way up, they soon found the girls and Onni in an enclave underneath a window. The window gave a glimpse of the Nottingham skyline in early evening dusk with the twinkle of streetlights just through the impending darkness.

"Hi, everyone, can I get anyone a drink?" Reed asked, but they all

86

replied no thanks. He sat on a chair alongside Euan, whilst the other three perched on the bench underneath the window.

"How's your presentation today, Reed?" asked Emily.

"Excellent. The client loved the vivid branding throughout. I left it with him to pick which option to go with. Glad that's finished, I can relax now," he responded. "Just to update everyone, the two goons visited us last night, offering to buy the fereter and map for ten grand. I turned them down. Sounds like whoever they work for has deduced it could be associated with Robin Hood. They spotted the fereter when Lynsey and Euan met at the cafe. Emily mentioned the feather-like symbol in the initial Facebook group messages. They must have some kind of monitoring software enabling them to track our conversations. Let's keep messages and social media posts to a minimum. That way, they can't track what we're doing," he outlined, pausing for breath before asking the group, "Is everyone still keen to go treasure hunting at the weekend?"

After a chorus of enthusiastic positive answers, he said, "If we find nothing, we could decide to sell them the fereter on Monday and I'll split it five ways."

"That's very generous of you, Reed. I appreciate that," Onni said as the others nodded their agreement.

"Em, I wondered if you preferred to go through the research before we discuss the other stuff?"

"I think it's better if Lynsey explains it. She's done more research than me."

Lynsey explained their thought processes on the locations, caves, and large stones before naming the key locations. "We've narrowed the list down to three locations: The Salt Cellar on Derwent Edge, Eagle Stone on Baslow Edge and Mother Cap near Millstone Edge," she said "plus another I wasn't too sure about, the Coach and Horses rock formation on Derwent Edge. I couldn't decide whether it was one rock or a cluster, so no harm in considering it, as we'll be close by, anyway. The problem is we couldn't link any caves to those areas. I decided if it was a known cave, any treasures would have been discovered already," Lynsey explained. Euan gave Lynsey a broad smile, as the work she had done impressed him.

"That makes sense," Onni said. "What do you think, Reed? You and Euan know the areas better than the rest of us."

"They all sound plausible if we consider there are unknown caves, although I'm not sure Derwent Edge has enough trees. We'll need the drone to help us. Is it ready, Euan?"

"Yes, it's updated, and I took it for a quick trial run yesterday evening. Works fine but not really successful in low light. Hopefully, we'll have a sunny day."

"Brilliant, are you coming over Friday evening or first thing Saturday?" Reed asked Euan.

"I'm coming over Friday after work. I'm planning on sleeping in the car so I can do a longer test on the drone before dark. Where are you thinking of parking?"

"In the Ladybower Inn car park. It's a reasonable size and close to Derwent Edge. Let's make it our first stop on Saturday morning. What do you think, Em?"

"Sounds good to me. What are you thinking of doing, Lyns?"

"I wasn't sure. I was waiting to see what everyone else thought of doing. What're you thinking, Onni?"

"I'm thinking the same as you, but I'm keen to start straightaway on Saturday. Does the pub have accommodation available?" he asked.

Reed opened up Google and found the website for the Inn and checked availability. They had two rooms available for Friday night. Onni and Lynsey confirmed they would come over on Friday night. Reed booked the rooms at the pub. "Great, I've booked them. That just leaves the equipment to talk about, Onni?"

"I checked through my old dig equipment box and gathered together trowels and brushes. I also have an underwater handheld metal detector from Norway and have put fresh batteries in. It's working fine now. It's not the most suitable one for our adventure, but it's the best we have available, as I can't borrow anything from work."

"Good, I've got my climbing gear in the campervan. Does anyone have any suggestions for other gear or equipment we might require?"

No-one had any other suggestions, so Reed ambled downstairs, returning with a full tray of drinks. They continued their conversation, speculating about potential discoveries the weekend could yield. Reed sat listening to the chatter from the other four and hoped the weekend's adventure would bring them some luck. He cast his memory back to the weekend when he discovered the fereter and wondered how it got there? Was it dropped in the fissure? Did someone place it there on purpose? Once they had finished their drinks, Reed suggested they walk up the hill to get a photo alongside the Robin Hood statue poised outside Nottingham Castle. A moment in time captured as a memory, defining the future perhaps?

Chapter 20

PEAK DISTRICT

*T*HE LANDSCAPE BUSTLED WITH *the greenery of spring in 1403AD, exploding into a riot of colours.*

The man had the remaining fereter to give to the lady in Hathersage, Marian. He carried out the last wish of his leader as he laid on his deathbed a few days ago. He had hidden some treasures in little-known locations his leader had frequented with the lady. Each fereter contained a map giving minimal indications of the concealed locations, but she would know. It became vital they didn't fall into the wrong hands. He had to make sure of that.

It was challenging to reach the last location, but having knowledge of the correct route made it simple. His horse whimpered as he climbed back on to the moor. Astride the black stallion, he traversed north, heading towards Hathersage. In the distance he could see black clouds gathering over Stanage Edge, drawing the light away. As he approached the gap between the moors, he recognised some of the sheriff's men coming up the hill. One let out a cry.

"Outlaw."

"Get him."

"Stop now."

The man pushed the horse harder, through the gap and onto Curbar Edge. He glanced over his shoulder and spotted five men hot on his heels. He had to keep ahead of them across the rocky edge, so he could lose them in the wooded valley beyond. A race against his enemy. The stakes were high. He had to emerge victorious. The horse's breathing became strained, and his heart pumped as they manoeuvred through the treacherous terrain. The wooded area appeared. He urged the horse for one final push.

With no forewarning, he lost his balance and tumbled off the horse, crashing onto the unforgiving ground with a resounding thud. A sharp sting of pain shot through his left leg, making him wince as he grappled with the discomfort. The horse had clipped a rock and lay stunned on its side; he shouldn't have pushed it so hard. Unable to walk, he looked behind, spotting the sheriff's men approaching. Their pace decreased when they caught sight of the man lying on the ground. He looked to his left and noticed the cliff edge close by, so crawled towards it, hoping to climb down away from them. The group of men had reined their horses to a stop. One approached him with his sword. Panic took hold as he realised his impending demise.

"Time to meet your maker, outlaw."

"Take him down."

"Off with his head."

"Kill him"

"Rip his heart out."

The sound of the sheriff's men's raucous chatter filled the air. The man crawled as quick as he could towards the rocky edge, pulling the fereter from his cloak. With his back facing the sheriff's man, he threw it down a fissure in the rock, hoping to hide it well. Seconds later, the sword penetrated his cloak. He lay there, soaked in blood as his life ebbed away. As his last breath escaped him, his mind lingered on the image of his leader, the unwavering champion of the people.

Chapter 21

COTGRAVE, NEAR NOTTINGHAM

FRIDAY

C OULSON STROLLED ALONG THE perimeter of his sprawling grounds after a thirty-minute workout in the gym. As he ventured outside, the bright hues of flowers and lush greenery greeted him. The smell of cut grass mingled with flower pollen to create a fragrant aroma. It took him about fifteen minutes to walk the perimeter. Enough time to check the security cameras, ensuring the property looked secure. It also enabled him to carry out spot checks on the gardener's work, stopping by the workshop for a quick chat. He returned to the house and sat in his favourite chair in the library with a cup of coffee. He sensed static electricity in the air, feeling a thunderstorm approaching.

Bentley arrived soon afterwards, joining his uncle in the library.

"How's the training going, Bentley?" he asked his nephew.

"Very well, I feel strong and with only a few weeks left before my fight, I'm concentrating on improving my jab speed,"

"Did you get me a ticket?"

"Not yet Uncle, I'll sort out a ticket nearer the time, just one?" he said.

"Yes, just one. Your aunty doesn't enjoy violence and can't see the point of it. Myself, I think it's a super way for young men to use their pent up aggression in a controlled environment."

"I enjoy it, makes me feel alive," said Bentley.

"Glad you do Bentley. You might have to get tough tomorrow. Don't let me down. I'm going to *The Safe*, sort out the cabinet ready for our guest, please. I'll be back soon," Coulson said.

He rose from his chair, making his way into the downstairs cloakroom before opening the sliding door with his retina scanner in the mirror. He descended the stairs, placing his hand on the door scanner and entered *The Safe*. Coulson donned some white gloves before picking up the silver goblet. He selected an appropriate sized wooden box lined with dark green velour. He placed the gleaming goblet inside. Every artefact came with an authentication certificate featuring Garcia's signature. He picked up the certificate for the goblet and laid it inside the box before returning to the library.

Coulson placed the artefact inside the display cabinet, close to the window, to utilise the natural light. He used it to present items to his clients. Coulson locked the cabinet and put the key in the breast pocket of the gilet he wore. He spotted Bentley sitting in the chair nearest the door, for security reasons.

Before long, the doorbell chimed, and the client arrived. Coulson greeted Justin Gadd on the doorstep and invited him in. He had become an important client and, being a CEO of a prominent London bank, had plenty of money to burn. They walked into the library. Settling in the comfortable chairs, Coulson offered his client a drink.

"How's business, Justin?" he asked.

"Our sales are increasing with the extra investment arm I added two years ago. Since we've moved away from the pandemic, our business is on the rise."

"Good to hear. I assume that will mean a bigger bonus for you?" said Coulson.

"I would think so. Profit margins are also increasing, having moved up by two percentage points. You have the Queen Victoria goblet ready for me, I see?"

Coulson passed Justin some white gloves, pulled out the key and opened the display cabinet, encouraging Justin to join him. He stood there, his mouth wide open at the goblet, reaching into the cabinet to retrieve it. As Justin held it, he stared in wonderment at the intricate stem, marvelling at the three tiny rubies encrusted within.

"I'm telling you, Eric, it's amazing and worth every single penny," said Justin.

"It's indeed a remarkable piece and to think Queen Victoria would sip wine from it most evenings," replied Coulson.

Justin placed the goblet inside the wooden box and checked the authentication certificate. Happy with his purchase, he closed the lid. All that remained was the last payment, having paid the bulk of it prior to today. Justin opened his banking app and sent the money, waiting for Coulson to verify receipt. Upon completion, Coulson poured them both a finger of Scotch whisky to celebrate. He believed in providing his clients a *'theatre experience'* when they purchased an item from him. He made it something to remember, even if they were only spending ten grand. They wanted to feel they were getting something unique.

"Thanks again Justin, I appreciate your business," said Coulson.

"This goblet will provide me with years of delight. I'm grateful for that. Thank you for providing another amazing artefact."

"Here's too many more, Justin."

They both downed their scotch in one go, shook hands, and Bentley showed Justin out. Coulson then turned his attention to the next matter in hand, the silver fereter and map he wanted to gain. A secure message waited for him from Pearson.

'Euan Spencer's car travelled to Nottingham and back to Sheffield last night. Several of the group were together in Nottingham. Making plans for the weekend?'

He mused on this whilst eating a light lunch of tuna salad. The profiles prepared by Pearson of each person lay on the table. He picked them up and read through, gleaning the key points, noticing Euan Spencer had a drone. He gave Ambrose a call just to make sure she was ready in case they needed to head off to the Peak District at short notice, also mentioning the drone in case she hadn't picked that up.

Chapter 22

LADYBOWER RESERVOIR, PEAK DISTRICT

FRIDAY

EUAN FINISHED HIS LAST job for the day around four thirty, heading home to assemble his gear for the weekend. After parking on the road outside his house, he removed all the boxes of electrical items from the boot of his Ford Focus Estate. Euan organised his work stuff to make it easy to use the vehicle at weekends, allowing room for his climbing gear and drone. He checked he had everything plus a spare battery pack for the drone. Euan grabbed his backpack, threw in a few clothes, and picked up some snack food to take for the weekend before having a shower. He planned to use the toilets at Heatherdene's car park for a wash down in the morning and utilise Reed's campervan for coffee. He checked the weather forecast, spotting a thunderstorm predicted for this evening. Time to make a move.

Euan arrived at the Ladybower Inn car park, checking to see if Reed and Emily were there. Unable to spot the campervan, he fired off a message.

Euan: *'Aye up mate, I'm at the car park. What time are you getting here?'*
Reed: *'We'll leave in fifteen minutes. See you soon mate.'*

Euan choose to wait until Reed and Emily arrived before testing the drone, as he only had half an hour to wait. Instead, he popped into the *Ladybower Inn* and ordered himself a pint of Stella. He liked this pub. It became one of their go-to spots for a drink and a bite to eat after a strenuous day of climbing, located just fifteen minutes from Sheffield. On a nice day, you can opt to sit outside and soak up the sun, or join the crowd of walkers in the busy bar area. As Euan waited outside for the others to arrive, he checked the menu. His mind wandered whilst he people-watched. Thinking about tomorrow's adventure made him eager. He loved this type of experience, usually with just Reed, but on this occasion, Lynsey would be present. Now that appealed to him, he thought, smiling to himself. Euan spotted the red campervan coming down the hill and waved as they pulled into the car park, then strolling across to join him.

"Started early, mate?" Reed asked.

"Why not? It's a lovely summer evening, perfect for a pint outside. Hi Em, how're you?"

"Fine, thanks Euan. Are you excited about the weekend?"

"Oh yes. The drone is ready for action. I want to try it out this evening. When are Lynsey and Onni getting here?"

"Lynsey said half seven. Why's that, Euan?" asked Emily, smiling.

"Looking forward to it. She's rather lovely. I think it's best we do the drone testing before they get here. Did you get the map, Reed?" Euan asked.

"Yes, I popped into the safe deposit building at lunchtime. Shall we get some food?"

"Sounds like a plan," Emily said, picking up the menu. After making their choices, Reed ordered the food and got another round of drinks. They sat outside eating and watching the sun edge towards the crest of Win Hill in the distance. A rainbow materialised to the east of Win Hill, a result of the rain coming from the north. A faint rumble of thunder rolled in the distance, causing the group to finish their drinks and wander over the road to the cars.

Euan picked up the drone, turned it on, made a few checks and manoeuvred it upwards with the remote control unit. As he piloted it over the inn, it gave a wide-ranging view, pulling in the green hillside behind the inn and the glistening water of the reservoir, all in glorious colour. With anticipation, they gathered around the control unit, their gaze locked on the screen.

"That's pretty clear, Euan," Reed said.

"It's not too bad. We can see the lie of the land and match it to the map if I send it high enough."

"If we get up early, we can check out Derwent Edge by ten before it's too busy. We need to be discreet using the drone, not draw any unwanted attention," Reed said.

"I agree," said Emily, "okay, that's the drone tested. Shall we get another drink whilst we wait for the other two to arrive?"

"My round," said Euan.

They sat outside, listening to the approaching thunderstorm. Sipping their drinks, they spotted the first streak of lightning over the Kinder plateau in the distance. They didn't notice Lynsey's car arrive until both she and Onni were waving at them from across the road. After greeting each other, Lynsey spotted the lightning in the distance.

"I checked the weather forecast earlier, so I've brought a digital recorder to capture footage of the lightning," Lynsey said.

"When the lightning gets nearer, I can send the drone towards it and get a bird's-eye view," Euan said, hoping to impress her.

"Oh, that'd be amazing if you could, Euan. Can you record it?"

"Yes, of course. I can capture up to fifteen minutes."

"That'd be so brilliant, thank you."

Euan watched Lynsey position her recorder on a sturdy tripod beside their table, adjusting the zoom to capture the electrifying lightning. He couldn't help but admire her curves in her leggings and vowed to chat to her as much as he could this weekend. The group continued to chat about the plans for tomorrow, agreeing to get to Derwent Edge by ten. It would mean leaving the cars in the car park and following the route up the hill, taking an hour to reach the summit. They planned to gather at the pub at eight o'clock in the morning for breakfast, and proceed together as a group.

"We've some amazing scenery in Finland, but this is stunning," Onni said.

"We're so lucky to have it on our doorstep," Reed replied.

"Despite living in England for four years, I haven't explored the Peak District yet. I'll try harder to come here more often after this weekend."

"You're welcome to come rock climbing with Euan and I one weekend if that's something you'd like to try?"

"I'm afraid of heights, Reed, so that's not something I'd want to do, but thank you."

"No problem, Onni. If you change your mind, let us know."

The gap between the lightning and thunder became shorter, with the latest flash appearing just behind Win Hill. It lit up the night sky, creating an atmosphere of excitement and menace. Lynsey checked her recorder and asked Euan if they could try out the drone now. They both popped over the road to Euan's car. As he opened the boot of the Ford Focus estate, his bag of clothes fell out, a pair of Transformers pants, with a hole in, fell onto the floor. He heard Lynsey laugh.

"Nice pants, Euan," she said, giving him a playful punch on his arm.

"Thanks Lynsey. Perhaps I need a new pair," he said, embarrassed, retrieving them and turning his attention to the drone. He soon had it in the air and moving towards Win Hill. The drone had a distance capability of over two kilometres, so Euan could manoeuvre it above the lower slopes of Win Hill. A dramatic flash of lightning lit up the sky.

"Wow, Euan, this is amazing. Are you capturing footage of the lightning?"

"Yes, I put it onto record before I sent it up. We can get a few more examples."

"This is so good. I need to speak to my manager and persuade him to purchase a drone. It would be a game changer for our research."

"You need to be careful. If the drone gets caught by lightning, it'll fry the electrics in an instant," Euan explained. As Lynsey leant in to view the small screen, Euan got a whiff of her perfume, increasing his attraction to her. He spent the next few minutes trying to impress her with his knowledge of drones, keen to get some brownie points in the bank. He eventually brought the drone down, not wanting it to get caught in either the lightning or impending rain. Plus, the battery had limited capacity and although he had a spare, it took time to recharge. They finished with the drone and headed over to join the others, Lynsey enthusing about how incredible the footage was. Euan's face had a broad smile, pleased he had garnered such an enthusiastic reaction from Lynsey and vowed to use that advantage later on in the weekend.

After more social chatting, everyone decided they should get an early night, as they had a busy weekend ahead. Lynsey and Onni headed to their rooms in the inn whilst the other three nipped across the road to their vehicles. Reed and Emily settled in to the campervan as Euan strode to his car. He unrolled his sleeping bag, retrieved the pillow from the boot and jumped in the back seat of the car, laying there watching the lightning flash as the rain begun. Reflecting on this evening, he felt pleased with himself for impressing Lynsey, deciding he would ask her out on a date during this weekend. His thoughts meandered to the exciting adventure that lay ahead the next day as he drifted off to sleep.

Chapter 23

COTGRAVE, NEAR NOTTINGHAM

SATURDAY

P EARSON HAD ARRIVED AT the country manor house just after eight o'clock. Last night, upon discovering the location where the campervan had become stationary, he wasted no time in informing Mr Coulson. This resulted in Mr Coulson sending Ambrose and Bentley off early this morning to get to the car park as quick as possible. Pearson double-checked the campervan tracking and confirmed it as stationary in the car park at Ladybower Inn. Also, checking for any ANPR data for Euan and Lynsey's vehicles, he found no further movements. They must be in the Peak District.

Pearson checked his watch and noticed the time edging towards nine o'clock and wondered if Ambrose and Bentley had reached the car park yet. He was keen to get *'eyes on'* the group, knowing it would increase their likelihood of intercepting something valuable today. Time to check in with Ambrose.

"Yes Pearson?" asked Ambrose.

"Just checking in to confirm your whereabouts, as the campervan is stationary in the car park."

"We're just going through a place called Hathersage, stuck behind a lorry, so it's taking longer than expected."

"Around fifteen more minutes until you reach the car park?"

"If there are no further traffic problems."

"Okay, let me know once you get *'eyes on'* our target."

"This isn't a military manoeuvre Pearson, knock it off!" Ambrose said.

The line went dead as Ambrose finished the call. Pearson went in search of Mr Coulson to update him. He found him in the library, engrossed in a phone conversation, forcing him to wait until he had finished.

"Yes Pearson?" asked Coulson.

"Just reporting in boss, Ambrose and Bentley aren't there yet. Traffic has held them up."

"I told her to get there before nine," he said, looking at his watch. "We're always behind the game."

"I've told her to call once she has a visual on the group."

"Yes, and keep me updated."

"Will do."

Pearson wandered off to the office and checked the social media accounts for the group. For several days, there was a noticeable lack of activity online. The four individuals had made zero postings. They must know they were being tracked. He busied himself with some other tasks, waiting for Ambrose to call and provide an update. The situation felt like a pressure cooker ready to explode. He was desperate for the phone to ring. Getting up for another cup of coffee, he jumped as his phone buzzed an hour after he had spoken to Ambrose earlier.

"Ambrose, have you found them?" he asked.

"They aren't here, Pearson! We've checked the pub, the car park and surrounding areas, but nothing."

"You've missed them, Ambrose. They must have headed off somewhere. Did you check with the landlord of the pub?"

"Of course I did. He recognised them and said they finished breakfast about half an hour before we got there. We've found all the vehicles parked in the car park."

"Are there many places they could have gone, Ambrose?"

"Pearson, they could be anywhere. There are shit loads of hills.

PARADOX OF THE THIEF

Ask Mr Coulson what he suggests we do?"

"Wait near the campervan. They may return. I'll ask him and let you know."

They ended the call, and Pearson went looking for Coulson, finding him still in the library.

"Ambrose got there too late and hasn't seen them yet. What should they do?" Pearson asked.

"They have to find the group and I don't care how they achieve it. Remind her we discussed one of them has a drone, so it's likely they'll use it. She has the binoculars, so tell her to use them," Coulson said.

"Of course, boss, I'd forgotten. It's illegal to use drones without permission. There can't be many about. I'll call her now."

Pearson hurried back to the office, picking up the phone to dial Ambrose, but it went straight to voicemail. He tried several more times and then remembered the satellite phone, using that instead.

"Pearson, what're we doing?"

"Mr Coulson said you discussed one of them having a drone. Look for it in the sky."

"Ah yes, I remember, of course. Leave it with us. I'll keep you posted," Ambrose said.

Pearson went back to tapping away on his laptop, concerned about finding the group. He pictured them digging up treasure right at this moment. Mr Coulson didn't like failure.

Chapter 24

DERWENT EDGE, PEAK DISTRICT

SATURDAY

R EED RALLIED THE TROOPS. He wanted to leave before nine o'clock with all their gear packed in backpacks and rucksacks. The puddles in the car park, caused by the previous night's rain, had almost evaporated with the breaking sun increasing the ground temperature. The group was halfway up the path leading to the Coach and Horses rock on Derwent Edge, and the sun's rays were already painting the landscape with warmth. A gentle breeze carried the distant chirping of birds. As they continued their ascent, the heat of the sun embraced their skin, reminding them of the beautiful day unfolding before their eyes. As Reed glanced back, he observed the sun climbing in the distance and noticed Onni struggling to keep up. Emily had dropped back to encourage him. Euan and Lynsey were behind him chatting about lightning and drones, impervious to everything going on around them. He stopped for a refreshment break, enabling Onni to catch up.

"How're you doing, Onni?" asked Reed.

"I'm struggling a bit, Reed. I'm not used to these hills. Back in Finland, I skied regularly, but I've only been trekking on foot occasionally since relocating to England. It's glorious. I'll go walking more," Onni responded.

"The journey back's less challenging. It's all downhill, making it easier for you. The other two locations are more accessible. Euan, you lead the rest of the way, mate," said Reed.

"Okay, will do."

They set off again, climbing upwards and before long they had reached the ridge. The group came to a halt, immersing themselves in the awe-inspiring sight of Ladybower Reservoir. Reed's eyes scanned the skyline, catching sight of a handful of climbers on the far-off edge. The gentle breeze carried the distant murmur of their voices. Even seeing the Coach and Horses rock formation in front of them, they still couldn't decide whether it looked like a cluster or an individual rock. Over thousands of years, the rocks underwent weathering, resulting in distinct rounded layers. The sight of these rocks appeared impressive. They concluded to include it and compare it to the map before moving along the ridge to the Salt Cellar. They walked away from the ridge, about a hundred yards over the moor, away from the main walking route. Euan unpacked the drone, started it, and sent it straight up. Reed retrieved the map from the hidden pocket of his backpack, ready to compare against the remote control screen. As Euan positioned the drone above the rock, they all crowded around the screen, trying to see if this matched.

"The rock's too close to the edge compared to the map," Reed observed, noting a lack of trees, too.

Emily's voice held a hint of annoyance as she exclaimed, "Just what I was thinking! This isn't the right place."

"All in agreement?" asked Reed.

Everyone agreed, so Euan brought the drone down and packed it away. With their backpacks on, they headed back to the ridge, making their way along to the Salt Cellar. It became hard going with lots of rocks to manoeuvre around and loose scree underfoot. Reed stopped on occasions to wait for the others to catch up, also taking time to check behind them. He had concerns which he hadn't voiced to the others. The possibility of the two goons following them here added an extra layer of tension to their already exciting journey.

He set aside that thought and continued with their journey to the second rock. Despite being weathered the same, the Salt Cellar boulder was less impressive than its predecessor. After reaching their destination, they stumbled upon a track diverging from the ridge, granting them seclusion from onlookers. Euan's drone ascended into the air again, its propellers creating a gentle hum as it hovered over the rock. Checking the view against the map, they concluded this wasn't a match either.

"Two down, two to go. I suggest we head back to the vehicles, take mine and Euan's. We'll drive down to Millstone Edge and Mother Cap. The car park's much closer to the boulder." Reed said.

"That's an excellent plan," Euan remarked.

They retraced their steps back to the ridge and continued along the main pathway, enjoying the panoramas of Win Hill above Ladybower Reservoir. Onni was too busy enjoying the views and tripped on a half hidden rock, falling to his knees, banging them both and scuffing his hand. After several minutes of cleaning himself up and ensuring nothing hurt, they continued on their way. Another half hour later, they reached the midpoint of the track down to the bottom, pausing for a quick refreshment break.

<hr />

Ambrose had spotted the drone an hour earlier whilst surveying the surroundings with the binoculars. She confirmed it as a drone and not a bird of prey. Ambrose and Bentley headed up the hill towards the area she had spotted it, stopping every few minutes to check for people coming down towards them. She felt cautious, not wanting to cross paths with the group and risk exposing themselves.

They stopped again. Bentley took his turn on the binoculars, scanning the hillside path and ridge. Reed's face appeared around a corner, causing him to signal to Ambrose to take cover. The group appeared at least a hundred yards away but coming towards them. He passed the binoculars to Ambrose so she could double check. She confirmed Bentley's statement.

"They've stopped Bentley. That gives us a chance to hide somewhere and follow them."

"Let's give that side path we passed earlier a try," Bentley suggested. "It leads to a rocky area."

They hustled back to the side path, heading to the rocks, and slipping into the shadows, maintaining a clear view of the main path. They waited in silence, watching for the group to appear. A few minutes later they came past, chatting away, unaware they were being watched. Ambrose felt relieved they had located them, but felt unsure whether they had found anything. She followed for now, keeping them in sight to see what their next activity was.

They tracked the group back to the car park, so she sent Bentley to the pub with the binoculars to observe whilst she sat on a bench, head down. Soon, two of the vehicles departed from the car park, heading towards the reservoir instead of Sheffield. She beckoned Bentley to come over to her car, handing him the keys and told him to follow them. Time to call in with an update.

"We've found them, Pearson. We spotted the drone and tracked them down. They've now left the car park and travelled further into the Peak District. I'm assuming they've found nothing, otherwise they'd have probably gone home," Ambrose said.

"Superb Ambrose, let me check the tracking app for the campervan's position. Oh, that's strange, it's showing as still at the car park."

"Well, I can assure you it's left. We're following them now."

"Hang on, let me refresh it. Nope, still showing as at the car park."

"Maybe they found the tracker?" asked Ambrose.

"Oh hang on, it's moving now. Seems we've got a slight delay."

"I hope this won't be an issue, Pearson."

"It shouldn't be, but we'll keep that in mind and adjust our plans if necessary. I'll let Mr Coulson know. Give me a shout when you've stopped."

"Okay will do," said Ambrose.

Pearson wandered off to give Mr Coulson the news, hopeful of a successful conclusion to the operation.

Chapter 25

MILLSTONE EDGE, PEAK DISTRICT

SATURDAY

E UAN PARKED HIS CAR next to Reed's campervan in the Surprise View car park, fortunate to get a space, as it appeared very busy. As he picked up his backpack from the boot, he noticed a grey Peak District Rangers vehicle near the entrance to the car park. He sidled over to Reed, pointing out the vehicle.

"We won't be able to use the drone without drawing attention to ourselves," Euan said.

"Oh shite. Maybe we should return later and explore Baslow instead?" Reed suggested.

"I think I can climb Mother Cap without too much trouble. It's pretty high, but should give me a sign of whether this area is right. If not, then on to Baslow Moor."

"Okay, Euan, use your harness and let's rope you up, just in case."

Euan checked the others had their bags and led the way up the path, through the rocky section. Clusters of birch trees lined the path, backed by layers of ferns around their trunks. As he scrambled up the granite rocks, he remembered Onni wasn't used to this terrain so paused for a few minutes to allow the others time to catch up. Once over the hard part, they pushed on to reach Mother Cap. This massive boulder resembled its name, with a distinct top section that looked like a cap. It looked about fifteen feet high and seemed easy enough to climb, thought Euan.

"I'm climbing the rock instead of using the drone," Euan said to the other members of the group.

"You also noticed the ranger's vehicle," Emily said.

"Yes, can you secure the rope around the rock if I throw it over Reed?"

"Yes, mate, chuck it over," Reed said.

They secured the rope, clipping Euan onto the rope with a belay device attached to his harness using a carabiner. He climbed the lowest edge, pausing, looking both ways, visualising the map in his mind. Not happy with what he saw, he climbed to the next level, repeating the process. After scrambling up the remaining section to complete the climb, he enjoyed a perfect view in both directions from the cap. Turning around so he didn't slip on the weathered rocks, Euan could see Padley Gorge in the distance. The views were sublime in the sunshine. He opened the channel on the two-way radio to Reed.

"This almost matches the map, although the tree area to the east appears flat and I can't spot anything suggesting there's a cave there."

"Does the distance between Millstone Edge, Mother Cap and the trees match the map?" asked Reed.

"I believe it does, mate, although I'm not sure anything resembles a cave looking from up here."

"What do you suggest?"

"It'd be an idea for us to walk through the trees together and see if anything catches our attention."

"Okay Euan, let's do that. Come down and we'll get going."

Euan made his way down, struggling a bit because he forgot to wear his climbing shoes. Part way down, his foot slipped on a patch of moss. He swung inwards, clattering against the rock. The girls below let out audible gasps, their concern clear. He finished the descent with no further mishap.

"Are you okay, Euan?" asked Lynsey, concern etched on her face. Then she looked at him, puzzled.

"Yes, fine thanks. That's pretty normal for climbing. I forgot to wear my rock climbing shoes. Their grip is better. You look puzzled, Lynsey?"

"You've got a lump of moss in your right ear, Euan."

"Oh," he said, pulling it out, feeling somewhat annoyed with himself for being such an idiot with Lynsey watching him.

"Euan, do you want to share your plan?" Reed asked.

"While the edge, rock, and trees are laid out similar to the map, my concern is the apparent lack of caves within the trees. I suggest we walk through the trees, maintaining a reasonable distance between us in a straight line. This'll allow us to cover the terrain effectively, increasing our chances of finding any caves."

The group donned their backpacks and moved towards the wooded area. Euan took the centre point, Emily and Reed to his left, with Onni and Lynsey to his right. They needed another radio, but Reed was excellent at whistling, so Lynsey and Euan had the radios. They made inroads into the trees, picking their way between rocks and boulders. Euan had seen nothing resembling a cave until he heard Reed whistle. He looked up, watching him beckoning them over. He radioed Lynsey to meet with Reed.

"What about this?" Reed asked, his finger pointing to a three-foot opening between some rocks. Euan fished out his head torch and shone it in the opening, which appeared large enough for one person to fit through. They mulled over what to do and decided Euan would go inside. He secured his harness, changed his shoes this time, while Reed tied the rope to a nearby tree. Lowering himself, Euan's feet met the ground six feet down, able to stand with just the top of his head visible. He knelt, using his head torch to survey the inside of the opening. The air felt heavy with a dank and musty odour. Clusters of moss clung to the walls, creating a damp and earthy atmosphere. Pressing the radio button, he said, "It's small. It doesn't open out at all. I can't see anything interesting. Can you pass me the metal detector?"

Onni reached for the handheld metal detector, passing it through the opening to Euan, showing him which button to press. They listened to the beeping sound as Euan scanned the inside of the opening. Neither the tone nor frequency changed. Onni shook his head and used the radio.

"There's nothing inside. The device will detect down to sixteen inches unless it's buried deeper?" Onni asked.

"I can't see any sign of previous digging," Euan said, scanning the floor with his head torch.

"Any movement in the rocks, Euan?"

"Doesn't appear to be. Let's leave this and try Baslow next. We can always come back later."

Euan climbed out of the opening, assisted by Reed. Disappointed, they packed up their gear and descended to the vehicles in silence. Once there, they agreed to drive to Nether End car park and grab a sandwich from the snack shop before heading up to Baslow Edge.

<hr />

When Bentley arrived at the car park, the only available space was next to Reed's campervan at the far end. They had lost track of the vehicles through Hathersage because of heavy traffic and arrived five minutes later. Ambrose instructed him to pull on to the side of the road instead, concerned they would get spotted. She passed him the binoculars and told him to search for the group whilst she waited for a parking space away from the campervan. He picked a position hidden behind a large rock to the side of the car park, scanning the horizon for a drone. No sign of a drone. Only birds.

"Ambrose, I can't see a drone. What next?" he asked.

"They can't have gone far. We only arrived a few minutes behind them. Check over the road first at that large rock. If you climb up, you might see them. If not, climb the hill behind the car park. I'll wait here and catch you up, text me your position. Have you got a signal?"

"Yes, I have. Okay will do."

Bentley crossed the road and walked towards the cluster of large rocks, scrutinising every person ahead of him. He pulled down his cap, putting sunglasses on, hoping if he ran into the group, they wouldn't recognise him. People were climbing a large rock, so Bentley followed suit to get a better vantage point. He surveyed the landscape with the binoculars; thinking about how picturesque it looked. He swivelled round in all directions, checking for signs of a drone. Still nothing. He checked the larger groups of people but couldn't see anyone resembling the group he looked for. One group of five were hovering around the head of Padley Gorge, but they were older. Time to return to the car park and climb up the hill.

Ambrose sat in the car outside the car park as he passed, so he updated her. He followed the main path upwards, ensuring he checked all people ahead of him. Just as he moved into an open area with a massive boulder, he spotted someone dropping from the top of the boulder with a rope attached. Dashing behind the nearest rock, he watched from a distance and confirmed it was the group they were looking for. He fired out a quick text to Ambrose to advise her. He watched from his hiding place as they moved off to the east and then spread out, searching the ground.

When the group united, he climbed further up the hill to improve his perspective on the situation by utilising the binoculars. He sent Ambrose another text, taking some photos as she instructed, zooming in to get more detail on what the group was doing. The group packed up and walked away towards the car park. He waited until they disappeared out of sight before scrambling to where they were. Bentley popped his head inside the opening, using his phone torch to provide some light. There were zero signs of digging or the movement of rocks, but he quickly snapped some more photos. Another idea came to him. He opened Google Maps on his phone and pinned the location. Just in case his uncle wanted to investigate this further. His phoned pinged.

Ambrose: *'They are leaving the car park. Get back here quick.'*
Bentley: *'I'll be there soon. They were inside an opening about six feet deep, got photos.'*

He hurried back to the car, sharing the photos with Ambrose. She called Pearson with an update before enquiring on the campervan's location, as they had lost them.

Chapter 26

BASLOW MOOR, PEAK DISTRICT

SATURDAY

REED MUNCHED HIS WAY through a tuna mayo sandwich, leading the group up Bar Road towards Baslow Edge. He pulled the cucumber slices out of his sandwich and dumped them in a bin. Reed disliked cucumber with a vengeance. Why did prepacked tuna sandwiches always come with cucumber? he thought. The climb was steep, so being mindful of Onni's lack of fitness and Emily's desire to take it easy, he set a comfortable pace. The tarmac road soon changed to a dirt track and then, once through the gate, it became more rugged. Gorse bushes and large rocks lined the side of the track as they climbed. Reed spotted Eagle Rock as the track levelled out on the moor with a flurry of purple flowered heather. They huddled together around the massive boulder, their eyes surveying the rock, its surface marked with many grooves from centuries of nature's bombardment.

"This is it. We should wait for walkers to pass before using the drone," Reed said.

"Yes, I'll get it ready here on the grass and then whip it straight up once we have a window," Euan responded.

They waited twenty minutes for the opportunity to use the drone, at which point Euan sent it up, ascending in to the sky. The group huddled around the screen again to check the layout of the land compared to the map. Positive noises came from each member of the group. "No question about it. It's a certain match," said Reed.

Euan manoeuvred the drone over the trees on a steep slope. It gave some optimism for finding a cave. It wasn't possible to see anything beneath the canopy of green, so Euan brought the drone down the hill in the direction they had arrived. Reed spotted a path leading into the trees on the drone screen.

"We should investigate the path that goes into the woods. Can you take the drone over the path?" Reed asked Euan.

"Nah mate, it'd end up smashing into a tree, its difficult to manoeuvre around branches."

"That's fair enough, so let's walk the lower path instead."

Reed split them into two groups with a radio each, with him and Onni up top, whilst the others followed the lower path. Reed walked along the top of the wooded area with Onni, keeping pace with the team on the bottom path. He paused, his body tense, his eyes scanning the area, vigilant for any sign of the two goons. The team on the lower path had walked further along. Reed lost sight of them through the riot of rocks and greenery. The radio squawked.

"Reed, are you there? We can't see you," Emily said.

"I've lost you Emily, let me move closer to the rock edge and jump up and down."

"Ah, got you, we're further along."

"Okay, I'm now moving that way. Have you found anything resembling a cave?"

"Nothing clear just yet."

"Let's carry on. There are some larger rocky sections further on," Reed said.

"Yes, I see. Wait until we get level with them."

Reed hurried along the top of the rocky ledge, with Onni following him. As he gazed down at the sheer rock face, he couldn't help but feel this appeared promising.

"Reed, we think there might be something below you," said Emily.

"I was thinking the same thing, Em."

"There's an opening going underneath the enormous rock face you're standing above."

"Can you climb up to it?" asked Reed.

"Euan thinks it's too steep, and it'd be easier coming over the top. Anchoring the rope to a couple of trees should be secure enough."

"Okay, yes, come back up to me. I'll stay in this spot where we'll climb down the rock face."

Reed, surrounded by the serene beauty of nature, conveyed the plan to Onni. As he arranged his climbing gear, the sound of rustling leaves filled the air. He took a moment to survey the breathtaking drop, feeling a rush of excitement. He secured the main rope around two sturdy trees. Soon the other group arrived and Euan put his harness, climbing shoes and safety helmet on. With smiles on their faces, the boys locked eyes, knowing full well what would unfold.

"Harness tight?"

"Check."

"Rope secure?"

"Check."

"Head torch on?"

"Check."

"Radio active?"

Silence.

"Em, you have the other radio. You're supposed to say check," Reed said.

"Oh sorry, I didn't realise. Say it again," she replied.

"Radio ready?"

"Check."

The boys fist bumped each other with a firework effect flourish afterwards. The other three laughed and gave them some applause with a whistle from Lynsey.

"Thanks," Euan said, winking at Lynsey and garnering a smile from her.

"I'll go over first Euan. See you ground side."

117

They watched Reed go over the edge, anticipation growing inside them.

"Impressive performance Euan," Lynsey said, warming to Euan's playful side of his personality.

"Aw, thanks. We like to entertain our fans," he said, smirking. The radio squawked again.

"I'm down Em, let Euan know. There appears to be a cave. The opening seems big enough to squeeze through," said Reed.

"Okay, we'll keep a lookout up here, making sure no-one gets too interested in what we're doing."

Ambrose held the binoculars steady as she surveyed the group, noticing Reed dropping out of sight. It was easy tracking the group from Nether End car park. They had just crossed the main road when she and Bentley arrived. It was a straightforward task following them a hundred yards behind, keeping out of sight but ensuring the group was always in view. Ambrose selected the higher route along Baslow Edge upon reaching the moor, to provide some distance between them and the group as they waited at Eagle Rock. After watching the drone, they were almost spotted as some of the group headed towards them. Once the group had reformed, Ambrose and Bentley took up a viewpoint near Eagle Rock. Close enough, but it gave them some suitable cover.

"They've discovered something, Bentley. Reed has just climbed down off the rock edge."

"About time. I was hoping for some proper action today."

"You always want to fight!"

"What's wrong with that?" Bentley said.

"Nothing I suppose. The ginger one has also gone off the rock edge. There must be something down there."

PARADOX OF THE THIEF

"Lets hope so."

Emily settled herself farther from the towering trees, basking in the gentle touch of the sun's warm rays. She closed her eyes, allowing the sights of nature to fade away. She listened to the distant chirping of birds and inhaled the earthy scent of the woods. With each passing moment, she felt the tension in her body loosen, her muscles relaxing under the soothing ambiance of the serene setting. She heard Lynsey tapping away on her phone and Onni talking to the boys over the radio, so she zoned out. Her thoughts turned to the map and wondered if it could be associated with Robin Hood? Would the boys discover any hidden treasures as they ventured deeper into the cave? A glint of something near Eagle Rock caught her eye, interrupting her thoughts. She couldn't see anything. Then it happened again. The sunlight seemed to bounce off a polished surface, resembling metal or glass.

Chapter 27

BASLOW MOOR, PEAK DISTRICT

SATURDAY

O NNI'S HAND CLENCHED THE radio, his knuckles turning white, as he crawled to the top of the rocky edge. Reed encouraged him to descend and look in the cave with them as the metal detector had beeped louder. Neither Euan nor Reed was sure of what they were doing and required Onni's expert help. As Onni looked over the edge, his fear of heights kicked in. He felt sick in the pit of his stomach. It looked a sheer drop of around twenty feet, like standing on top of a two-storey building with a flat roof. Very scary. Reed beckoned to him, but his eyes glazed over and his brain became clouded with fear. The rocks were slippery and covered in moss, making him worry about how he could manage the climb.

"Onni, I'm coming up," said Reed over the radio.

"Okay."

Onni watched Reed ascend the rock, using cracks in the sheer cliff face to get hand and footholds. Before long, reed stood next to Onni, telling him to relax. As Reed rummaged through Euan's backpack, Lynsey came over, having spotted Onni on all fours, asking, "What's going on?"

"Onni needs to come into the cave with us. The metal detector is beeping, but we don't know what we're doing and need him to help."

"Onni, do you think you'll be able to handle that?" asked Lynsey.

"I'll try, but it's very scary for me."

"You can only do your best, but imagine the secrets inside the cave."

"Yes, I want to go."

As Onni stood up, Reed began fitting Euan's spare harness on to his body, feeling the tightness of each strap. Reed briefed him on how to descend and asked him to repeat the instructions. Onni passed the radio to Emily. They walked to the edge. Reed clipped Onni onto the rope with the belay device, whilst Euan waited at the bottom. Onni approached the edge, avoiding looking down and keeping his focus on the rugged rock face. He moved one foot down six inches, then the other six inches whilst gripping the rope with his hands. Sweat poured off his brow, stinging his eyes as it dripped into them. He edged his way lower, encouraged by Reed, Emily and Lynsey at the top and Euan below him.

Half way down, his foot slipped, and he swung in towards the rock face. Panicking, he put out a hand to hold himself steady against the rock. He gripped the rope with only one hand, causing it to feed out fast, his body descending with a sense of urgency. With a sudden jolt, he found himself in a crouched position, his hands aching from holding the rope. The smell of dust and rope fibres filled the air, a reminder of the intense effort exerted. His foot, the only thing keeping him from plummeting, strained to maintain its grip, pressure and tension coursing through his leg.

"Don't panic Onni, stay clam" Euan said.

"You're fine, just relax for a minute," Reed said from above.

He held his position, then followed Euan's instructions on how to straighten out and continue downwards. Euan coaxed him to the ground. He felt an enormous sense of relief to put his feet on solid ground. Before he knew it, Reed stood beside him, having shimmied down at a rate of knots.

As Onni squeezed into the cave, he smelt damp with a faint whiff of charcoal. Their head torches cast a bright, piercing light, cutting through the darkness, revealing the space before them. It stretched back about thirty feet, curving towards the rear, creating a sense of depth and intrigue. As they ventured further in, a tingling sensation of anticipation crept up their spines. Reed's finger extended toward the distant rock, drawing Onni's attention to a small yet distinct object etched into the stone at the rear of the cave. As he drew nearer, a feather came into view, its markings tangible against the rough rock.

"Oh, wow!" Onni said.

"It's the right place. The symbol matches the one on the map."

"Especially as the metal detector is beeping, there must be treasure here."

"That's what we thought."

Onni grabbed the metal detector and scanned the cave, waiting for the beeping to increase and the red light to flash. There, nestled in the shadows, a disorganised heap of small rocks attracted his attention. The anticipation urged him closer to explore the mysterious pile. Between the three of them, they eased the rocks, one at a time, until the ground became visible. Nothing there. The ground felt solid with no signs of disturbance, but the metal detector beeped louder, although still not at full volume. Onni reached for his tools Reed had brought down, he began digging in the area with his pickaxe. After seven inches of digging, he stopped to recheck the metal detector; the sound increasing in volume, with the red light flashing faster with every turn. After he had dug down over a foot, his pick axe hit something hard, exclaiming, "I've found something."

"What is it?" asked Reed.

"The pickaxe hit something hard. I need to excavate around it first before we go any deeper."

"Shit me Onni, this is exciting," said Euan.

Onni's trembling hands prompted them to pause and gather their composure. They took a moment, savouring a sip of water to ease the palpable tension. Onni widened the hole he dug with his trowel, piling up the earth to the side. Reed radioed an update to the girls as Onni and Euan scraped more earth away. A glimmer of gold appeared in the hole, causing all three lads to gasp in astonishment. Onni beavered away with his softer tools, brushing away earth from the gold, uncovering more of the artefact that lay in the ground. After several minutes, they uncovered it so Onni could lift the artefact from the hole.

Under the glare of their head torches, they marvelled at the intricate details of the gold crucifix in Onni's hands. The object measured around ten inches from the top to the bottom and was about six inches wide. It's captivating appearance enhanced by a circular shape at its centre with an encrusted emerald, that caught the eye. Speechless, all three gazed upon the crucifix until the crackle of the radio disturbed their thoughts.

"Any news lads?" asked Emily.

"We've found a gold crucifix with an emerald," said Reed.

"Oh wow, that's amazing. We can't wait to see it."

"We'll be up top soon."

Onni finished cleaning up the crucifix as best he could, passing it to Reed to put in his harness pocket when he spotted Euan filling the hole in.

"Stop Euan," he exclaimed. "Before we fill the hole, it's important to check there isn't anything else there."

"Oh sorry Onni, I didn't think."

After Euan had cleared the hole, Onni grabbed the metal detector and checked again. The metal detector emitted loud beeps and the red light flashed. Their eyes met, exchanging glances of anticipation.

Onni, his hands covered in dirt, used his trowel to excavate deeper as the earth released an aroma of dampness. Once again, he struck a hard object and, with careful work using the brush, he unearthed a silver item, extracting it from the hole. Another silver fereter.

"This could be another map."

"Let's open it and see."

"Why don't we wait until we get in a clean environment, so if there is another map, the damp atmosphere can't taint it," Onni suggested.

"You're right, Onni," said Reed.

Euan put the fereter in his harness whilst Onni checked the hole again. This time, the metal detector didn't react. They filled the hole, compacting the soil as tightly as possible, then piled the rocks back onto the ground, making it look as though it had been there for several hundred years.

Onni needed to ascend the rocks, which, with his confidence boosted from discovering the treasure, he felt much happier about. He started the climb beside Reed, his friend offering him detailed guidance on where to put each limb. After exerting some effort and encountering no mishaps, the lads reached the summit of the sheer rock face.

<hr />

Emily held the crucifix as she stared at it in awe, admiring the emerald. They all exuded compliments about the crucifix, wondering how old it could be? Who it belonged to? How much it might be worth?

"It's incredible, Reed. I can't believe we've found something so beautiful. It's heavy. Well done all of you, especially you Onni, for your efforts climbing when you were so scared," said Emily.

"Thanks, Emily."

Emily turned over the crucifix, inspecting the rear of the artefact.

She brushed some dirt away and felt some indentations beneath her fingers. As she wiped away the remaining earth from the surface, her eyes strained to decipher the faint word - *Tooke*. The letters, though fragmented in places, showed with a surprising clarity, like ancient relics emerging from the depths of time.

"Hey, everyone, check out the word on the back!"

She pointed it out to the others, and Onni responded first. "That's the archaic spelling for Tuck. I think this crucifix belonged to the Friar," he said.

Emily imagined the echoes of monks chanting their prayers with the flickering candlelight casting eerie shadows on the walls of their place of worship. Shaking those thoughts aside, she passed the crucifix to Reed for safekeeping. A wave of euphoria washed over the group, their collective excitement crackling. The air buzzed with energy, as wide smiles plastered across their faces. It felt like the moment surpassed their wildest dreams, leaving them breathless with joy.

"Reed, it's that blonde woman coming towards us," Emily gasped.

A wave of panic washed over the group, their eyes widening as their hearts pounded in their chests.

Ambrose approached the group and spoke to Reed.

"Looks like we meet again."

"How'd you find us?" he asked.

"That's irrelevant. You look as though you've been busy today searching for treasure and got lucky."

"We've found nothing."

"I can see something silver sticking out of his pocket," Ambrose said, pointing her finger at Euan. "is that another fereter?"

"You were spying on us over by Eagle Rock. I noticed the

sun reflecting off something. I bet you were using binoculars," interjected Emily.

"Maybe we were, maybe we weren't. My boss is still interested in the fereter. The offer of ten grand remains on the table."

"Not interested."

"Fair enough," Ambrose said, adjusting her feet into a fighting stance. A thrill of excitement moved through her body like a shiver.

Chapter 28

BASLOW MOOR, PEAK DISTRICT

SATURDAY

A FTER EMILY'S URGENT WARNING, Reed had put the metal crucifix in Lynsey's backpack. He felt relieved the symbol of faith was now hidden. The approaching duo had no idea what he had just done. Reed leaned in and whispered to Lynsey.

"You're the quickest runner, Lynsey. If the situation calls for it, run back to the campervan with Emily. She's got the keys."

"Okay," she whispered.

As Ambrose took up a familiar stance, Reed considered his options. The atmosphere grew tense, with an air of apprehension. The sight of furrowed brows and clenched fists hinted at an impending clash.

"Emily, Lynsey, go now, run," Reed said.

Reed watched the girls hurry away whilst the young lad opposed Euan. Onni stood there surprised by the sudden turn of events and Reed cajoled him to join in.

"We're going to need your help here, Onni," he said.

"I'm right behind you, Reed."

Ambrose made a swift leg sweep move towards Reed, attempting to take him down, but he spotted it and avoided it with her boot just clipping his shin. As her weight had shifted to her rear leg, he responded with an elbow throw-by at her shoulder, connecting and pushing her backwards. Reed stood his ground whilst Ambrose moved forward with a punch towards his face, followed by a kick to his hip. He recognised the moves and realised Ambrose was skilled in kickboxing. The punch had been a red herring, and the kick connected, causing him to stagger backwards. Onni jumped in with a punch towards Ambrose's shoulder, but he moved too slow as Reed watched her grab his wrist, twisting him to the floor and he banged his head on the ground. He looked over at Euan, who had blood running from his nose. The young lad was dominating Euan and looked an accomplished boxer. Reed realised he had started off too complacent, expecting an easy victory.

"Looks like we've the upper hand," Ambrose said.

"We're not finished!" Reed replied.

"Ten grand for the fereter. Or we take it for free, after we mess you guys up proper."

"The fereter's ours. We found it."

"It doesn't belong to you, though, does it? It is the landowners' property and has to be recorded with the authorities, otherwise it's worth jack shit to you," Ambrose retorted.

Reed had to listen to Ambrose's constant goading whilst defending his position, glancing over at Euan, struggling. Onni was still reeling from the force of the impact when he hit the ground a few moments ago, struggling to regain his balance. Reed's mind swirled, unsure of what course of action to take. He need to remove Ambrose from the equation and help Euan, otherwise Bentley would take the fereter off him. The key principle of Jeet Kune Do *"Using no way as way; having no limitation as limitation"* sprang into his mind. Time for some serious moves, so he pulled out his favourite one: a single leg takedown, knowing kickboxers don't enjoy going to the ground. He moved forward to encourage a punch or two, avoiding them, then stepping back, hoping for a kick to come. Sure enough, Ambrose fell into his trap and went for the kick. Reed grabbed her foot, twisting and locking it, causing her to overbalance. She smacked straight into the ground, face first, Reed jumping on her quick as a flash, putting her arm in a lock. Gasping for air, he gripped her arm, his heart pounding in his chest. He fought to focus, taking in the smell of his exertions and the sounds of his ragged breath. He regained his composure, feeling a sense of control return as his breathing steadied.

"Now, who has the advantage?" Reed taunted, a sly smile playing on his lips.

Just a grunt from Ambrose as Reed observed Onni rising from the floor. He felt they were now in control. Then bang! With a resounding thud, he tumbled off Ambrose, the impact of a hefty punch reverberating through the air. Bentley had delivered the killer blow. He hit the ground and his head spun from the force, feeling a kick to his side, then a blow to his back. His eyes searched for Euan, spotting him laying prone some fifteen feet away. Bentley held the fereter with glee, having grabbed it from Euan's harness pocket. They had lost. The two goons jogged off down the hill, their footsteps echoing against the rocky terrain with the prize gripped in their hands. Reed surveyed the scene before him as the fog in his brain dissipated.

"Euan, you okay mate?"

"Just about Reed."

"We need to warn the girls."

Reed snatched his phone from his pocket and dialled Emily.

"Em, they've beaten us up. We didn't stand a chance. Where are you?"

"Oh Reed, we'll come and meet you guys."

"No, don't do that. They're heading down the hill back towards the car park. You need to leave there now, go to Curbar Gap car park. We'll meet you there," said Reed.

"Okay, on our way now."

Ambrose stopped at a bench part way down the hill, needing time to catch her breath.

"Well done Bentley, you were awesome up there."

"Thanks, the training is paying off, although my trainer won't be happy about the cut knuckles."

"Let's phone your uncle and give him the positive news."

She took a moment to relax and get her breath, then dialled Mr Coulson.

"Ambrose, I'm hoping you have some positive information to share with me."

"Yes, boss. We found them, observed them for a couple of hours whilst they investigated a cave and moved in when it looked like they were celebrating. They found another silver fereter, so I offered them ten grand again. The two girls ran off, so we ended up battling the three lads. Bentley was brilliant. We got hold of the fereter."

"Excellent news Ambrose. What does it look like?" he asked.

"Rectangular with hinges, sealed with wax around the edges, with a simple feather symbol on one side."

"That's superb Ambrose. Well done, both of you. I'm out tonight, but keep it safe and come over to the house tomorrow at lunchtime. I know it's Sunday, but I'll put on a barbeque."

"Thanks boss, I'll tell Bentley," said Ambrose.

"I'll speak to Pearson and let him know," Coulson said, finalising the conversation.

Ambrose and Bentley wandered off down the hill towards the car park, pleased with their efforts for the day.

Chapter 29

CURBAR GAP, PEAK DISTRICT
SATURDAY

E UAN'S NOSE THROBBED, BLOOD trickling down his face, staining his shirt and trousers. The metallic scent of iron lingered in the air, mixing with the musty odour of sweat. His body ached all over as he struggled to walk across the moorland path, avoiding the many rocks and stones. He felt devastated, his heart sinking as he recalled the young lad snatch the silver fereter from his harness pocket. The precious artefact could hold another hidden map, teasing him with its secrets.

The three of them stumbled towards the car park at Curbar Gap, receiving many strange looks from walkers, but none offered any help. Euan watched Reed, his face contorted in pain, hobbling along beside the unsteady Onni. The silence between them was crushing, each aware of their failings in the struggle of losing the fereter. As the trees surrounding the car park came into view, his spirits lifted, remembering the crucifix they secured thanks to Reed's quick thinking.

"We may have lost the fereter, but we have the crucifix," Reed said.

"That's true," Euan replied, his voice tinged with disappointment. He sighed, the weight of his words hanging in the air. Euan's eyes dropped, his gaze filled with regret, as he muttered, "Sorry for losing the fereter."

"Listen mate, you've nothing to be sorry about. We're all in it together and the young lad is an accomplished boxer. He would've taken me out even with my Jeet Kune Do skills."

"Maybe Reed, maybe not."

"They're superior to us with better skills. We must find a different approach to get the silver fereter back."

"I'm on board with that. Not sure if the girls will agree after they see our injuries."

"I'm not sure either, Euan. I'm not used to physical violence like that," Onni said.

"Fair enough Onni."

They reached the road, crossing it and looking for the campervan, spotting it parked on the far side.

———◄O►———

As they trooped over, Reed detected concern on Emily and Lynsey's faces. They were a mess. Blood, bruises and injured limbs, although nothing appeared broken.

"What the hell happened, Reed?" Emily gasped.

"They were better than us," he said, his head bowed.

"You told me you could handle yourself!"

"The young lad's a skilled boxer and knocked down Euan before turning his attention to me as I struggled to restrain the woman I pinned on the ground. They stole the fereter and ran off."

"At least we have the crucifix," interjected Lynsey, pulling it from her backpack.

"True, but the fereter may contain another map," Reed said.

"We need to forget about that. You can't go getting beat up again," Emily said.

"But that's not fair Em, we found it. I want to retrieve it somehow."

"Well, unless by some miracle you gain some boxing skills, Reed, that won't happen. We've no information about who they are, where they live, or anything else."

"Not yet, but I have an idea."

"You can park your ideas for now, as I'm not getting involved in anything else illegal," Emily said doggedly.

"We should save this conversation for another time, when we've reflected on today's events," Euan said.

Nodding in agreement, a hushed silence fell over the group. Reed asked Emily to help clean him up while Lynsey did the same with Euan, washing dirt and blood from their faces and hands. He watched Euan's face with its stupid grin from being close to Lynsey again, expecting him to ask her out, but he appeared to have lost his nerve. He would mention it to him another time. They all relaxed in the camping chairs whilst Emily busied herself tidying up before sharing out some beers from the tiny fridge.

"I want to express my thanks to everyone. Although the day has finished on a disappointing note, we had an amazing time. Friar Tuck's gold crucifix is nothing short of astonishing," said Reed. "I propose we meet again this week to discuss what to do about the crucifix. Does everyone agree?"

The other members of the group responded with murmurs of agreement. As the night drew in, Reed lit some candles as they sipped on their beer. Savouring the cold, refreshing taste from his bottle, his eyes watched Lynsey pass round the ancient crucifix. Everyone gawped in awe and wonder, as the flickering candlelight danced upon the crucifix, casting a mesmerising glow which enveloped the group.

Chapter 30

UNKNOWN CAVE, BASLOW MOOR

G OLDEN LEAVES ADORNED THE *landscape shed from trees in the autumn of 1396AD, decorating the ground with their vibrant tones.*

The fire crackled as the flames danced around the logs, keeping it ablaze for the six people enjoying the warmth. The rocky sides of the cave drew in the heat, which would keep the space warm during the night, helping to ensure the group survived. Their leader had marked the cave as his, etching a feather on the rear wall. Earlier, the archer had taken down a red deer and now one of its legs spluttered as the fat oozed out, roasting over the open fire. The minstrel plucked the strings of his lute, adding tales of honour and valour to the melodic tune he created.

"Time's up."

"For the evil to crumble."

"We shall prevail."

"Against the law."

The friar listened to the minstrel's song, but needed some space for his thoughts. He rose from the floor, stepping outside the cave, gazing at Gardom's Leap across the valley, the moonlight shimmering on the wet rocks. He enjoyed this location. It gave him a sense of serenity, helpful in connecting with his god. The gold crucifix weighed heavily around his neck tonight as they had lost a brother in a skirmish with some of the sheriff's men the previous day. They had taken revenge, though, making sure none of the soldiers returned to Nottingham. His leader called the friar from within the cave as the food was ready. His stomach had been grumbling. He was ready to feast.

"Tooke, the meat is ready."

The friar gave prayers for their fallen brother, and the group of six tucked into the venison. They relished its rich taste and aroma. Green vegetables picked by their leader's companion accompanied the venison. The group of six had formed formidable opposition to the Sheriff. They challenged his laws and stood up for the common people. Most evenings they would go their separate ways, but tonight they joined up at one of their many secret locations, unknown to the authorities. They had a plan, crafted by the ingenuity of their leader, to snatch some of the Sheriff's prized possessions. Patience was the key to the plan unfolding to a successful conclusion.

Chapter 31

Cotgrave, near Nottingham

Sunday

COULSON HAD PREPPED HIS chef to work today, as he was having a barbeque party with his team. Their reward for recovering a silver fereter. As this was the second one, his thoughts considered it may be a treasure trail of such. He hoped it would lead to a stash of treasure, making him even richer. The gate buzzer sounded. He granted access to Ambrose. Soon he would get to see the fereter, hold it and open it, his excitement building. The others had already arrived.

"Come in Ambrose," he said. "Let me look at the fereter, please."

Ambrose pulled the object from her bag and gave it to Coulson.

"This feather symbol's what the elderly professor talked about. Where'd they find it?"

"Not sure, boss. We couldn't see exactly where they went without getting too close and revealing our position. Bentley tried looking on Google maps at the satellite pictures, but it's just a big hill with rocks and trees. They dropped over the edge with harnesses using a rope."

"It's possible there might be a cave there we can explore. It'd be wise to enlist the help of a climbing expert to assist us."

"Neither myself nor Bentley have those skills, but we know where the group was."

"Sure, no problem. I'll find someone and we can meet them later this week. Let's open this fereter. I need to make a quick trip to *The Safe*, won't be long."

Ambrose walked off to join the others on the sunlit patio, where the aroma of sizzling burgers filled the air.

Meanwhile, Coulson ventured into the cloakroom, activating the secret panel to reveal the door. He descended the staircase, the sound of his footsteps echoing around him, until he reached *The Safe*. He donned his gloves and cleaned up the fereter, polishing it and used the correct knife-like tool to break the wax seal. Easing it open, he observed the scroll inside with intense interest. He unfurled the scroll and laid it open on his workbench. The ancient parchment had several distinct markings. Positioned at the top of the scroll was a jagged edge. Just below it, there sat an arch that looked like a cave. A wavy line inside the arch. On the bottom left, a group of squares resembling a cluster of buildings. On the bottom right, a more prominent rectangular shape, completing the intriguing map.

The map evoked a sense of adventure and hinted at some treasure lost deep within the depths of a damp cave. Coulson's knowledge of the Peak District was confined to a handful of pubs, leaving him reliant on Pearson's help to unravel the whereabouts of the location. He rolled the scroll up and took it upstairs with him to join the others outside on the patio.

"Look what's inside the silver fereter," he said, unfurling the scroll.

"Oh wow, that's ancient," Bentley said.

"It is, my boy. We need to decipher this location, Pearson," Coulson said, pointing to the cave like marking with the small wavy line.

"I know what I'll be working on in the next few days," Pearson replied.

"Come here early Tuesday to go through your suggestions. I'll take a photo of the map now as I'll keep it in *The Safe*."

"Yes, boss."

Everyone gathered around the table, looking at the map, amazed at what they stole. The conversation continued around the fereter and map whilst the smell of burgers, sausages and prawns on the barbeque delighted their taste buds. With their plates piled high, they dived into the mouthwatering feast cooked by Coulson's chef. The quality of food rewarded them for their exceptional work yesterday.

After enjoying his food, Coulson wandered off to get out his extra-special aged brandy he kept for these occasions. Eager for what lay ahead after the difficulties of obtaining the map.

Chapter 32

SCREWED SOFTWARE, CENTRAL SHEFFIELD

MONDAY

REED BOUNCED INTO THE office early, eager to see Phil and tell him everything that had happened on Saturday. Yesterday, he'd been thinking about getting the second fereter back. He felt disappointed in himself for underestimating his opponent. This made him more determined to retrieve it. Jeet Kune Do taught both the mental and physical aspects of conflict. On Saturday, he lacked in the mental side. He popped to the coffee machine to get his cappuccino ready to crack on with his day at the office.

Reed had arrived early to make a phone call to his mate Euan, wanting to discuss his idea without Emily listening in. After the caffeine hit, he felt ready and picked up his phone, dialling Euan.

"How're you feeling, mate? How's the nosebleed?" he asked.

"Yeah, not too bad, thanks, the nose is feeling better, pleased it's in one piece."

"I wanted to know your thoughts on our next steps. I think we can discuss the crucifix decision with the rest of the team. Are you free tomorrow evening? I'm pretty keen to get the second fereter. What do you think?"

"Tuesday evening's fine with me. I want to retrieve the fereter too Reed, but as you said on Saturday night, we must approach this situation shrewdly. We need to be prepared because the two goons are stronger than us and I don't fancy becoming smashed avocado again."

"On that Euan, I've had some thoughts. I'm having a chat with my mate Phil today, as he's got contacts in the programming world. His friend is a bit of a hacker, so I'm wondering if we can use him to help us get some information on the goons."

"That sounds like an excellent idea, Reed. I've been thinking about how to enhance the drone. Plus, I've been designing a mini UGV."

"What's an UGV mate?" asked Reed

"An unmanned ground robot which doesn't need to be controlled by a remote if you pre-program it in advance. I can arm it with mini arrow-like bolts and smoke canisters. Listen, I've one job this week, so I can put in some hours developing both them," Euan said.

"Oh mate, sounds amazing."

"It's critical we uncover the identities of the two goons finding the employer of these individuals and locate the fereter," Reed responded.

"I'll leave that one with you. I'll come over tomorrow evening. Does Emily know?"

"Not yet. I wanted to check with you first. Yes, come over. I'll get Emily to speak with Lynsey and Onni. We can start by discussing the crucifix. Once we've addressed that, we can shift our focus towards a fereter recovery plan. Speak later Euan."

Reed made a mental note to call Emily on her lunch break, aware not to send a message, as he felt certain their messages were being monitored. The two goons locating them in the Peak District on Saturday suggested they were being followed, which concerned him.

As soon as Phil stepped foot into the office, Reed motioned for him to come closer. He talked Phil through the action that took place on Saturday. He pulled out the crucifix to show him. The emerald sparkled underneath the office lights in the middle of the gold cross.

"Wow Reed, this is incredible. I can't believe you've found this. The jewel sparkles. It must be worth a fortune. What's the plan for it?"

"I don't know yet Phil. I'm going to discuss with the others tomorrow. It belonged to Friar Tuck," he said, turning over the crucifix to show the inscription etched on the back. "I need your help on something else, mate."

"What's that?" Phil asked.

"These two goons followed us. They must have a way of tracking us, as well as monitoring our messages. This is bothering me. I know you've got a mate who's a bit of a hacker, so I wondered if you could speak to him and see if he can help us understand how they followed us. Second, we need to identify the two goons that confronted us and stole the second fereter."

"Okay, Reed, I'll drop him an email in a minute. Jed knows how to penetrate secure systems. If he shows me, I can then help you."

"That'd be brilliant if you could. I feel disappointed we lost the second fereter because it could contain another map."

"Sounds right, Reed."

"I'm going to the safe deposit box at lunchtime to put the crucifix in there. I don't want them taking that as well. Fancy coming along?"

"Yes, we'll talk about any information Jed has provided by then."

"Let's get to work. Talk to you at lunchtime."

Both Reed and Phil went back to their desks and starting working, beavering away so they could take an extended lunch break.

———— ◄O► ————

Lunch time soon came around. Reed grabbed his phone, calling Emily, suggesting they should meet tomorrow evening, so could she get in touch with Lynsey and Onni to come over to theirs. She said she would.

Reed picked Phil up on his way out of the office, walking through Central Sheffield towards the safe deposit box building, as Phil updated Reed on his email conversation with Jed.

"Jed believes you'll find a tracking device affixed to your campervan. You should check it tonight when you get home. They'll have identified phone numbers of everyone involved, tracking messages and social media activity. You should refrain from posting anything helpful to them. He also suggested there may be listening devices or cameras put inside your homes. It'd be advisable to check your house for any unusual objects. According to Jed, installing a camera in the corner of a photo frame is easy," Phil said.

"We thought they might track our messages and social media, so've stopped posting anything related to the map or fereter. I didn't think anyone would track my campervan, but that would explain why they appeared from nowhere. It felt like they'd been observing our every move throughout the day and waited for when we discovered the crucifix. Fortunately, they didn't see that. Having seen how they attacked us Saturday, I guess they could've also broken into our house and placed a surveillance device. They know where we live."

"You better do some thorough checking tonight, mate."

"I will," replied Reed.

"To trace the two goons, Jed needs information to begin the search, like a photo or mobile number or car registration."

"I don't have any of those, but Euan spotted their car at The Peaks University on Tuesday last week around eleven because he phoned me. Do you think they'll have security cameras there?"

"I'd think so. Can you describe the car? Then maybe Jed can hack into the CCTV system."

"Let me call Euan and see what he remembers," Reed said, pulling out his phone, calling Euan, and explained what they were trying to do. "Euan said they left about a minute after him. He has a blue Ford

Focus, reg YY18 EEU. He said their car was a black Audi A3, four doors, hatchback and low-profile tyres. Is that description enough?"

"I'll send it over to Jed and see what he can find."

They reached the safe deposit box building, where Reed placed the crucifix inside his box alongside the map. They wandered back to the Screwed Software office, picking up BLT sandwiches on the way before returning to their individual workstations.

<hr />

Later that afternoon, Phil called Reed over to his workstation.

"Jed has come up trumps, mate," he said, pointing at a photo on his screen. "Is that the woman?"

"That's amazing, Phil, it is. How did he find her?"

"He said the security in the university's systems was weak. Once he breached the firewall, he cracked the password for the CCTV system and found the car leaving when you said, just after Euan's. He located the vehicle's owner, Maria Ambrose, which was a simple task. Told you he's superb at this stuff."

"That's brilliant. We need loads more information, though. Who's the young lad? Who do they work for? Where's the fereter? Do you think he would be prepared to help us?"

"I'll put it to him and see what he says, Reed."

Chapter 33

COTGRAVE, NEAR NOTTINGHAM
TUESDAY

PEARSON HAD ARRIVED EARLY, as instructed by Mr Coulson. He sat in the office, reviewing the information he'd found out about the map. It took him all day Monday to research Robin Hood caves in the Peak District and surrounding areas, coming up with a list of ten locations. Unfortunately, he didn't possess enough knowledge about the Peak District and only had one suitable match with the map. Mr Coulson had retrieved the map earlier and placed it on the table. Pearson passed a copy of his notes to Mr Coulson, who took several moments to read them.

"There are too many locations for us to check every single one, Pearson. Can't you narrow it down any further?" Coulson asked.

"I don't have enough knowledge of the rural areas. We could do with some help from somebody who does," Pearson replied.

"Maybe. Let's go over the places you consider most likely."

"The first one's quite an obvious one. It's a place called Robin Hood's Cave on Stanage Edge. It seems to fit with the map, but I don't know what the large rectangular marking is. The smaller squares could be the town Hathersage."

"Isn't that place well-known? Is it likely to have any artefacts remaining in the cave?" Coulson asked.

"Yes, unlikely. I examined the remaining rocky edges in the Peak District, but none seemed to have caves that were immediately apparent. There are plenty of caves in the Peak District, although none quite match the location on the map."

"What about this one, Pearson, Reynard's Cave?"

"It's in rugged terrain. The entrance is high up the slope of a valley in Dovedale. There's a river in the valley, but no appropriate markings on the map, making me question its validity."

"I understand your thoughts. There isn't any sign of a large river on the map. We should discount that one. What about this one, Thor's cave?"

"Similar reasons. It's close to a large river, but no marks for a river on the map."

"What about the Robin Hood tree? Any caves near there?"

"It's known as the *Major Oak,* but I can't see any caves near it. There isn't a tree symbol on the map, which makes it unlikely, even though it's a prominent location for Robin Hood. It's become synonymous with the legend's presence, but I discounted that as well."

Coulson fired question after question at Pearson. "I know a pub called *'Robin Hood Inn'.* Are there any caves near that?"

"There might be an unknown cave. I came up empty-handed on my exhaustive search on Google. Where they found the second fereter on Saturday has no known caves in that area either. Perhaps we need to search for undiscovered caves."

"Yes, that'd make more sense, Pearson. I'd be astounded if any buried artefacts remained inside of mapped caves. We need to inspect the cave where they discovered the second fereter before deciding on which locations to check next."

"How do we go about checking these locations, boss? Are you sending Ambrose and Bentley?" Pearson asked.

"Yes, they also need a person who has climbing skills to accompany them. I know someone suitable, but need to check her availability. I'll set up a meeting for Thursday evening, as I want Garcia to join us and study the fereter. In the meantime, conduct some more research. Try to find out what action the group is planning next," Coulson said, concluding the conversation.

Pearson retrieved his laptop from its bag. He stayed in Mr Coulson's office for a while longer whilst he researched further and checked on the movements of Reed and his group.

Chapter 34

FULWOOD, SHEFFIELD

TUESDAY

E MILY SET UP THE laptop in the lounge with Euan and Reed beside her, with Lynsey and Onni joining via Zoom at the university cafe. They believed it would be easier than driving on the M1 again. Emily took the lead in the discussions, as Reed had a sore throat. She planned to update everyone on the discoveries from Monday before discussing the crucifix.

"Hi everyone, hope you've recovered from the eventful weekend. Before discussing the crucifix, I wanted to just update everyone on what's happened since. Reed's been talking with his mate Phil at work. He has a friend called Jed, who is very proficient at hacking software. He suggested someone has tracked us, not necessarily the two individuals, but maybe someone else. We've checked some things he suggested. Reed discovered a tracker underneath his camper van, which is now removed and placed on the floor, so they think the campervan is still sitting in the driveway. He searched the entire house, finding a tiny device in the lounge, so they've been recording our conversations as well. That's a bit of a concern because it's quite possible you may also have a listening device somewhere in your flat, Lynsey. Can you check your flat soon?" detailed Emily.

"Yes, of course, Em. I'll do it this week," Lynsey replied.

"They're also monitoring our messages and posts on social media, as we thought, so they've learned about the first fereter that way. Another thing worth mentioning is Jed has identified the woman, and her name is Maria Ambrose. This brings me to the crucifix and what action we should take. What are your thoughts on this Onni? You're the one with the expertise?"

"We should contact the Finds Liaison Officer for Derbyshire and arrange a meeting. This has to be done within fourteen days of finding the crucifix. They would need to complete documents and carry out tests on the artefact," he said, pausing before continuing. "They'll evaluate the artefact, analysing its authenticity, which can take up to ninety days. Robin Hood's significance will be vital as it's prepared for auction, with museums competing to own it. I know several museums will want it and the price will be quite high, but until we speak to the Finds Liaison Officer, I don't know exactly how high."

"Has anyone considered we should sell it to a private collector?" interjected Reed.

"We shouldn't even consider that option as it's against the law," said Emily

"I understand your point, but I believe it'd be more valuable if we took that approach."

"But who'd we sell it to?" asked Onni.

Reed nodded and replied, "Yes, that's the tough part."

Lynsey voiced her opinion, saying, "I agree with Emily. We should take the lawful route."

"Okay, I understand the three of you are keen to follow the law. Let's do that. Are you going to contact the Finds Liaison Officer Onni and set up a meeting?"

"Yes, I'll do that. In addition, I'll work out a cover story. Doing so will enable me to gain some professional credit. I'll contact them and let you know."

"Apart from that, Euan and I have devised a strategy to regain the fereter. We've already talked it through with Emily," Reed said.

"It's fair to say I agree with this now, especially how underhand these people have been, beating you up, planting trackers and listening devices. They've been inside my home. That's pissed me off big time. So yes, I agree with Reed. We should aim to get back the second fereter," said Emily.

"The plan is myself and Phil will meet his friend Jed, the hacker, tomorrow lunchtime and discuss how to track down these individuals. Find out who they're working for. Then, we can try to locate the fereter. Euan has some suggestions to be better prepared as they are stronger than us. Do you want to share your ideas, Euan?" said Reed.

"Yeah sure, you know we used the drone at the weekend, well I can adapt it to use a jamming frequency on GPS signals and Wi-Fi signals. I've also been working on an unmanned ground vehicle. The UGV is like a small robot. The military uses this type of vehicle, but on a bigger scale, mine is smaller with all-terrain wheels. My machine resembles a travel bag, similar to those carried onto airplanes. Its high axle provides stability, allowing for effortless manoeuvring even on challenging terrains. I can adapt it to carry things like smoke canisters and mini arrow-like bolts that'll give us some extra defence if we ever encounter the two goons again. By the end of the week, I believe I'll have everything set up and ready."

"That sounds creative, Euan," said Lynsey teasingly.

"Thanks Lyns, appreciate that. I do my best," Euan replied, his cheeks flushing as the rest of the group smiled knowingly.

"We'll work on the hacking software and gadgets at our end. Onni, you get a meeting lined up with the Finds Liaison Officer, if you let Reed know when," Emily said.

"Yes, of course I'll let you know and try to give you at least a day's notice. Are you bringing the crucifix to Nottingham?"

"That would be the plan. I'd go to the safe deposit box, pick it up and then come straight over to you. I assume the Finds Liaison Officer will keep it secure?"

"Yes, that's right Reed, once you give them the crucifix, they'll store it in the safe."

"Okay, we have a plan. Thanks for your help everyone and let's continue our little adventure. We should meet up for a meal on Friday evening. Everyone like Indian?" asked Emily.

Everyone agreed to that, so Emily ended the zoom call, wandering into the kitchen. She grabbed three bottles of beer, returning to the lounge and passing two to the lads. They sat sipping on their cold beer, discussing the crucifix and their plan to get the second fereter back as the night drew in.

Chapter 35

SCREWED SOFTWARE, CENTRAL SHEFFIELD

WEDNESDAY

P HIL HAD BROUGHT HIS personal laptop to work with him. He needed it at the meeting with his friend Jed in the cafe at lunchtime. Jed would analyse the technology options to gather further information about the individuals who had taken the second fereter. Phil and Reed had a catch up conversation with their morning coffee earlier in the day. The time edged towards lunchtime, Phil checked he had his laptop with him as they headed out to meet Jed at the local cafe.

"So what's Jed like?" asked Reed.

"Well, mate, he's nerdy, but without a doubt, he knows computers and systems as he's been hacking them for the last ten years."

"He did an outstanding job discovering who the blonde woman really was. Let's hope he has additional information for us."

"He emailed me last night and said he'll give me a copy of his hacking software system. I can use it for free since he has a heavy workload in the upcoming week. I can help you guys."

"So pleased you're helping us Phil, excellent having you on board the team. I'll give you a cut of the money, if we make any. You can spend it on your bike."

"That'd be amazing, mate. I expected nothing, so that's nice of you."

"No problem, mate."

As they entered the cafe, they saw Jed sitting in the corner, his back against the wall with his laptop open. The cafe exuded a certain charm with captivating designs that adorned the walls, immersing visitors in a Gothic ambiance. Phil smelt the cooking as various aromas wafted across from the kitchen area. Jed appeared wiry, with his unkempt fringe obstructing his vision, while a faint tremor in his left eye betrayed his cautious nature. His hands danced across the keyboard at lightning speed. His eyes remained fixed on the laptop screen, unaware of the bustling cafe around him. Phil and Reed approached him. After introductions, they got straight down to business.

"I've carried out more analysis on this character, Ambrose, and have an address for you," said Jed.

"Oh wow, that's amazing," Reed said.

Jed eyed him, never comfortable with praise. "It's easy. I'm going to show Phil how to do it."

"Here's my laptop, Jed. You said you're going to transfer over the software," Phil said.

Jed whipped out a cable from his backpack sitting on the floor, attached it to the side of his laptop and ushered Phil to put his laptop on the table, connecting them with the cable. He clicked the *'transfer'* button, watching as the progress bar filled up across the screen. The computer hummed as the data transferred. Whilst they waited, the waitress appeared, taking their orders for lunch, with all three of them choosing an English breakfast.

"That's all transferred now. Let me show you how to log into the system and how it operates." Jed said.

Phil and Reed watched as Jed's fingers whizzed over the laptop, opening up this software hacking system which would enable Phil to dig up information on the other characters following them. Jed explained about the decryption processes and how to delve deep into the depths of social media. He showed Phil how to hack into systems, bypass firewalls and access CCTV recordings. Then their food arrived steaming hot, looking appetising. They tucked into their full English breakfasts. Reed outlined what had happened over the course of the previous week and how they lost the second fereter. Jed jumped in with some suggestions.

"You now have the home address for Maria Ambrose, so you should put a tracker on her car. Then you can see what places she visits. At some point she's likely to visit her employer, then you investigate land registry to identify who owns the property. Take things step by step."

"Like a digital detective?" Reed asked.

"Yes, pretty much, hacking isn't legal, but once you've got some basic information, you can delve into any person's social media activities, check car records, look at their phone messages and any property records putting together a profile."

"In order to reclaim the second fereter, we need to gather a substantial amount of information. I appreciate your help, Jed."

"Yeah, no problem, pay for the lunch. That's a thank you."

"Of course, no problem." Reed said.

They finished their food, grabbed their laptops and headed out of the cafe, Jed going his own way. Phil and Reed heading back to the Screwed Software office. They discussed Jed's advice. Phil said he would crack on tonight, looking for further information. Reed said he would speak with Euan about getting a tracker and putting it on the woman's vehicle. Perhaps Lynsey could do it as she lives closest to Ambrose, in Nottingham.

Chapter 36

COTGRAVE, NEAR NOTTINGHAM

THURSDAY

C OULSON FINISHED HIS EVENING meal of crayfish arrabiata, enjoying the heat and taste of his favourite meal, prepared by his chef. He expected several visitors soon to plan out exploring the unknown cave and Robin Hood's cave on Stanage Edge. His intention was to be involved in this himself, supervising the activities. The front gate intercom buzzed. Pearson was waiting to come in. He thought to himself, Pearson is always the first person to arrive for meetings. He activated the entry button so the gates would open and Pearson drove up the drive in his old Mini Cooper. Once Pearson settled in the library, where Coulson held all his meetings, he disappeared downstairs to *The Safe* to collect the fereter and ancient parchment.

Returning upstairs to the library, Coulson put the silver fereter and map into the display case. The one he used to show his artefacts. Within the next few minutes, the other visitors arrived. Coulson kicked off the meeting.

"Thank you all for coming. Before we begin, I'd like to introduce a new member, Wendy Markham. Wendy's a proficient rock climber, working as a manager at Blacks in Derby. She'll join us investigating the unknown cave and Robin Hood's cave at Stanage Edge. Welcome, Wendy."

"Thanks very much, pleased to meet you all and I'm looking

forward to the adventure," she responded.

"I'll take part in the Saturday exploration, looking in the caves. I'm going down the rock face with you Wendy, so if you can bring additional equipment to facilitate that please. We'll head up to Baslow Moor first, explore the unknown cave there, examining its surroundings. I want to see inside the cave and film it for future reference. After that, we're going to Robin Hood's cave at Stanage Edge. You don't need to come, Garcia. Ambrose and Bentley, you can join Wendy and I. Let's hope we find another fereter or treasure. Pearson, any more news or thoughts on the map?"

"No, boss, I can't find any other suitable locations matching the markings on the map. The only thing I can add is the larger rectangular block in the bottom right corner may well be called Carl's Wark, which I spotted on Google Maps, although it's a ruin now."

"Yes, that's a ruin. I've passed it on walks in the Peak District," interjected Wendy.

"Oh, great! It seems like we're in the right place. However, I'm concerned, as this cave is famous. It makes it improbable there's anything inside. In terms of equipment, I'll bring a metal detector and archaeological tools in case we have to do any digging. Any other thoughts, anyone?"

"I assume you're going to bring all the climbing equipment and gear that's required, Wendy?" asked Ambrose.

"Yes, I've got my harness, ropes, climbing shoes, head torch, and other accessories. I'll bring the lot."

"Excellent Wendy, thank you Ambrose. Bentley, I'll pick you up first thing Saturday morning. I'll have the Jaguar F-type, as Mrs Coulson is taking the Porsche Cayenne for the weekend to her sister's in Dorset. Ambrose, you pick up Wendy and we'll meet you in Baslow at Nether End car park at nine thirty."

"Yes, boss."

"Pearson, anything to report on the group?"

"Nothing, no social media activity, the campervan hasn't moved and no conversations of note to report."

"Okay. Garcia, come over here. I want you to have a look at this fereter and give me your thoughts on it, please."

Coulson and Garcia walked over to the display, donning white gloves, the Spaniard viewed the fereter inside and out. He concurred with Coulson's view that yes; it could be six or seven hundred years old and constructed from silver. He was also aware the feather symbol may be associated with Robin Hood. Coulson beckoned the remaining members of the group to look at the map and study it. Wendy agreed with Pearson's view. It looked like Robin Hood's cave, as she had plenty of climbing experience at Stanage Edge and knew the location well. The group continued to have discussions about the location and the plan for Saturday morning, whilst Coulson poured everyone a special brandy.

The meeting concluded with everyone departing, leaving Coulson to enjoy another glass of his special brandy in his favourite chair in the library. He sat staring at the feather symbol on the silver fereter and wondered if it was a trail to some treasure. He pondered if there could be another one inside Robin Hood's cave? If that is indeed the case, how is it possible it has remained undiscovered in the 21st century?

Chapter 37

PEAK TANDOORI, CHESTERFIELD
FRIDAY

R EED AND EMILY WALKED through the centre of Chesterfield towards the Indian restaurant they had booked for the team. For a moment, they stopped to admire the famous crooked church spire, its distinct shape dominating the town's marketplace. As they took in the sight, a gentle breeze brushed against their skin. Friday night always bustling with people, their laughter and chatter coming from the neon signed pubs. Taxis zoomed by, their tyres screeching and engines rumbling. The smells of food from the restaurants intermingled with the pubs as they strolled along the high street. Chesterfield is close to the Peak District with many tourists during the summer months, adding to the lively atmosphere in the town.

They found the *Peak Tandoori* just off the main street. Entering it, they had arrived first and ordered a drink at the bar. The restaurant exuded an enchanting Indian ambiance, adorned with vibrant hues painted across the walls, while a few street-art pieces added an authentic touch. Red table cloths adorned each table, their rich colour adding a touch of elegance. The hum of conversations and clinking of cutlery added to the social atmosphere. Reed was thankful he had made reservations ahead of time. A few minutes later, Euan arrived. Phil followed soon after him, then Lynsey and Onni, after their trip up the M1 from Nottingham. They took their seats and Reed introduced Phil to the other members of the group.

"If each of us can provide an update on their tasks from Wednesday evening," Reed said. "Did you want to go first, Onni?"

"Okay, yes. We're meeting the Finds Liaison Officer next Tuesday at three o'clock, Reed. If you're available on that day, can we meet at the University and bring the crucifix with you? We'll need to complete the paperwork with him. I've said you found the crucifix, and I'm assisting you in the process as a friend."

"Yes, I can meet you then. Any more thoughts on the valuation?"

"If we get several interested museums, you might get one hundred thousand for it."

The waiter approached the table. A notepad and pen in hand, ready to jot down the hungry patrons' orders. He waited, a gentle smile on his face, as the group deliberated over the menu. Once the ordering was complete, the waiter walked away as Reed suggested Euan updated everyone on his drone and UGV.

"Before I start, I've got a present for you Lynsey," Euan said.

"Oh Euan, that's kind of you," she replied, smiling as Euan passed a small box to her.

"You're welcome, Lynsey."

Lynsey's face changed when she realised what it was, giving Euan a playful punch on the arm. "How to disappoint a girl, Euan!"

Euan laughed. "It's a tracker for you to put on the woman's vehicle. If you could get this on to the vehicle either tonight or tomorrow morning, we can track her movements. Phil has the app on his phone. He'll get a notification if the vehicle moves. That's correct Phil?"

"Yes, that's right," Phil said.

"It didn't take me long to complete the upgrade on the drone. If we can bring the drone down to a low enough level, I can jam GPS, mobile, radio, and Wi-Fi signals. But it's limited by its flight time. The battery restricts this, so I'm getting a bigger one. I've made progress on the UGV which I tested yesterday evening in the park. It can navigate various terrains, I can also program it to search for specific targets. Enhanced features include installing a canister that can billow smoke from the rear. Two barrels affixed on opposite sides holding five small metal bolts, resembling arrows, can reload themselves after being fired. These bolts fly at a speed of ninety miles per hour but limited to a range of just thirty yards. All ready for action," Euan detailed.

"Brilliant, thanks Euan. Phil, do you want to update us on what else you've found out using Jed's software?"

"Yes Reed. I've got more pictures of the woman from her social media. She's into Muay Thai kickboxing, but I can't find anything else useful," said Phil.

"I thought she was a kickboxer based on her moves on Saturday," Reed interjected. "Have you linked her to anybody else yet?"

"No, not so far. If we can get some tracking data on her travel patterns, then that might lead us to who she's working for."

"Oh, that's disappointing," said Emily

"Yes, it's disappointing. It takes time to put together a profile of a person," Phil said.

The conversation muted as the waiter brought their starters. The aroma of the food filled the air and with mouths watering, they couldn't resist indulging in the dishes that lay before them. All the starters disappeared within minutes, with the waiter returning to remove the plates. Reed continued the conversation. "We need to gather more information about the woman's employer before starting surveillance."

"Let's hope the vehicle tracker gives us some helpful clues," Euan said.

Their main meals arrived as the conversation shifted to more mundane topics, such as work and rock climbing. After finishing their meal, the group walked outside into the night, deciding on another drink at a local bar.

On this bustling Friday night, the streets were alive with many revellers. They settled on a lively music bar, where the melodies enveloped them from outside. Inside, the pounding beats resonated in their chests, merging with laughter and chatter. They completed the night out with a round of shots before departing. Reed said goodbye to Lynsey, confirming she planned to attach the tracker to the women's vehicle on her way home. She intended to do this undercover of darkness.

Chapter 38

SOMEWHERE IN THE PEAK DISTRICT

SATURDAY

A MBROSE HAD SET OFF at seven thirty as she had to go via Belper to pick up Wendy before heading towards Baslow. They navigated their way through Matlock with its myriad of tourist shops, restaurants and fish and chip takeaways. The increase in traffic resulted in a stop-start journey through Matlock Bath. Ambrose couldn't help but think they should rename the place Gridlock. A picturesque valley unfolded in front of them as the sheer rock cliffs towered over the main road. The sound of rushing water floated in the open window as the meandering river Derwent dictated the road's direction. Ambrose checked the estimated time of arrival on the sat nav. She realised they would be around twenty minutes early, which suited her. A relaxing journey is better than rushing to reach the destination, she thought.

"Do you know Matlock, Wendy?" asked Ambrose of her passenger.

"Yes, pretty well. There are a couple of climbs here I've completed. It's excellent for a hill walk, especially if you add in Cromford and there is a national trail, *The High Peak Trail*, which is well-known for climbers, called Black Rocks. It's one of my favourite climbing places, as there's never much wind, unlike some climbs in the Peak District." Wendy said.

"How do you know Mr Coulson?" Ambrose inquired, keen to

learn more about the recent addition to the team.

"He's a friend of my dad's and asked if I could help, knowing I'm a keen climber. This first cave. Do you know how they accessed it?"

"They just tied ropes around a couple of trees and disappeared over the edge. We couldn't see exactly what the group was doing. We were too far away, hidden behind Eagle Rock."

"It's not one I'm aware of, but there are loads of small caves in the Peak District. What's he expecting to discover in the cave?" asked Wendy.

"Not sure. He seems to think there may be some markings on the cave wall linked to Robin Hood. He also wants to investigate the spot they found the fereter."

"I thought Robin Hood was just a story?"

"I also had my doubts, but he thinks there might be some truth to it. The map implies something along those lines. Perhaps we might uncover some treasure in the second cave."

"That cave isn't big. I've only stepped inside once, but perhaps there's another entrance tucked away in the rear."

"Who knows? We're going to be early. Fancy stopping to grab a quick cup of coffee beforehand?" asked Ambrose.

"Yes, please,"

Ambrose had spotted a garage with coffee to-go, so she pulled over. They picked up a coffee and carried on their way, still likely to be fifteen minutes early.

Coulson had picked Bentley up at just after eight o'clock. They were navigating their way to Baslow in the Peak District. The roar of the engine of the Jaguar F-Type echoed through the air as it zoomed by. The powerful sound reverberated, turning heads, drawing admiring glances at the sight of the stylish car in motion. Its go-faster stripes complemented the bodywork, a striking shade of red, catching the eye. The rear spoiler added a touch of sophistication as well as enhancing the car's aerodynamics. He would often race the vehicle on a track day at Donnington, enjoying the thrill of speed.

They approached a stepped junction, and Coulson could see Bentley was enjoying the ride. After navigating the junction, with one car in front and a straight stretch ahead of them, he put his foot down. Dropping into fifth gear, he swung the vehicle into the right-hand lane to overtake. G-force from the unexpected move threw Bentley back in his seat as Coulson overtook the car and raced ahead, hitting eighty miles an hour in under ten seconds. The engine purred as the car flew down the straight section with ease. It wasn't long before another junction beckoned so Coulson braked hard to bring the speed down, the squeal of the brakes counteracting the engine growling as he dropped to a standstill at the give-way sign.

"How's that Bentley? Enjoy the bit of extra speed?"

"Superb, uncle, loved it."

"I feel the same way. The thrill of speed is hard to find elsewhere."

"Other than knocking someone out and winning a boxing match," Bentley said.

"Yes, you're right lad, if you're successful enough, you can have your very own sports car."

"I intend to. If I win my next fight, my manager said I could be in line for a British belt challengers fight."

"Brilliant, you stick to training hard and success will come. Don't forget my ticket," Coulson reminded Bentley.

"No, I won't. I'll sort it out next week for you, I promise."

"Looks like some bends coming up. Shall we test the tyres on this beast?" asked Coulson.

"Go for it, uncle."

Coulson dropped gears as he lent into the first corner, hitting the gas. The tyres squealed as it pulled forward, gaining traction and shooting through the chicane. After throwing it around a couple more corners, they reached the main road, heading from Chesterfield into Baslow. Joining the traffic, they settled back into a more mundane tempo for the rest of their journey.

Earlier, Phil had received a notification on the tracking app showing Ambrose's vehicle had moved north from her home in Nottingham. He spoke to Reed on his way to Derwent Edge with Euan to do a climb that morning. They had waited until Ambrose had stopped in Belper before deciding what to do. Phil's second phone call to Reed had yielded the same answer.

He watched the tracker app as she continued her journey north on the A6 after her stop and correlated that with Google maps to get a likely destination. Phil concluded, guessing her destination was pointless. He realised she could drive all the way to Manchester using the A6. As time crept by, he watched the tracker turn off the A6 at Rowsley, passing through the Chatsworth Estate. The app transfixed him, updating it every few seconds, waiting to see if the little green dot stopped. Then the realisation hit him, Ambrose was going to Baslow, the scene of last week's altercation. Several minutes passed before the vehicle came to a stop in Nether End car park. He waited awhile, making sure the vehicle had become stationary before calling Reed.

"Aye up, mate, she's stopped. You will never guess where?"

Reed hesitated for a moment, then blurted out, "Baslow."

"Spot on, Reed. They must have found another cave somewhere close."

"Bloody hell Phil, you're right. Euan and I will need an hour to get to Baslow's car park. We're in the middle of setting up for a climb, but it'll take thirty minutes trekking downhill to the car."

"Okay, I'll get on the bike and if I motor, I might get there in fifteen minutes. I know what she looks like, but if I can't see her, I'll wait for you guys."

"If you don't mind Phil, that would be awesome, mate. Euan has the drone. We can use it to trace her."

"Right, on my way. See you soon."

Phil pulled on his sleek black leathers, the supple material hugging his body. He secured his helmet, the click of the strap echoing in the garage as he manoeuvred his powerful bike out onto the road. Inside two minutes, he raced out of Chesterfield as fast as he dare watching for any police around.

Once on the A619 to Baslow, he opened up the Suzuki GSX-R-1000, its guts roaring into life. The bike's sleek profile, glinting under the sun, allowed him to weave through traffic, its powerful engine purring with each twist of the throttle. The rush of wind filled his helmet as he manoeuvred the bike, catching the faint scent of exhaust from the cars he passed. He zoomed through the winding curves, embracing the sights of the undulating Peak District landscape. He felt the adrenaline pumping through his veins, conquering everything the scenic terrain offered.

Phil's phone sat in a secure cradle on his bike handlebars with the tracker app open. He glanced at the app, still no movement as the time crept past nine thirty. He still had a couple of miles to reach the car park. With hope in his heart, he longed to reach the destination in time. His goal was to spot the blonde woman and trail her, no matter where she ventured. Phil had no concerns about being seen. She didn't know he existed, never mind being a friend of Reed's.

He roared into Nether End car park a couple of minutes later, scanning the area for the blonde woman he had seen on his computer screen earlier in the week. No-one resembled her. He was too late! After parking the bike and removing his helmet, he trudged around the car park looking for the vehicle, finding it tucked away in a far corner. The vehicle looked empty. No-one inside. As he made his way back to his bike, a wave of disappointment washed over him.

The sound of cars rushing past filled the air, a constant reminder of the time slipping away. He couldn't help but feel the weight of regret settle upon his shoulders, a tangible reminder he had missed his chance. Phil glanced back at the Audi as he sat astride his bike. His eyes caught sight of a red Jaguar F-Type sports car parked just a couple of spaces away. This vehicle emitted an unmistakable aura of opulence. Could this be the person who employed Ambrose, perhaps?

Chapter 39

Baslow Moor, Peak District

Saturday

W ENDY SET A BRISK pace up the hill towards Baslow Moor, having walked it many times before, Mr Coulson keeping in step with her all the way, probing her about rock climbing. They stopped at the gate two thirds of the way up the track, waiting for Ambrose to join them, having stopped to remove a stone from her shoe. Wendy noticed Mr Coulson had various tools in his backpack, which she assumed were archaeological, that he may need if they find anything interesting today. She gazed up at the bright expanse of the cloudless sky, relieved she had remembered to bring her sunglasses. As the sun intensified, its rays shimmered against her vision, casting a warm golden glow over everything she looked at. She noticed a common buzzard soaring through the air, riding the invisible currents of rising warm air. Its majestic wings were outstretched as it let out a high-pitched screech.

The group pressed on towards the moor, their eyes scanning the path ahead. The gravel mixed with jagged rocks jutting out from the ground added an element of precaution to their journey. As they reached the summit of the track, Wendy's eyes focussed on Eagle Rock, its presence dominating the landscape. The vibrant colours of blooming yellow gorse bushes and purple heather created a picturesque sight. Wendy couldn't help but feel a sense of tranquillity amid such natural beauty. She waited for Ambrose to guide her towards the Wellington Cross. They followed the main path as it drew further away from the rocky edge.

"This is where we had the scuffle, wasn't it Bentley?" Ambrose asked, stopping a hundred yards from the cross.

"Yes, just here. They used these two trees to tie their rope to," he pointed out after consulting his pin on Google maps.

Wendy ventured to the precipice of the rock, her eyes straining to see the vertical drop spanning about twenty feet. She set about putting her gear together. Soon she was ready to descend. Mr Coulson had his harness on. She clipped him up with a belay device and a carabiner, encouraging him as he went over the edge. Wendy followed afterwards, enabling her to give him instructions on foot and hand holds. It didn't take long to descend. They unclipped from the rope and switched on their head torches, ready to squeeze through the cave entrance. Once inside, they drank in the damp musty air, like smelling salts needed to clear their heads.

"What are you searching for, Eric?" asked Wendy.

"Call me Mr Coulson when the others are around, Wendy. I'm looking for any etching on the cave walls."

Wendy watched Coulson scan the inside of the cave. The head torch light bounced off the rough, textured sides of the wall, illuminating the earthy floor.

"There Wendy, can you see it?" asked Coulson, pointing to the rear wall of the cave.

"Oh, I see. It's like a feather," she said.

"Yes, it's supposed to be Robin Hood's sign. It's brought back memories of an elderly professor's words many years ago. Let's search the ground, finding the spot they discovered the fereter."

Wendy headed over to the curved rear wall and Coulson scouted around the floor, checking the rock faces for any cracks. No apparent signs. Then she noticed the pile of rocks which, on closer inspection, had disturbed soil around the edges. Wendy showed Coulson and together they moved the rocks. Coulson used his metal detector to scan the earth, but nothing happened. No beeping, no red light. Satisfied there was nothing there, he piled the rocks back up, careful to cover all the disturbed soil. Wendy watched Coulson retrieve his Go-Pro to record the inside of the cave, focussing on the etching.

"Right, I'm all done Wendy. Let's get up top and move onto the next cave where there might be some of Robin Hood's treasure, hopefully."

"Yes, Mr Coulson."

Wendy guided Mr Coulson back to the top, where Ambrose and Bentley waited, standing there chatting. They packed up their climbing gear, heading towards the track to start the descent back to the vehicles. Onward to the second cave, Wendy's curiosity piqued. Maybe this one held the key to unlocking the mystery.

———◆O◆———

Euan, Reed, and Phil found themselves nestled in a hollow, encircled by rugged rocks beneath Baslow Edge, shielded from the flow of hikers near Eagle Rock. They met Phil at the car park, where they took photos of the Jaguar F-Type car, recording the registration for use upon their return. Hidden in their secluded spot, Euan activated the drone, its propellers whirring as it soared into the sky. He scanned the surroundings, searching for a glimpse of the blonde woman, Ambrose. Euan's heart raced with anticipation as he controlled the drone, feeling the metal controller beneath his fingertips. He soon found her standing watch in the shade of the trees where the fight had happened last weekend. The young lad with the exceptional boxing skills kept her company. Because of the bright sunlight, they had difficulty seeing the screen on the remote control unit. However, Euan came up with a clever solution by creating a small shelter over it using a waterproof jacket.

"They look like they're waiting for someone to meet them," said Phil.

"Looks like it. Let's wait. Can you zoom in any further, Euan?" asked Reed.

"I'm on maximum zoom mate, I could drop the drone further down, hang on."

Euan piloted the drone closer, but not too close. They spotted some movement behind Ambrose, seeing two people coming into view over the crest of the rock edge.

"Record this, Euan. We can see the person in charge," said Reed.

"One is a young girl with climbing gear. The other is an older man. I bet he's the mastermind behind all this," said Phil.

"Yes, spot on Phil. It seems likely he owns the Jaguar."

They watched the group pack up their gear and head towards the downhill track. Realising Ambrose's group would pass close to them soon, Euan attempted to pull down the makeshift shelter. The arm of the waterproof caught on a rock and as Euan tugged it, it collapsed on top of his head. His fingers caught the control thumb stick, which manoeuvred the drone into a dive sequence, heading for Reed, who had moved around the corner. Euan struggled to see what was happening as he heard Reed shout at him. He corrected the drone and brought it to the floor beside Reed, but time had run out. The group strolled within fifty feet of him. He couldn't move now. He laid down on the floor, his heart racing, and pretended to be asleep with the waterproof over his face. Phew, that was close.

Once the Ambrose group had passed by, he stood up with mud splattered over his clothes and hair. Reed came round the corner laughing. Reed, Euan, and Phil scuttled their way down the track, careful not to be seen by the leading group. Euan marvelled at how the roles had reversed within just a week. His mind buzzed with the intriguing shift that had taken place.

Chapter 40

Hathersage, Peak District

Saturday

C OULSON JUMPED INTO HIS sports car back at Nether End car park and fired up the engine. Bentley joined him. He sped off, leaving Ambrose in her Audi to follow them as they drove towards Stanage Edge. He increased speed on the open stretches of road, the powerful Jaguar engine growling, manoeuvring round the sharp turns, the tyres gripping the road with a satisfying squeal. Wind rushed through the open windows, the smell of asphalt blasting their senses, as they raced towards their next stop. They planned to park at Hooks Carr car park as it looked the closest to Robin Hood's cave, but as they neared it, the volume of cars parked on the side of the road dismayed Coulson. The Peak District's vistas were more popular than he imagined. Where have all these people come from? Coulson thought. On reaching the car park, it was full. He paused for a few seconds, deciding against parking his car on the side of the road. He wanted to avoid getting stuck in any mud.

"Bentley, let Ambrose know I'm going to the next car park – Hollins Bank," he fired at his nephew.

"Yes, uncle."

They raced to the next car park, finding this also jammed with vehicles and people milling around. He felt his frustration building up and sensed the prickling heat of agitation crawling under his skin. Determined to remain calm and in control, he instructed Bentley to message Ambrose once more, "Tell her to move to the furthermost car park."

They reached this inside a minute and again, the only option was to pull onto a grassy bank. Coulson sat there pondering. The situation hadn't unfolded as he intended. If he couldn't park his car, then logic said there would be lots of people milling around, making it difficult to carry out a full survey of the cave. He took a few seconds to relax and realised they should come back later when they could park, which would also mean less chance of being interrupted in their investigation. By now Ambrose had caught up to him and awaiting instruction. Coulson fired off a quick message.

Mr Coulson: *'Ambrose, too many people around, lunch in Hathersage and come back later.'*
Ambrose: *'Okay, I'll follow you.'*
Mr Coulson: *'Scotmans Pack Country Inn.'*
Ambrose: *'Thanks.'*

Coulson turned the sports car around to return the way they came, following Bentley's instructions to arrive at the pub in under five minutes. When they got out of the car, he noted the brown tourist sign pointing towards Little John's Grave in a nearby church.

He wanted to visit this before they had lunch. He told Bentley to get a table and order some drinks, passing him his debit card. Coulson strode off with purpose, leaving his companions behind at the bustling pub. As he made his way towards the old church, the gravel path crunched beneath his sturdy boots. At the churchyard, he approached the weathered headstone with curiosity. Coulson ran his fingers over the carved letters. A sense of wonder washed over him as he pondered whether the headstone was a tourist gimmick or a genuine testament to someone's life.

He returned to the pub, bumping into a biker in leathers as he entered, then sat down with the others to enjoy a leisurely lunch.

He planned to return to the car parks later in the afternoon, hoping there would be fewer people.

As Reed, Euan and Phil loped down the hill towards Nether End car park in Baslow, they noticed the Jaguar F-Type speeding off whilst Ambrose's Audi eased out onto the main road.

"That must be the older man's sports car. Let's track the Audi. If it's in the same location as the sports car, then we've found the mastermind behind their illegal activities," said Reed.

"I've got the registration plate, so I'll get straight on it when I get home. Let's follow them. I'll keep track and you follow me," Phil said.

"Okay, let's do it."

Phil followed the tracking, but he found himself about three minutes behind. No need to get up close. The Audi wound its way up towards Stanage Edge, then stopped, so he eased off and pulled into Hollins Bank's car park. Reed and Euan pulled in just behind him, looking around in case Ambrose spotted them. Reed wound the window down.

"Where are they, Phil?" he asked.

"Further up the road, they've stopped, lets give it a minute and then head their way."

Phil eased the Suzuki to the junction with the main road, with Reed just behind him, spotting a sports car flying towards him. He checked the tracking device. The Audi was moving towards him, and flapped his hand at Reed to hide. He turned and watched Reed and Euan duck down out of sight just as the red Jaguar flew past, followed by the black Audi. Phew, that was close, he thought. He waited another minute, then turned left to follow the vehicles as they headed away from the car park towards the town.

The tracker stopped in a pub car park, so Phil found a parking space a couple of streets away. Reed and Euan caught up, parked near Phil, then set off on foot towards the pub. They saw both the Jaguar and the Audi in the car park. They stood out of sight, checking for any of the group, but seeing nothing, they sent Phil into the pub as no-one in Coulson's group knew who he was.

Phil wandered in to the white walled pub with ivy on the exterior walls and wooden beams in the ceiling. Scanning the clientele, he spotted the blonde woman at a table near the bar. Phil rolled up to the bar and, while pretending to queue, he managed a couple of covert photos of the group. One was missing. The older man wasn't there. He scanned around again, not seeing him, and presumed he had gone to the toilet.

He shuffled towards the exit, ready to leave and, whilst still checking out the members of the Ambrose group, he bumped into someone coming through the door. The older man. Phil panicked. He completed his exit in a hurry, returning to the other two lads to update them.

Chapter 41

STANAGE EDGE, PEAK DISTRICT

SATURDAY

COULSON CHECKED THE TIME on his Rolex to correlate it to Google's interpretations of how busy it would be at Robin Hood's cave. He decided they should head back to one of the car parks around four o'clock. They arrived at Hooks Carr car park, finding two spaces.

Coulson checked the contents of his backpack, which included a mini pickaxe. He ensured the other three were ready before ascending the hill towards Stanage Edge, which would lead to the cave. He checked the photo of the map on his phone and, satisfied it all matched, continued upwards. Wendy had advised him over lunch it looked easy to descend to the cave from the top and wouldn't require any climbing gear. He surveyed the landscape ahead, the vibrant bracken interspersed with large rocks and boulders, like croutons in a green salad. He marvelled at how nature had evolved, suspecting though six or seven hundred years ago it would have looked similar except for the tarmac roads and car park. As Wendy pointed out the cave in the distance, he spotted the sheer cliffs. The height of the cliffs made his heart skip a beat, and he felt a sense of relief they weren't climbing up to the cave.

As they neared the rocky path to the edge, Coulson found himself ahead of the others, Ambrose behind him. Wendy was walking with Bentley, no doubt chatting about rap music or something, as youngsters do nowadays, he thought. Struggling to ascend the irregular rocks and boulders, he reached the summit. As he turned around, the vista captivated him with the sprawling landscape laid out in front of him. The insistent breeze brushed against his face, carrying with it the distant chirping of birds. It stretched for miles in all directions, the haze of the sunshine creating an almost surreal feel to the panoramic. The activity of walkers was unmistakable, generating trails like an army of ants.

When the other three had joined Coulson, the group continued north along the ridge, bounding over rocks, avoiding puddles and boggy ground. Before long, they reached their destination and, glancing at his expensive watch, Coulson noted it was five o'clock. He felt pleased with himself having delayed the plan as now no-one mingled around the cave or the path to it.

Coulson dropped on to the path and headed to the cave entrance, stopping beside it to put on his head torch. He stooped to enter it. The front of the cave appeared dry with no over-whelming damp smell as the double entrance allowed the wind to flow through the cave. The depths of the cave, where the solid rock transitioned into damp earth, piqued Coulson's curiosity. He felt drawn to the recesses, where the faint sound of dripping water echoed and the air carried a distinct, earthy scent. Once his eyes had adjusted to the gloom, which contrasted with the brightness of his head torch, he beckoned Wendy to join him.

"Tell Ambrose and Bentley to wait outside the entrance. We don't want anyone coming in and disturbing us," he said.

Wendy passed on the instructions whilst he moved to the back of the cave, scrutinising the walls for any markings. He drew a blank on the first scan. He stopped and took a moment to draw a deep breath and apply his many years' experience working on archaeological digs. A few moments later, he spotted some faint lines carved in the rock at the rear of the cave just above the earth line. He grabbed his trowel, moved some earth, and formed a mound away from the wall. With each trowel movement, more lines were unearthed. He removed one of his brushes from his backpack, clearing the lines on the wall. There it stood, the unmistakable feather sign, confirming they found themselves in the correct location.

"Wendy, look over here."

"Another feather sign confirming this is the correct place," she replied.

"Let's bring out the metal detector."

As Coulson scanned the wall and ground, he monitored the red indicator light and tuned his ears into the beeping sound of the equipment. The tone increased. Almost too faint to hear, but his trained ears picked it up. He had a top of the range OKM metal detector that could detect gold down to forty feet. It flashed something up on the screen as he zoned in on the location beneath his feet. He checked the screen, turned the beeping off, and listened as his ears picked up something else.

A faint plip, plip, reminiscent of water trickling down into a tranquil pool. Coulson had spotted small streams flowing over rocks as they walked along Stanage Edge, noticing how they ran down through the cliff edges. Inside his backpack, he found his collapsible walking pole, which doubled as a probe. Using it, he poked around on the ground. After several attempts, it pierced the earth, in the cave's corner, left of the feather symbol on the wall.

"Wendy, can you come here, please?"

"Yes, Mr Coulson?"

"I'm on to something, but I need some help to dig," he said, showing her where the handle of the walking pole stuck proudly out of the solid ground. He passed her the mini shovel whilst he put on his knee pads and started digging with his pickaxe. Wendy shovelled the damp earth to the other side of the cave. After several minutes of excavation, the walking pole became loose and then dropped out of view. Coulson's heart jumped a beat.

He knew from his experience they had found something. Before long, he had excavated a hole. Despite his head torch, the void below remained shrouded in impenetrable darkness. A damp, earthy smell rose from the hole as he peered into it, making him hopeful. He pointed the metal detector down through the hole. It beeped louder, the red light flashed faster, and the screen more vibrant, showing several spots of interest. He needed to dig a hole big enough to enable him to descend into the damp darkness below.

After several more minutes of digging with his pickaxe, he hit a rock at the side. This narrow passage wouldn't be wide enough to squeeze through, though. As he worked his way around the edge of the rock, it soon became apparent this was a separate boulder about the size of a large suitcase. Coulson cleared the surrounding soil, isolating the single boulder wedged in place, stopping access to the space below. As he stood there, a surge of conviction washed over him. The rock seemed placed there on purpose, evoking a sense of intrigue. He couldn't help but wonder what secrets lay hidden below. After pondering his next step, he retrieved his crowbar from the backpack and levered the rock, to no avail. Wendy assisted him. They moved it a fraction, but not enough.

"Bentley, can you come in here please?" he shouted. "Can you use the crowbar? You're stronger than me. I'll help Wendy move it when it's loose."

"Yes, of course."

The sound of metal against stone echoed through the cave. The smell of earth and sweat mingled as beads of perspiration formed on their brows. Coulson and Wendy strained alongside Bentley, and after fifteen minutes, their determination paid off as they moved the boulder. A sense of accomplishment washed over them as they stood before an opening big enough for a single person to descend into.

"Well done, you two, brilliant effort," Coulson said, enthusing with his praise.

"Do you want me to descend?" asked Wendy.

"No, I'll go down. I need you and Bentley to hold the rope, keeping me secure. One of you tell Ambrose what is happening and under no circumstances is she to allow anyone inside the cave."

———— ◄O► ————

Coulson put on his harness and helmet, getting out his Go-Pro and attached it to his chest. He strapped on his archaeologist's belt, ensuring all tools were secured. He spotted a pool below, in the darkness, as the head torch light reflected from the gloom. With his metal detector slung over his shoulder, he was ready to descend. Wendy and Bentley fed the rope down as Coulson descended into the darkness below, his head disappearing out of sight.

"Stop, I've reached the pool. Let me test the depth before you go any further," he shouted up.

Coulson picked up the walking pole laid propped against the wall, half in the water, and prodded around. The pool felt two feet deep. He asked to be dropped until his feet hit the bottom of the pool with the water coming up above his knees. He turned on the metal detector, scrutinising the restrictive oval space which looked around twelve feet wide, and spotted the dripping water into a side of the pool. Coulson pointed the detecting equipment towards the pool. It went crazy, beeping and flashing like mad. The pool was dark, hindering his visibility. After all, it had been centuries since light would have reached this water. Rummaging around in the pool, his hand hit something hard and round, like a tree branch. He picked it up and pulled it from its dark hiding place. A wooden quarterstaff, almost fully intact. With two gleaming gold ends, one flat and polished, the other displaying a dangerous sharp point. His mind cast back to the tombstone earlier. Could this be Little John's quarterstaff? He was gobsmacked. He touched the gold spike, elated with his find.

Time to get practical. The ancient hardwood had been preserved by spending centuries submerged in water, shielded from oxygen and light. He would need to embark on the delicate task of restoring it. The wood, cradled in his hands, exuded a subtle dampness, its texture cool and smooth against his fingertips. Aware of its vulnerability, he took care to safeguard the wood's integrity. Coulson remembered his training from years gone by, pushing aside the elation of his find and putting the metal detector to work again. In the underground space, he directed the equipment towards the poolside, where a mound of soil was located. The beeping, flashing, and signal on the screen showed something metal buried there. He dug up the soil and before long, he discovered another silver fereter. The same as the previous one with a feather symbol and sealed with wax.

"Wendy, Bentley, pull me up. I've got some things to show you."

They pulled Coulson up and watched in amazement as he rose from the hole, like a resurrection, clutching a six-foot pole with gold ends.

"Oh wow, what's that?" asked Bentley.

"If I'm correct, this is Little John's quarterstaff."

"That's just incredible, Mr Coulson," Wendy said.

"It is Wendy. I've also found another silver fereter. Our next step is to make the cave appear untouched. Let's start by replacing the boulder. Then we can pack the surrounding soil before heading home for a celebration."

They manoeuvred the boulder back in position and replaced the soil the best they could, although it left a small hole at one side. As Coulson emerged from the dark cave, the sunlight bathed his face, highlighting his triumphant smile. With a flourish, he displayed his discovery to Ambrose, who marvelled at the glimmering object. The sound of their eager voices echoed through the air, mingling with the whistling breeze. The group retraced their steps onto the edge and descended the hill back to the cars. A sense of euphoria amongst them. Their efforts today had been worthwhile.

The three lads had found Ambrose's car and the Jaguar but as the landscape was open moorland up towards Stanage Edge, they had parked at the Hollins Bank car park, enclosed by trees. They arrived in time to see the group walking up to Stanage Edge, so positioned themselves in a large cluster of trees to the north of Robin Hood's cave. Euan prepared the drone, its propellers humming as it soared into the sky, scanning for the quartet of individuals. High in the sky, the drone could be mistaken for a bird swooping on the warm air currents. Euan soon found the group, training the drone on them, spotting two and then a third member disappear inside Robin Hood's cave. They waited in their secluded place, observing Ambrose standing outside the entrance to the cave.

After eighty minutes of observation, they watched the other three emerge from the cave. Euan lowered the drone for a better view. As they peered at the screen, a faint glimmer caught their attention from an object grasped by the older man.

"Can you get a better view, Euan?" asked Reed.

"I'll have to drop it down further, Reed. They could spot the drone."

"We need to move closer and observe the group."

Euan dropped the drone, the group coming more into focus. Then they spotted the quarterstaff with a gold top to it, being clutched tight in the older man's grasp.

"Look at that," Phil said.

"It's a pole with a golden tip."

"Is the pole metal? It looks dark."

"Could be. It's hard to tell from here. Can you record it, Euan?" asked Reed.

"Yes, I'll do a few minutes, then we can check it later, zooming in on the laptop."

Euan hit the record button as they looked at the group's discovery, feeling miffed it wasn't them. Disappointment rippled across the three of them as they trudged back to the car park, with some grainy drone footage to console themselves with.

Chapter 42

Stanage Edge, Peak District

*T*HE SUMMER WARMTH CONTINUED *into the early evenings in 1397AD, the warm air currents utilised by soaring birds of prey.*

The giant stood at the entrance to the cave on Stanage Edge, observing the group of horsemen heading in his direction, his quarterstaff clutched in his hand. They had arrived in the bustling town in the valley below earlier that day. They sought him out amidst the clang of hammers emanating from his smithy. The townsfolk had alerted him whilst taking part in the morning prayer. The sheriff's men had arrived in force, as they had done on previous occasions, looking to capture him. Frequently, he followed his leader, the archer, to different locations across the land, evading the soldiers' efforts to capture them and causing a lot of trouble to support the poor people of the region. This time, he was alone.

He counted five figures huddled together in a group way below him, their presence almost swallowed by the vastness of the surroundings. Determined to capture the soldier's attention, he clambered up to the edge, the rough texture of the surface scraping against his palms. Standing tall, he positioned himself against the backdrop of the sprawling skyline with his quarterstaff. Casting a striking silhouette. One man spotted him and pointed. They galloped further up the hill until they reached the foot of the sheer cliffs. As they dismounted, one man took the reins of the horses and held them whilst the other four continued on foot, hauling themselves up the rocky path until they reached the top. One soldier shouted.

"It's the blacksmith."

"Let's take him."

"Your time is up."

Their voices carried with the blustery wind across to Little John and a smile crept across his face, confident he could take all four of the soldiers. Their polished armour, adorned with the emblem of the sheriff, shimmered in the sunlight. The metallic scent of the armour blended with the earthy aroma of the surrounding moorland. The soldiers approached him, stepping over boulders, avoiding crevices and spreading out to attack him on three sides. He stood tall, waiting. One soldier came in from the side, but Little John swatted him with his quarterstaff, like he was a fly. The man staggering backwards and fell over a rock. A second and third soldier then moved in unison, waving their swords around in front of him. Little John waited for the exact moment, using his quarterstaff to knock one sword back before swirling it around to hit the third soldier in the face with the blunt end. He felt the sharp edge of the fourth soldier's sword strike him in the shoulder from the other side. Blood oozed from the wound as his arm throbbed. He needed to finish the fight quick.

Fuelled by the pain of the injury, Little John whipped the staff around and used the sharp end to pierce the third soldier's chest as he stumbled towards him, still reeling from the blow to the head. He swung the staff above his head, arrowing in on the second soldier, who had reclaimed his sword from the ground. A quick smack across the arm with the quarterstaff made the panicking soldier drop it again. The fourth soldier rushed in, requiring a nimble sidestep which belied his bulk. Little John jumped up onto an adjoining rock, avoiding the sharp metal blade, bringing the staff down onto the soldier's arm. Time to finish this, so with a couple of swift movements, he stabbed the fourth soldier in the leg and followed through with another blow to the second soldier's head, knocking him unconscious. He eliminated the two downed soldiers without hesitation.

Little John strode over to the first soldier, who struggled to get away, grabbed his collar, dragging him to the cliff edge. With a thunderous voice, he hollered at the fifth soldier, his words slicing through the air. He propelled the first soldier over the precipice, the rush of wind against his face mirroring the surge of adrenaline coursing through his veins. The fifth soldier panicked, letting some horses go, mounting his own steed as he galloped off with much haste. The blacksmith stood, surveying the bloody scene with a triumphant smile. Another victory against the forces of evil.

Chapter 43

SCREWED SOFTWARE, SHEFFIELD

MONDAY

P HIL BOUNDED OVER TO Reed's desk when he entered the Screwed Software offices on Monday morning, his eyes filled with anticipation and a wide smile on his face. The sound of keyboards and ringing phones created a buzz of productivity. The smell of freshly brewed coffee wafted through the room. Phil was eager to share his findings with Reed.

"I've some news for you, Reed," he blurted out.

"I hope so Phil because I'm still pissed off they've beaten us to the next piece of treasure and clue."

"Well, mate, listen to this. I persuaded Jed to help me yesterday. We spent the day searching and finding out as much information as possible about the individuals we encountered on Saturday. We know about Ambrose. I now have her mobile number. She's not active on social media and sends very few messages, nothing really to help us. The older guy is Eric Coulson. I traced his car registration to get his name. On Saturday evening Ambrose's car went to a massive house in the country in Cotgrave, just south of Nottingham and guess who owns it?"

"Eric Coulson," Reed said.

"Spot on Reed. He has a history of being an archaeologist, as I found many references to his younger days on various dig sites, but nothing for the past ten years. I wondered what he's been doing in the last decade. Acquiring artefacts and selling them on the black market is my guess. Nothing on social media for him."

Reed listened to Phil's detailed explanations of what he had found out, getting more interested as it went on.

"The young lad's name is Brandon Bentley. He's Eric Coulson's nephew. He's a boxer, as you suspected, just turned semi-pro, with a big fight coming up in a few weeks' time, according to his Instagram page. I have phone numbers for the trio and set up a notification system using Jed's software for any messages or social media posts. We can be straight on them."

"Perfect, playing them at their own game," said Reed.

"We are mate. The downside is I can't find anything on the young ginger haired girl. Zero social media links to her from any of the other three."

"Well, you've made a cracking start, Phil. We just need one of them to trip up. Or we could conduct surveillance of Coulson's house, let me think about that. Thanks so much for doing all that."

"Happy to help. My weekend's been the most exciting for decades!" Phil said.

Phil returned to his desk, chuckling to himself. He planned to carry out some more research during his lunch break. He had a strong desire to uncover as much information as he could. They had to find the third silver fereter and its ancient map.

Chapter 44

COTGRAVE, NEAR NOTTINGHAM
MONDAY

C OULSON HAD PLACED AN order for a powerful dehumidifier, anticipating the change it would bring to the damp hardwood of Little John's quarterstaff. He hoped restoring the hardwood would succeed, enabling him to get a large sum of money for it. On returning to the manor house on Saturday evening, he had placed the staff in the fishpond wrapped in hessian cloth to stop the fish from nibbling on it. The key was keeping it submerged for now. He had seen what happened on a previous archaeological dig near La Paz in Bolivia on the banks of Lake Titicaca. Deep in the murky depths of the lake, a discovery of ancient spears etched with Mayan symbols had laid hidden on the lake bed. The inexperienced workers left the wood to dry in the sun. As a result, the wood disintegrated. He couldn't bear the idea of Little John's quarterstaff ending up in a similar situation.

The backstop solution if he wasn't able to revive the hardwood would be to recreate the quarterstaff using the gold end pieces. These alone would be worth a tidy sum. He imagined the quarterstaff taking pride of place in one of his clients' grand hallways after they had coughed up substantial funds to purchase it from him. His estimation of value was several hundred thousand, maybe half a million pounds, if he could get a couple of buyers bidding against each other.

Yesterday, he had opened the third fereter and discovered another scroll with a treasure map. He couldn't help but think this discovery was turning into something incredible. The map revealed a winding river flowing from the south to the north, forming gentle bends. A feature of the ancient map was a crude forest marking on the east side with a large half-closed arch sitting in the middle of the forest area, plus a tiny square with a wavy line inside. The arch had some depth to it, suggesting cliffs or massive rocks. He examined the map inside the library's display cabinet again, still unable to determine its location. He needed to see how Pearson was getting on with the puzzle.

"Pearson, have you made any progress with the map?"

"No, boss, it's proving to be very difficult," Pearson responded to Coulson's phone call.

"Keep digging Pearson, we need to find this next place. The treasure might surpass the quarterstaff's value."

"I'll keep at it Mr Coulson."

"Do Ambrose and Bentley know you've uploaded it to the secure message system?"

"Yes, they do."

"Okay, ensure no-one downloads the photo or sends it to anyone else. Call me when you have something," said Coulson.

"Yes, will do."

Coulson reached for a book from the shelves in his library, delving deeper into the tale of Robin Hood. The pages described the weapons used in medieval times, whilst the promise of further treasure permeated his thoughts. He always carried out further research during archaeological digs and saw no reason to change his approach now. Coulson cast his mind back to Ambrose's description of the fight and how they retrieved the second fereter. A fleeting thought crossed his mind. Reaching for his phone, he dialled Ambrose.

"Ambrose, a question. When you confronted the group on Baslow

Moor, did you notice anything else other than the fereter?"

"Do you mean some other treasure?" she asked.

"Yes, anything gold?"

"No, nothing, just the silver fereter."

"Didn't you say the girls ran off once you got there?" questioned Coulson.

"Yes, that's correct. I assumed they were running away from the fight," replied Ambrose.

"Could they have had some treasure?" asked Coulson.

"I saw nothing in their hands, but they both had backpacks on, so yes, I suppose they could've hidden it in one of their bags."

"It just seems absurd we've found the quarterstaff plus a fereter, yet they only had a fereter. My guess is they found something. I'll speak to Garcia and get him to keep his ears and eyes open," concluded Coulson.

Seated in the library staring out of the large windows, Coulson realised the group must have stumbled upon a discovery. They would have concealed it from Ambrose. He knew they would report the discovery to the Finds Liaison Officer in the future. Perhaps he should pre-empt it, as they would have no other avenues to gain the true worth associated with the discovery.

Chapter 45

THE PEAKS UNIVERSITY

TUESDAY

REED RETRIEVED THE CRUCIFIX from his safe deposit box in Sheffield during his lunchtime. He then drove down the M1 to The Peaks University to meet with the Finds Liaison Officer. He sat in his car in the university car park, contemplating whether they were doing the right thing? Reed had a gut feeling he could earn more money by selling the artefact on the underground black market. Wealthy collectors would pay a significant amount for something like Friar Tuck's crucifix. Emily insisted they followed the law. Euan and Phil agreed with his viewpoint. However, the other two, Lynsey and Onni, believed Emily was right. They were bound by law in their jobs at the university. Reed closed his eyes and thought about the journey to this point, the discovery of the fereter, the map inside, finding the cave location, fighting with Ambrose and Bentley and seeing Coulson with the other artefact. He sighed. He resigned himself to the path they had all agreed on.

Reed grabbed his backpack, which had the gold crucifix hidden inside. He headed towards the archaeology department to meet Onni. They greeted each other and entered the sterile meeting room where the Finds Liaison Officer introduced himself as Mike Miller. He looked in his early fifties, balding on top with glasses and wearing a green, mottled jumper.

"Onni tells me you're a friend of his and found a gold item in the

191

Peak District about ten days ago?" asked Mike.

"Yes, that's correct. I was doing some rock climbing with my friend, as we often do on the weekends and discovered a small cave. We investigated it as we had head torches with us and found a gold crucifix buried beneath some stones," Reed said, pulling the crucifix out of his bag. "With an emerald, and an unusual word on the reverse, '*Tooke*.'"

Mike Miller picked up the crucifix wearing white gloves, rotating it, using his eyeglass to get a better view of the inscription and the emerald. He must have spent five minutes scrutinising the artefact without saying a word. He laid it down on a piece of white cloth.

"This is an incredible item, Reed, without doubt an amazing find. My initial estimate of age is around six or seven hundred years old, being of gold and a genuine emerald. The inscription on the back makes it interesting. I'm not sure how strong your history is, but it's the old English word for Tuck, so I suspect it belonged to Friar Tuck. He's a mythical figure in the tale of Robin Hood. Folklore often contains kernels of truth. If it's genuine, which I've no reason to doubt, then several museums would be interested in this piece."

"Oh wow, that sounds brilliant," Reed said, pretending to be surprised. "What happens now?"

"To begin, we'll complete the registration paperwork. Afterwards, I'll take the crucifix for analysis and safekeeping. Once we've verified it, we need to contact the landowner to make them aware it was found on their land. We then go to auction with the bidding process, any interested museums putting forward their offers. The auction lasts for a maximum of ninety days. Once the winning bidder makes payment, we'll pay you your share."

"Where will you keep the crucifix?" asked Reed.

"It's held in our safe here at The Peaks University."

"Who's got access to the safe?" asked Onni, feigning innocence.

"Just myself and the manager, Garcia," responded Mike.

Reed's face dropped, as they knew Garcia wasn't honest after the bag search incident. Coulson could have an easy way to steal it!

"Do any artefacts ever go missing from the safe, Mike?" Reed asked.

"Never. Why do you ask?"

Not wanting to disclose any further information, Reed said, "Just wondered. What do you think the gold crucifix is worth?"

"Maybe fifty thousand pounds, as this could have historical significance," Mike said.

"Oh, I thought it would fetch a higher price."

"Unlikely, face value without the name on the back it may be worth twenty thousand, but I'm betting on the link to Friar Tuck being a powerful pull."

"I'm curious," Reed asked, "how much would end up being mine?"

"We have testing to pay for plus analysis work, then the remaining amount will be apportioned between yourself and the landowner," said Mike.

"That's disappointing. What if I wanted to keep the gold crucifix for myself?"

"I'm sorry. I can't let you do that. The law is explicit on ancient artefacts or relics over three hundred years old. They're an integral part of our nation's history and should be accessible for everyone to view. It'll be on display in a museum somewhere," Mike said.

Reed had nothing to say in response. He tried to catch Onni's eye, but Onni evaded his gaze. I knew we were mistaken to follow the law, Reed thought. Mike Miller went through the paperwork, worked out the latitude and longitude of the cave, and finished up with requesting Reed's signature, which he obliged. They wrapped up the meeting and Reed trudged back to his campervan, disappointed for the second time in the past few days. The exhilaration of the discovery waned, but he had an idea so called Euan.

"Hey mate, the Finds Liaison Officer reckons fifty grand tops for the crucifix before their fees, and guess what? We have to split it with the landowner!"

"Oh Reed, that's disappointing. Everyone's invested their time and effort. We'll receive about four thousand pounds each. I suppose that's a decent sum of money," Euan said.

"Yes, true mate. I've got an idea. Are you busy tonight?"

"No, what've you got planned?"

"I'm in Nottingham. I'm going to look at Coulson's property. Fancy meeting me there with your gadgets?"

"Hell yeah, mate, I'm on my way home. I'll be with you in an hour and a half."

"Brilliant, Euan. Oh, one more thing, when are you going to ask out Lynsey? There's no doubt she likes you."

"I know. I never feel the time is quite right, so end up panicking."

"Just do it, Euan," said Reed.

"Yes, I will."

"Okay, see you soon."

Reed then fired off a message to Emily.

Reed: *'Hi Em, bad news from the meeting. I'll update you when I get home. Be back around eight as I'm catching up with Euan.'*

Emily: *'Okay, see you soon.'*

After spending some time contemplating how to gain the next map, he took a break and searched for a takeaway pizza restaurant. He intended to grab something to eat for them, before driving to Cotgrave on this leg of his journey.

Chapter 46

COTGRAVE, NEAR NOTTINGHAM

TUESDAY

E ARLIER, COULSON HAD JUST finished his late afternoon cup of Earl Grey tea when his phone rang, the sound cutting through the silence of the library. He picked it up, his fingers tapping on the smooth surface of the table. It was Garcia on the line, his voice somewhat guarded as he relayed the news of Reed's visit to the Finds Liaison Officer today. Coulson had leaned back in his chair, closing his eyes for a moment, imagining the gold crucifix in his hands. Garcia then confirmed he believed it to be genuine, having seen it. Coulson realised he had missed the chance to offer money to Reed Hascombe and summoned Garcia to join him at the house immediately on the pretext of showing him the quarterstaff.

Coulson and Garcia sat in the library as the early evening sunshine brightened up the dark room. He relayed the adventure from the weekend, but only focussed on Stanage Edge and the quarterstaff.

"Tell me about the crucifix situation Alejandro," asked Coulson.

"Well, there was a meeting earlier between Mike Miller, the Finds Liaison Officer, Reed Hascombe, and Onni Jarvinnen. Mr Hascombe brought in the gold crucifix, which he found in a cave in the Peak District. Mike showed it to me to get my opinion before we put it into the university safe. It's an amazing gold piece with a beautiful emerald and the inscription '*Tooke*'. We both think it's genuine and belonged to Friar Tuck, but we've yet to carry out tests to validate it."

"Mmmm, that's interesting. So this Onni fella has been helping Hascombe?"

"Although I haven't had the chance to speak with him yet, I believe there's a possibility he has. He's a diligent worker and quite capable. It would surprise me if he broke the rules."

"You break the rules, Alejandro. Why wouldn't anyone else?"

"Hmm, true."

"Which brings me on to my next point. I need you to break the rules again. Your reward will be substantial and well worth your efforts. Get me the crucifix," Coulson said, being firm.

"I can't do that. I'll lose my job straightaway," Garcia stammered.

Coulson suggested, "Stage it as a robbery, as the university will have insurance cover."

"I don't feel comfortable with your idea, Eric."

"I thought you wouldn't. Maybe I need to find someone else?"

"I think that's unfair. I've helped you a lot, but you're pushing me beyond the limit."

"And I've helped you a lot, Alejandro. The money I've given you is enough to buy a house in Spain!"

Garcia paused, his eyes scanning the room as he thought, the faint scent of old books lingering in the air. How could he know that? This was becoming too difficult. He had to buy himself some time.

Garcia stated, "I'll think about it and devise a plan. Can I look at the quarterstaff now?"

"Yes, of course. I urge you to come up with your plan soon. The quarterstaff is in the fishpond whilst I wait for a dehumidifier to arrive. It's been underground in the dark and immersed in a pool for centuries, so it's quite fragile. Follow me."

They went outside to the fishpond whilst the daylight remained. Coulson pulled the quarterstaff from the pond, unwrapping it for Garcia to look at. The sun's warm rays danced upon the gleaming gold end pieces, as if casting a spell. They both felt the powerful spiritual pull of the ancient item. Coulson imagined the countless battles it had witnessed and the lives it had taken. He could almost hear the echoes of past clashes and the distant cries of warriors.

"This is special, Eric," Garcia said.

"Do you agree it would have belonged to Little John, especially considering where I found it?" asked Coulson.

"Yes. Once restored, we should carry out the aging tests. Do you have another treasure map?"

"It's inside. I'll show you. Let me replace the staff back in the pond."

Coulson wrapped the quarterstaff in its hessian protection, lowering it into the fishpond. They returned to the library. Coulson showed Garcia the next map locked away in the display case close to the window.

"We think it's probably deep in the Peak District again. Do you have any suggestions for locations?"

"I don't know the Peak District. Shall I take a photo and do some research?"

"No. I don't want it getting into anyone else's hands," Coulson said, with emphasis on the word 'No.'

"Okay, sorry, I can't help with that," replied Garcia.

"Fine. Once you've figured out your plan to get the crucifix, let me know," Coulson said.

He guided Garcia towards the front door after concluding their business, before making his way back to the library. He settled into his plush leather chair, deep in thought, on how to uncover the whereabouts marked on the map. After several minutes of thinking, he took a break and headed downstairs to visit *The Safe*, intending to return to the library afterwards.

Chapter 47

COTGRAVE, NEAR NOTTINGHAM

TUESDAY

R EED HID IN SOME bushes in the country lane about fifty yards from the entrance to Coulson's manor house, waiting for Euan to arrive. A white Skoda Octavia estate had passed him seconds after entering the large evergreen bush. He watched, eyes fixed on the vehicle as it rolled up to the imposing gate. Along with the ten-foot brick wall, the gate presented a barrier to Coulson's property for unwanted visitors. The metal ironwork gate had an intricate design. It opened with a low creak, granting the vehicle access. As the gate closed behind it, a faint scent of exhaust wafted towards him, mingling with the smell of pizza waiting to be eaten. Reed spotted Euan strolling up the lane after leaving his car further down the road. He popped his head out waving and together they sat in the bush, eating the pizzas Reed had brought with him.

"Euan, it's time to get the drone flying," Reed said.

"Hang on, just one more piece to finish," Euan said, downing the remaining cold slice of pepperoni pizza. He rummaged through his backpack to retrieve the drone and prepare it for flight. With a soft hum of propellers, it soared above the ten-foot wall, ascending higher and higher into the expanse of the sky.

"Look Reed, he's got CCTV cameras on the inside of the wall. The house looks immense, expensive, worth quite a few million," Euan said.

"Makes me sick. He got the goons to steal the fereter when he already has this! How close can you get?"

"Pretty close if everyone is inside. What're we looking for?"

"Anything that can help us get the next map, mate."

"Let's scope out the house. Hopefully, we can find something to help," Reed said.

Euan piloted the drone around the top of the ivy-clad house, noting more cameras on every side of the property, the red Jaguar F-Type parked in front of the palatial frontage of the house. They detected movement at the front door, Euan moving the drone further upwards, out of sight, ensuring it couldn't be heard. Reed observed two figures emerging from the house through the flickering screen of the remote control as the front door swung open. Coulson, he knew, but the second was unknown. The pair meandered towards the fishpond, its water reflecting the orange hue of the setting sun. Coulson reached into the water of the fishpond and retrieved a long pole.

"Shit me Reed, that's the same thing we spotted him with on Saturday. What's it doing in the fishpond?" Euan asked.

"Don't know. Look at that reflection," Reed said. "It must be gold."

"Pity I can't get a closer look without them hearing or seeing the drone."

"Don't risk getting too close, Euan."

Reed and Euan watched as Coulson and the other person finished looking at the pole, placing it back in the pond before returning inside the house. They continued watching the house as the second person exited the property, got in the white Skoda, and drove towards the gate. Reed and Euan, still inside the bush, held their breath as the vehicle passed close by them.

"I've got an idea Euan. Why don't we climb over the wall? We could steal the pole from the pond."

"There are far too many cameras, Reed. He's covered the entire property with them. We'll get seen."

"Can't you try out the jammer function you've built in to the drone?" asked Reed.

"I can try, but the battery only has ten minutes' charge remaining and I don't have a spare with me. Can we enter and exit in time?"

"I could if you stayed here."

"Excellent idea. Let's grab a rope so you can climb over the wall," Euan said.

Reed retrieved a rope from his campervan and spotted a suitable point to climb over the wall. He tied it to a nearby tree, pulling himself up the wall. He sat atop the wall, gazing at the country house in the distance, working out a route to get to the fishpond unseen. Euan activated the jamming functionality on the drone. The surveillance camera closest to Reed started flashing with a small red light, showing it had lost connection with the base unit in the house.

Reed put his thumb up to Euan and dropped from the ten-foot wall, rolling into a sprint-ready position. He ran towards a clump of oak trees close to the far corner of the house, his black hair flowing in the wind. The oak trees would give him some cover close to the house as the fishpond sat at the front of the property. He had set the timer on his watch for ten minutes, enabling him to monitor how much time he had left. Once inside the cluster of oak trees, he checked the watch; two and a half minutes gone already. Lights illuminated the two rooms he needed to bypass in order to reach the fishpond. Hugging the wall, he scurried beneath the windowsill of the first room, glancing in the window, seeing a grand piano beside a luxurious leather sofa positioned in front of a gigantic television. Another reminder of this man's wealth.

Reed crept along the wall to the next room, about to bob down below the line of sight, when something caught his eye. A glass display case close to the window backdropped by dark wooden shelves full of books. This must be the library, he thought, observing the plush leather chairs, large hardwood table and high ceiling. He couldn't believe his eyes. There, in the display case, was another map, similar to the one they had discovered two weeks ago. Without hesitation, he pulled out his phone and snapped off a few photos, making sure he zoomed in. Reed smiled. He had stumbled on this by accident. They were back in the game. Perhaps Coulson hadn't worked out the location yet, he thought. The two-way radio crackled and Euan barked.

"You've under five minutes left Reed, hurry."

Before Reed could answer, he spotted some movement in the library's doorway and, aware he stood right up against the glass, bobbed down out of sight. His heart rate increased as the adrenaline kicked in. What if he had been spotted? Reed made a quick decision. He didn't have sufficient time to reach the fishpond, resorting to crawling back along the wall in order to avoid being noticed. He crouched underneath the lounge window and scurried back to the clump of trees.

"Now on my way back, Euan."

"Roger that," came Euan's swift response.

No time to discuss anything he needed to move, and quick. He sprinted flat out across the lawn, dodging between flowerbeds, and reached the perimeter wall. With his heart pounding, he checked his watch. It showed less than thirty seconds left. Reed grabbed the rope and pulled himself up, but in his haste, he lost his grip and fell back down. Taking a deep breath with twenty seconds left, he ascended the rope again and his hands reached the top of the rough wall. A loud beep beside him propelled his last push. The camera reconnected with the master unit. He pulled his legs up, swung over the wall, detached the rope and raced to the bush to join Euan. He gulped in deep breaths, slumping to the floor.

"Bloody hell, Reed, you left that late. Where's the pole?"

"I couldn't reach the fishpond in time. Someone came into the library as I stood looking in the window. But look what I got!" Reed said. He pulled out his phone and showed Euan the photo of the map in the glass display unit.

"Another map, well done mate, we're back in the game. Who wants a wet, dirty pole anyway?" Euan said.

"You're right. We just need to figure out the exact location. I suspect the visitor Coulson had earlier was also studying the map, assuming he didn't know the location. We should assemble the team and brainstorm ideas for the weekend."

"Yes mate, tomorrow or Thursday?" asked Euan.

"Don't know yet. I'll let you know. I'll get some pictures printed out, but I won't share it with anyone. They'll still be tracking our messages, according to Jed."

They wrapped up the scouting mission and headed back to their vehicles. Reed's mind whirred as he made his way back to Sheffield. With each passing mile, Reed's earlier disappointment faded, replaced by a growing sense of satisfaction at how the day had unfolded. He enjoyed this adventurous lifestyle, loving every minute of every challenge.

Chapter 48

THE PEAKS UNIVERSITY

WEDNESDAY

A LEJANDRO GARCIA SAT IN his sparse office, deep in thought, considering his conversation with Coulson the previous evening. Coulson didn't say the words, but the implication appeared obvious. If he didn't carry out Coulson's demands of stealing the crucifix, he felt pretty sure there would be some retribution involving the loss of his job. He always visited Coulson to discuss artefacts, so no one could pin anything illegal on him. He racked his brains, but consequences of the fact that he brought a couple of items into the department for testing on a weekend dawned on him. In those early days, the allure of money had become irresistible whilst the prospect of future consequences never crossed his mind.

Garcia pulled out his phone and checked his banking app to see what level of savings he had. Did he have enough funds to return to Seville? As he pondered, his mind shifted its focus back to the crucifix. Was there a way to do this? He jumped up and wandered through the department, looking for Onni, finding him evaluating a pile of coins.

"Onni, can you spare me a few minutes in my office, please?"

"Yes, Mr Garcia," Onni said as they headed back to Garcia's office, closing the door behind them.

"I need to ask you why you were involved with Mike Miller in yesterday's artefact find meeting?" Garcia asked.

"Reed is a friend of mine. He's new to this, so suggested I'd sit in with him."

"How do you know him?"

"Through a mutual friend who works at the university."

"I see. Do you remember the incident the other week? When a member of staff entered our department with an item not documented on the register? Was that you?"

"No, Mr Garcia."

Garcia stared at Onni without answering. He looked uncomfortable. Onni's hands jiggled as he shifted twice in his seat. He felt sure Onni was involved. Then an idea exploded in Garcia's mind, make Onni the fall guy.

"Okay, thanks Onni. I think I'm going to put you in charge of testing the crucifix. We start next week once Mike Miller provides the clearance. We have covered everything for the moment. Thank you for your time."

"Thank you for the opportunity, Mr Garcia," said Onni, exiting the office.

The hum of the air conditioning helped Garcia ponder his plan. The glow of his monitor displaying the camera feed reminded him of the watchful eye on the entrance to the safe. He imagined the weight of the crucifix in his hands, cool and smooth against his skin. He could hear Onni's retreating footsteps in the corridor as a plan formed in his mind. Garcia envisioned himself slipping away, leaving the site on an urgent errand whilst Onni carried out the ageing tests. This would stop Onni from returning the crucifix to the vault, giving him no option but to place it in the general storage area. Garcia would return later in the evening and retrieve the artefact. The plan, though deceitful, appeared to be the perfect solution.

Chapter 49

CENTRAL CHESTERFIELD

THURSDAY

REED HAD ORGANISED ANOTHER evening out for the team in Chesterfield as it sat halfway between Nottingham and Sheffield, easier for everyone to get to in an evening. This time, they opted for a Thai restaurant. As they approached it, they spotted two homeless men sleeping in the doorway of a large shop. Huddled together in their worn-out sleeping bags, they shivered on the cold pavement, their tatty cover offering little comfort. Desperate for any kindness, they pleaded with passersby, their tired voices blending with the passing traffic. Their scruffy flat cap lay on the pavement, hoping for the clink of coins to bring them a glimmer of hope. Emily stopped. She pulled out a five-pound note, laying it on the grey cap.

"Thank you, miss," one man said, grinning a toothy smile.

"You're welcome. Get some food with it, please."

They walked further into town and, once out of earshot of the homeless men, Reed passed a comment.

"That's a waste Em, they'll only spend it on booze or drugs."

"Don't be so assuming Reed, some people need kindness and help. By displaying acts of kindness, we can show them good-natured people exist in this world. There'll be some extra money coming our way, so what is five pounds to us?"

"When you put it like that, Em, I guess you're right."

Reed's mind wandered to the country estate of Coulson, picturing the grandeur and wealth surrounding him. He contrasted this with the sight of the homeless men lying down in the shop doorway, but dismissed the notion as they approached the restaurant, the aroma of delicious food wafting through the air. They were last to arrive, the other four were chatting among themselves. The waiter guided the group to their table and left them to peruse the menu, promising to return soon for drinks orders. The restaurant provided a subtle ambiance with the golden buddha statues on display throughout.

"Thanks for coming again, everyone, especially at such short notice. Euan and I had another little adventure on Tuesday night, visiting the house where Coulson lives. To recap, Eric Coulson is the mastermind behind the two goons. He lives in a huge, impressive country manor near Cotgrave. I would guess all paid for by stealing artefacts and selling them to other rich people. We watched him holding a large pole he found at Robin Hood's cave on Saturday, which looked like it has gold decorative ends. Phil thinks it might be Little John's quarterstaff. I have a question for you, Onni. Why would he keep it in the fishpond?" Reed said.

"I assume it's wooden and if it's lain in water for centuries, there is every chance the wood has been preserved but if you bring it straight out into the light and a warmer atmosphere, then it'll dry out quicker than it should, making it likely to disintegrate," Onni explained.

"So he needs to keep it wet until he can control the moisture extraction?" interjected Lynsey.

"He needs a room with a dehumidifier. This will control the moisture content and stop the wood from disintegrating. Our university has equipment for that purpose."

"So, if your manager is involved with Coulson, he might do it for him?" asked Reed.

"If he did, they'd have to record it because it'll take several days, and Coulson would end up losing the quarterstaff to the authorities."

Euan asked, "Could that have been Onni's manager we saw on

Tuesday evening?"

"Yes, I suppose it could have," replied Reed.

Onni took the pause in the conversation to update the team on some news, "yesterday, my manager, Garcia, called me into his office. He asked about when Euan and Lynsey brought the first silver fereter to me. Once again, I denied it. However, he then informed me I'd be involved in testing the crucifix. I'm quite pleased with the assignment since it's the first time he's asked me to do something. Normal procedure is for my team leader to assign my tasks."

"Onni, that must be satisfying for you. I'm pleased you're involved."

The waiter came to the table to take their drinks orders, all artefact talk ceased until he returned to the bar. The restaurant, with its soft lighting and gentle hum of chatter, wasn't too busy. They had a cosy table tucked away in a corner, ensuring their conversation remained private. Reed retrieved a handful of photo prints from his bag, the glossy paper reflecting the overhead spotlights. He passed the photos around, explaining they were of another map that Coulson held. They studied the photos, their eyes scanning every detail. The conversation hushed as they pored over the images, searching for any clues of the hidden location on the ancient map. A river running south to north, the expanse of woodland, the strange half-closed arch in the middle of it.

"This is the first time you've seen the map, Lynsey and Onni. We couldn't figure out the location. Does anyone have any thoughts?"

"I've not found anything on Google maps resembling it," said Phil.

"I can't think of any caves big enough in the Peak District," said Euan, pointing to the large arch shape in the middle of the wooded area.

"Oh, I thought it looked far too big to be a cave when comparing it to the previous map," said Emily. "Could it be a natural amphitheatre, like a big rock horseshoe?"

The group fell into silence, deep in thought after Emily's words.

Clapping her hands out of the blue, Lynsey startled those around her. She gasped in excitement.

"I know where it is. I had a race a month ago around a town called Crich and there's a large rocky horseshoe shaped area in the middle of some woods there. It's on a hillside and I thought how lovely it appeared with the sun shining in between the trees."

"Show me where on Google maps?" asked Phil.

"Oh, hang on, I need to pull up my run on Strava."

Lynsey coordinated her run with Phil's Google maps and found it near a place called Whatstandwell, also spotting a track called Robin Hood Road running through the block of woodland.

"It's not obvious on Google maps. It's obscured by the tree cover. Are you sure Lynsey?"

"I remember it clear as day. It made quite an impression on me, and at the time I thought it resembled a natural amphitheatre. Thanks for the memory jog, Em."

"Wow Lynsey, that's amazing," said Euan, giving her a congratulatory clap on the shoulder.

"Ah, thanks Euan," she responded, leaning towards him with a nod of her head. Reed wondered when his mate would ask her out. He needed to have a word with his friend again, before he loses the opportunity.

"Anyone interested in going on another adventure this weekend?" Reed said.

The air filled with a chorus of enthusiastic positive responses. Ice cubes clinking against the sides of the glasses resonated throughout the restaurant as the waiter navigated around the maze of tables carrying a tray of beverages, ready to jot down their food orders. The group continued discussing the potential map location and making plans for Saturday. They agreed to meet early, at eight o'clock in the morning at Whatstandwell train station car park. The excitement became palpable as their food arrived, tucking into an array, including fragrant Thai prawns, shredded beef, and red chicken curry. The many aromas adding to their building sense of adventure. This time they would be better prepared, planning on having more than one lookout and Euan's UGV ready for action. Reed just hoped they weren't too late. Maybe Coulson had already got to the next lot of treasure before them.

Chapter 50

CENTRAL NOTTINGHAM

FRIDAY

PEARSON HAD ARRANGED ANOTHER Zoom call with Coulson and his team for lunchtime to go through an update on the map and his findings. He had researched countless caves and rock cliffs, but none seemed to align with the map. However, a glimmer of hope emerged as he considered Cresswell Crags, where the legendary Robin Hood may have lived in a cave. He set up the online meeting room and logged in. He waited for the other two to join him. Coulson's face appeared, followed by Ambrose's, so Pearson started the meeting off.

"I'm still struggling with the likely location for the map, Mr Coulson. I've narrowed it down to a place called Cresswell Crags."

"Why Cresswell Crags?" Coulson asked.

"Well, it features two long stretches of rocky cliffs which could have been a complete section six or seven hundred years ago. In between the cliffs, there's a lake with a river flowing through it. The area also has multiple caves, each one named. One is called Robin Hood cave, although they're a favourite spot for tourists and rock climbers," outlined Pearson.

"I understand. Is it your best idea?"

"Yes, at the moment."

The screen blipped as a fourth person joined the meeting: Wendy Markham.

"Ah, Wendy, thank you for joining us, I thought your knowledge of the Peak District would help," said Coulson, as he held up the map to the camera, "this is the map Wendy, there's a river with forest and a large arch or cave amid the wooded area. Pearson thinks it could be Cresswell Crags. Are you familiar with that area?"

"Yes, I know it. They often have climbing classes there."

"I thought it looked more of a horseshoe shape than an arch," Ambrose interjected.

"Maybe. It's difficult to tell. The parchment is old and faint," Pearson admitted. He felt embarrassed for not being innovative. His fingers tapped on the keyboard at speed, finding a new potential location.

"There's a Horseshoe Quarry in Middleton, but reviewing online pictures, the cliff faces look straight."

"I know that place well. I've often thought the name didn't fit," said Wendy.

"Do some more research on it, Pearson. Wendy, the map also has a tiny square marking in the middle of the arch, or horseshoe, with a wavy line through it," said Coulson.

"A thought just occurred to me. I know another place that might fit but it's not in the Peak District, it's near Whatstandwell. There are large rocky cliffs there, but I'm unsure if any caves exist," said Wendy.

Pearson carried out a quick Google review while the others were talking.

"I can't find anything on Google maps Wendy, it appears to be just woods. There is a Robin Hood Road which runs straight through the area, though."

"You won't see it from above because the entire area is woods."

"Okay, team, I think we need to check out both locations tomorrow. Let's head to Horseshoe Quarry first. Meet there at nine o'clock. Afterwards we'll try Wendy's suggestion. I don't think it's Cresswell Crags Pearson, that has already been excavated for relics.

I'll pick up Bentley and Ambrose, you pick up Wendy again. Let's hope one location is right. Pearson, any further information on the other group? Any conversations or social media activity?" said Coulson.

"I'm getting nothing at all, Mr Coulson, the campervan hasn't moved either. It's like they know we're tracking them," replied Pearson.

"Let's assume they've worked that out. At the moment, we're ahead of them. Let's keep it that way. Make sure you're available to help remotely Pearson."

After the meeting, Pearson started investigating both locations. He wanted to gather as much information as possible to help the team. Despite his efforts, he made little progress. Google proved to be of little help, offering only detailed climbing routes at Horseshoe Quarry.

Chapter 51

Whatstandwell, near Matlock

Saturday

R EED SAT IN THE front of Euan's car as they pulled into the
car park at Whatstandwell train station just before eight
o'clock. They were there first. With Emily's help, they unpacked
the climbing gear, the drone, and Euan's UGV. The roar of a Suzuki
engine caught Reed's attention as Phil spun into the car park, pulling
up beside Euan's car. Soon afterwards, Lynsey's car arrived with
her and Onni. The six friends gathered around Reed with their
backpacks and equipment, ready for another day of adventure.
Reed gazed across the undulating hills on the other side of the
A6 road, their peaks shrouded in a hazy morning mist. The distant
calls of birds sounded in the still air, while he caught the smell
of wildflowers. A sense of anticipation tingled in his skin as he
pondered what adventures awaited them today. At least it's dry after
last night's heavy showers, he thought. A rumble in the distance
made Reed question himself, but realised a train was approaching
as the tannoy announced the eight thirteen to Derby.

"Lynsey, can you lead the way? Everyone ready?" Reed asked.

After positive confirmations, the group trooped over the railway
bridge and onto the canal footpath before turning left towards
the bridge over the road. After the rain last night, the ground felt
squelchy and damp as Reed walked, with patches of mud sticking
to his shoes. The canal teemed with an array of birds, swimming,

foraging for food, and gliding in the sky. Passing under the bridge, they noticed another two cars pull up into a layby beside the canal. Reed felt on edge, checking if Coulson or any of his crew were inside the vehicles. They weren't. He remained mindful of the disastrous outcome of their previous quest for treasure, the memories of their misfortune etched in his mind. Determined not to repeat their past mistakes, he didn't intend to be caught out again, his senses alert to every sight, sound, and smell that might show danger.

Reed stayed at the back and watched as Lynsey led the group over a bridge spanning the canal and into a wooded area where the track started a steep climb. As they weaved between the canopy of trees, the track unveiled a steel gate, which they passed through. Emerging on the other side, they found themselves on Robin Hood Road. The track continued its ascent, disappearing into a wooded area. Reed's eyes caught sight of another track veering off to the right. Lynsey stayed focused on the main track and ignored the alternative path. As they continued their ascent, the path grew muddier. Reed heard rushing water, its powerful current cascading over rocks hidden within the thick foliage. Turning a corner, their eyes were drawn to the magnificent sight of towering rocky cliffs jutting above the track.

Lynsey ignored another pathway leading off to the right and continued on to the next turn, which opened out into a large wooded clearing bordered by rock cliffs. Reed gazed in awe as he beheld the immense cliffs, their towering grandeur marred by deep fissures and jagged cracks. Evidence of past rockfalls created a sense of danger and intrigue. Clusters of rocks, covered by a velvety blanket of green moss, only deepened the enigma of the place. The trees created a broad canopy explaining why the cliffs weren't obvious from above on Google maps. It looked like a natural amphitheatre, but Reed felt unsure whether he would class this as a horseshoe, so reached for the map in his backpack to check.

"Is this it Lynsey?" he asked.

"Yes, it's pretty impressive," she replied.

"It is. An almost surreal place, although I'm not sure it matches the map."

"Oh, why's that?"

"It's not a horseshoe shape, more of a crescent or half circle. I can't see the small square block. Unless rockfalls have covered it over the centuries."

The others gathered round Reed, pouring over the map, scanning the area and comparing it to their expectations, trying to make sense of the puzzle.

"It doesn't look quite the same," admitted Phil, "but shouldn't we check the area, anyway?"

"Yes, we should. Can you do it, Onni? I'm going to check out the other area we passed. Em, can you and Lynsey move down the hill and check for walkers heading up? Phil, you go up the hill and check for passersby. Euan, can you help Onni? I'll return in a few minutes," Reed said.

As the others headed off to do their tasks, Reed strode off to the smaller area he had spotted just below this one. The rocky cliffs fascinated him. He concluded there were no obvious climbing holds, the sheer rock faces weren't popular with climbers. As Reed stepped into the second location, the gentle caress of sunlight seeping through the lush foliage resembled fairy dust twirling in the air. This looked promising, but upon turning the corner, the rocky cliffs just disappeared into a mound of moss-covered rocks only a few feet high. It also looked too narrow to contain even a small square of rocks. Disappointed, he wandered back up the hill to the original clearing. He sought Phil and found him standing on a small wooden bridge spanning a rushing stream in the dense woods.

"Phil, that area isn't right either. It's too small and the cliffs are separate, not a horseshoe shape. Can you pull up Google maps?"

"Of course, we're here," he said, zooming in on the wooded area.

"What's that?" Reed asked, pointing to an area further east.

"It looks like some more rocky cliffs."

They both peered at Phil's phone, zooming in and out, peering at the satellite views and the pathways.

"The access to that area looks like it's the other pathway I spotted earlier. We should try it if Onni has found nothing."

"It could be a possibility, Reed."

Reed headed back to the main clearing to check on Onni and Euan, hoping for some news.

"Any luck?" he asked

"No, nothing yet. We've scanned the ground and cliff faces twice, just this section in the dip to try," said Onni.

Reed waited whilst his friend finished his detecting activity. The tone on the machine remained constant and the red light didn't flash once. Disappointment lingered, even Euan looked glum, Reed thought.

"This area isn't the correct location, nor does the area next to it look right either, although we should scan it to be sure," Reed said.

"Yes, I think you are right," replied Onni.

"There's a third area to check whilst we're here. We found it on Google maps using Phil's phone. I'll tell the girls."

Reed pressed the button on the two-way radio. He tells Emily and Lynsey where they are going to search next. The three lads picked up all their gear and moved to the second area to carry on metal detecting. Reed watched on. He checked his watch. This was taking far too long. He was still concerned Coulson and the goons could turn up anytime. After another twenty minutes, Onni finished his sweep of the area with the same result: nothing. Reed walked up the hill to collect Phil and together they headed down to meet up with the girls. At the junction by the road with the alternative path, they headed up the fresh track. The positive outlook an hour ago now diminished.

They rounded a sharp bend. In front of them, the entire area opened up, with rocky cliffs towering on three sides. As they stepped into the area, the radiant sun vanished behind a thick cloud. This unexpected change in lighting cast a gloomy shadow over the surroundings. It dampened the mood, but as they surveyed the area, excitement grew.

"Oh wow," Reed exclaimed.

"This is a horseshoe shape," Emily said.

"There's a square in the middle," exclaimed Onni.

"This matches the map. We should start detecting right away," Reed said.

Reed instructed Phil to position himself up the main walkway and sent the girls below the road next to the gate, taking the two-way radio with them. Onni strode over to the square block of rocks, only about three levels high. Everything was covered in moss and surrounded by mounds of earth. The structure appeared to be a diminutive building, its collapsed state clear. However, its limited height showed it would not have provided enough room for an individual to stand upright. Perhaps it was an animal shelter? Or maybe the outside walls had been higher than it suggested now, thought Reed.

Almost instantly, the metal detector beeped, and the red light flashed as Onni started scanning the collapsed building. Reed and Euan hurried over to Onni. Between them, they started moving the rocks from the top. Reed paused for a moment before telling the girls they needed to be on their guard. The lads toiled, their muscles straining as they heaved away the massive rocks. The shrill beeping of the metal detector grew louder, resonating through the air, guiding their efforts. With each passing moment, the rough boulders transitioned into soft soil and pebbles, making their work lighter. As the three lads laboured on the excavation, the hole deepened below the level of the rocks they had observed from the outside, making it obvious they would need to dig down at least three feet. The two-way radio squawked.

"Emily to Reed, come in."

"Yes, Em?"

"There's a group of elderly walkers coming up the hill. Let's hope they follow the main track, but it might be wise to be quieter for the next few minutes."

"Okay, will do. Thanks."

The outside walls were now above their knees when the next scan of the metal detector yielded an almost constant beeping noise. They stopped and Onni prodded around with his pickaxe. Reed took over as Onni looked tired, striking something metallic. He cleared the soil using the trowel and discovered a silver object, another fereter, like the other three. He waved it in the air with a triumphant shout. Remembering what Onni had done on their previous adventure, he grabbed the metal detector to check if anything remained. It continued to emit a loud, constant beep. Euan jumped in and between them, they flung out more soil and small stones with their hands. Then a glimmer of something.

Their diligent efforts revealed a gleaming treasure, its golden hue catching the sunlight. With meticulous care, they brushed away the layers of dirt, unveiling a regal chain shimmering in the light. Reed's eyes widened as they gazed upon the artefact, a sense of elation flooding his thoughts. The chain comprised several larger pieces of gold joined by chunky gold links and a main centre piece of a castle emblem. Reed grabbed the two-way radio and informed the girls, who appeared with Phil in tow. The group was ecstatic with their find.

"What do you think, Onni?" asked Reed.

"Look at the main centre piece. This looks like Nottingham castle to me. I think this belonged to the Sheriff of Nottingham. It would have been his civic regalia."

"Oh wow. That's incredible. Maybe Robin Hood stole it. It'd be worth a lot of money to a collector."

"We should declare it as a find, like we did the crucifix," Onni said.

"Not this time, Onni. I've an alternative idea about how we should make use of this treasure."

"You could go to prison Reed if you don't," said Emily.

"No-one'll know, lets talk about it later after I've shared my idea. We need to fill the hole in and leave, as I'm worried Coulson and his goons will turn up."

The girls walked back down the hill to keep watch while the four lads filled in the large hole with the soil and smaller stones. They kept the large moss-covered stones aside to place on the top, which should cover their tracks. They had almost finished bar two large boulders when the two-way radio crackled.

"Reed, it's Coulson. He's coming up the hill with the blonde woman and the young lad. They're only about fifty yards away from us," squawked Emily, panicking.

"We've almost finished. Come back here and let's hide. Maybe they'll follow the main pathway."

Reed placed the last large rocks on top of the square mound. All six of the group hid behind an outcrop just in case Coulson and his team wandered into this area. As they waited, Reed suggested to Euan to get his UGV ready for action. He watched as Euan prepped the small vehicle, checking the smoke canisters and loading bolts ready to fire. This time he put both the fereter and the civic regalia in Lynsey's backpack, confident she could outrun anyone in case of trouble.

Chapter 52

WHATSTANDWELL, NEAR MATLOCK

SATURDAY

As Bentley walked up the hill with his uncle, Ambrose and Wendy, he reflected on the morning's events so far. Their journey to Horseshoe Quarry proved fruitless. The area had confirmed his uncle's suspicion that the quarry had only been active in recent times. He had been further impressed by Wendy with her knowledge of different climbs and techniques. He acknowledged the time he had spent in the Peak District over the past few weeks had been enjoyable with its breathtaking scenery and picturesque villages. Speeding around winding bends in his uncle's car also added to the enjoyment.

They ascended the wooded hill near a location known as Whatstandwell, guided by Wendy. Bentley's eyes caught sight of two girls standing next to a polished steel gate in the distance. The girls dashed uphill, disappearing from view. As he walked, he felt a small stone nestled inside his shoe, causing a sharp pain with each step.

"I'm going to stop, Ambrose. I've got a stone in my shoe. Carry on without me. I'll catch you up," Bentley said.

"Okay, don't be long."

Bentley leaned against the rough bark of a towering tree, the faint scent of damp earth filling his nostrils. With a sigh, he knelt down and untied the laces on his once-pristine Nike trainers. He felt annoyed as he examined the now-dirtied shoes marred by dark smudges and clumps of mud. Determined to salvage their appearance, he plucked a handful of green bracken from the ground and wiped the grime away, though traces of dirt remained clinging to the trainers. I'll give them a thorough cleaning once I'm home, he murmured to himself. As he finished securing his laces, his gaze drifted up the sloping hill, straining his eyes, but the figures of his companions were nowhere to be seen.

Bentley arrived at the gate, easing through, and crossed the road ahead of him. After twenty metres, the track forked, although the left appeared to be the more obvious route. He hesitated whilst pondering which direction to take, hearing some voices coming from the right-hand path. He went that way. Following a sharp ninety-degree turn, his gaze fell upon a group of people standing ahead of him. He recognised Reed Hascombe and the familiar faces of the others.

He shouted as loud as he could, "Ambrose, I need help. I've found the group chasing the treasures,"

Euan spotted Bentley straightaway. With his eyes fixed on his target, he manoeuvred the UGV, its mechanics hummed as he positioned it in front of the group. Euan's heart raced, adrenaline surging through his veins, as he readied himself to fire a bolt. He spoke with authority to Bentley, "If you don't let us pass, I will shoot you."

"What with? You don't have a gun," Bentley replied, almost laughing.

Euan edged the UGV forward and, with no further warning, he shot a bolt from the mini vehicle towards Bentley, missing him on purpose. The mini-arrow flew into the rock behind the young lad. He stood there smiling with Bentley open-mouthed at what had just happened. The lad didn't move, so this time Euan aimed straight at his leg, firing a bolt into his calf. Bentley screamed, clutching his leg, firing out expletives. Euan strode forward and punched Bentley in the face. His connection generated a spray of blood which exploded from the young lad's nose. Perfect revenge for two weeks ago, he thought. Bentley crumpled on the floor amongst the rocks and moss.

"Come on, everyone, we need to leave straightaway."

He watched as the rest of the team bundled past Bentley, hurrying down the hill back to the car park. As they descended, Euan used the smoke canister to engulf Bentley and mask their direction of travel. He continued to send the smoke out of the UGV behind him as he raced down the hill. It created an ethereal blanket weaving between the trunks of the trees. This will slow them down, Euan thought. After everyone had reached the vehicles, they stowed their gear in the boot of the cars. Reed ensured he retrieved both the civic regalia and the fourth silver fereter from Lynsey's backpack.

"Wow, Euan, that was superb, mate," said Reed.

"Thanks, it all worked a treat, so pleased we got away with both items."

"You put some venom into the punch," Lynsey said, jumping into the conversation to praise Euan.

"My revenge for the previous fight, the little upstart," Euan said, his words laced with triumph as Lynsey grinned at him.

The two vehicles went in opposite directions as they left the car park. Every member of the group was desperate to make a quick getaway, keen to put as much distance as possible between themselves and Coulson's team.

———————◆O◆———————

Back up the wooded hill, Coulson was surveying the rocky cliffs after leaving the main track. The area was an appealing sight, with its towering cliffs and a dense canopy of trees casting shadows all around. It was easy to envision this location being a haven for thieves and outlaws in the 14th century. He felt uncertain about the correctness of the location when compared to the map, although the landscape appeared more fitting than Horseshoe Quarry. As he scanned the ground near the base of the towering cliffs with his metal detector, a blood-curdling scream pierced the air.

"What's that noise? Where's Bentley?" asked Coulson, spinning round and looking down the hill towards the source of the noise.

"Sounded like someone screaming. I'll look," said Ambrose.

"We'll all go. Is that smoke through there?"

The trio rushed down the hill, returning to the main path. A dense blanket of smoke engulfed the area, obscuring their vision and filling the air with a pungent smell. Navigating through the hazy veil proved challenging, making every step uncertain.

"Bentley?" shouted Coulson.

"I'm here, uncle."

A voice sounded off to their left amid the blanket of smoke. Bentley appeared in front of them, hobbling, in serious pain.

"What happened Bentley?"

"Reed Hascombe and his friends were here, up that path. They had a robot-like thing that shoots bolts and clouds of smoke," he said, showing them the bolt in his leg.

"We need to get you to hospital, lad. Which way did they go?"

"I'm not sure. I couldn't see because the smoke obscured them."

"Damn those people, they're annoying me. Ambrose, get after them. They may have gone down the hill to the car park."

"Yes, boss. I didn't see a campervan in the car park," she said.

Coulson pulled out his phone and called Pearson, asking for an update on the campervan and the other vehicles.

"The campervan's still in Sheffield. Euan Spencer's car left Sheffield this morning at around seven. It headed towards the Peak District. Lynsey Dewhurst's car travelled up the M1. Then, it headed towards Ripley on the A610."

"Anything since Pearson?"

"No, nothing boss."

Between Coulson and Wendy, they helped Bentley limp down the hill back to the car park, his pain obvious to see as he moaned and groaned all the way. It took an inordinate amount of time as lingering smoke on the hillside made them check every step to avoid any trip hazards. They reached Ambrose at the car park. She explained the other group had left.

Coulson took Bentley to the Accident and Emergency hospital department in Nottingham right away. On the drive back, Coulson's grip on the steering wheel tightened. His injured nephew's leg still dripped with blood. With each passing mile, his anger grew as he realised Bentley's upcoming fight could now be in jeopardy. It was only a few weeks away. His thoughts drifted to the other group, who may have discovered another valuable item of treasure, and maybe another fereter. He felt frustrated as things had turned unfavourable, casting a shadow over his efforts. Time for some drastic action!

Chapter 53

Nottingham Castle

*T*HE BITTER WINDS WHIPPED *around the castle as the winter chills continued unabated in 1398AD, creating clusters of ice in every corner.*

The Sheriff of Nottingham was enjoying his lavish New Year's feast, taking place in the grand hall of his castle. A sense of grandeur filled the air as the room filled with excitement. Raucous laughter echoed off the walls, intertwining with the melodic tunes of lively songs. The grand hall emanated a cosy warmth as the crackling flames from two colossal fireplaces danced at opposite ends of the immense room. In the centre, a gigantic oak table commanded attention adorned with succulent roasted hog and an abundance of intoxicating mead. Candles lit the dim corners of the room. A minstrel filled the air with melodies. The Sheriff enjoyed a feast and would invite local peasant girls to entertain his heads of office and high-ranking soldiers. Guards stood on duty by the entrances in case of intrusion by the archer and his ragtag band of men.

"Fetch me another goblet of mead," instructed the Sheriff.

"Yes, sir."

"Minstrel, play my favourite song."

"Of course."

The Sheriff had his eye on a pretty redhead girl who kept smiling at him. She would be his conquest this evening. He grabbed her by the hand and they danced for a while amongst the throng of revellers, his civic regalia bouncing against his chest as he moved. He felt loath to remove it. It signified his power as the ruler in this region of England. The redhead girl brought him more mead, but he didn't notice her drop some crushed mushrooms into the goblet as his drunkenness increased. Time for her to entertain him.

"Come with me, peasant," he said.

"Yes, sir."

"Up here."

"I'm coming, sir," said the redhead girl.

He led the girl up the stairs to his chamber, with the goblet clutched in his hand. The chamber was another haven of luxury, with bear and wolf skins covering the stone floor and bed as the soft fur created a warm atmosphere. The raging fire crackled, casting dancing shadows on the walls. Its warm glow illuminated the space, offering both light and comforting heat. The redhead girl started dancing whilst the Sheriff sat on the edge of the bed watching. He felt tired. He wasn't as energetic as he used to be, age was taking its toil on his body. The Sheriff had ruled for almost two decades, with a tight grip, except for the pesky archer and his band of outlaws.

The girl undressed him, removing his civic regalia, his woollen top and under garments. He sat there topless whilst she removed his breeches. His eyes became droopy, struggling to keep them open. Without warning, the redhead girl grabbed his civic regalia and slipped out of the room, like a fleeting shadow in the corner of his eye. Unable to keep his eyes open any longer, he succumbed to the impending sleep. His last thought struck him like an arrow. The redhead girl must be a member of Robin Hood's band of outlaws, as he realised she had tricked him!

Chapter 54

COTGRAVE, NEAR NOTTINGHAM

SUNDAY

C OULSON BUSIED HIMSELF IN *The Safe*, checking on Little John's quarterstaff and how the delicate operation of removing moisture from the hardwood was proceeding. In several days, he would know if the wood had survived the traumas of centuries underground in a dark cave, devoid of light and oxygen. He had a few interested clients already. He had set a valuation of £350,000. It would be ideal if I could also get the gold crucifix, he thought. He finished his checks and headed upstairs to his favourite room, the library.

Coulson entered the spacious room stacked with books as old as the eighteen hundreds. He spotted the gardener looking in the window, staring at the map in the glass display case. He had a lightbulb moment. Perhaps Reed's group had discovered some treasure yesterday the same way, by seeing the map through his window? He called Pearson.

"Pearson, I've an urgent job for you. Look through the last seven days' CCTV footage on the outside cameras. I'm looking for anyone getting into the garden."

"Okay, that'll take me a couple of hours. I can set it to stop when there is movement and review each instance. Do you think someone entered the grounds?" asked Pearson.

"I'm unsure, but I've just had a thought. Let me know if you find anything. Start from Friday and work backwards."

"Yes, boss."

Aware he had heard nothing from Garcia and having been busy with the events of the past day, his next phone call was to Garcia.

"Alejandro, update me on your plan to get hold of the crucifix," he said.

"I spoke with Onni Jarvinnen on Wednesday and whilst he didn't outright admit to being involved, it became clear from his response and body language he was," said Garcia.

"Good, and the plan?"

"I've informed Onni he'll carry out the authentication tests on the crucifix. This'll happen on Tuesday. I'll retrieve the crucifix from the safe and entrust him with completing the work. Towards the end of the day, I'll fabricate an emergency at home and rush off, leaving him with the artefact. With no other options, he'll have to secure the crucifix in the general storage area. The area has a simple padlock which bolt cutters can easily snap. I'll need one of your people to break in and remove it. Onni will take the blame for the loss, not me," said Garcia, confident in his idea.

"Alejandro, it seems you're getting used to the unpleasant side of artefact trading. However, neither Ambrose nor Bentley will be available to break in. You'll need to do it yourself."

This threw Garcia off balance. He wasn't expecting to carry out the burglary.

"You have an access card, Alejandro. Neither of my team can gain entry as easily as you. I wish you luck with your plan. Let's hope it works."

"Okay, I'll have to work out how I carry this through."

"One last thing. What figure do you expect a museum will offer for the crucifix?" asked Coulson.

"Mike Miller suggested around fifty grand, but I think it could be more."

"Thanks Alejandro. Keep me posted on the plan."

Coulson sat down in his luxurious chair, his eyes drifting to the ceiling, something he did out of habit when he needed to reflect on a tough decision. An idea formulated in his mind. Reed Hascombe seemed eager to gain some treasures, so must have felt disappointed with the crucifix's valuation. Coulson knew he could get £250,000 for it from a private client. He needed to make an unrefusable offer to get hold of whatever treasure they had found yesterday. The decision felt obvious. He would offer them £100,000 for the treasure and any additional fereter. He called Ambrose.

"Ambrose, I've an urgent job for you. I need you to go to Sheffield and make Reed Hascombe an offer. Go up to a hundred grand for whatever treasure they've found, including a fereter, please."

"Before I make any concrete offers, I'd need to understand what treasure they possess, and if there's another silver fereter," said Ambrose.

"Yes, you'll need to be creative and if you get it for less than one hundred grand, you'll get a bonus of twenty-five percent of the saving."

"That sounds fair. When shall I present them with the offer?" Ambrose asked.

"Now. I need to stop them from finding anything else," replied Coulson.

"Okay. How is Bentley?"

"The doctors said it's just a flesh wound and will heal fully in two weeks. He's still in pain but should walk pain-free in a few days," said Coulson, with frustration.

"I wondered if we should just break into their house and just steal whatever treasure they found?" asked Ambrose.

"Yes, I thought that. The problem is we don't know which person has it. There are at least four options. Let's carry out the offer process and see their reaction."

"Okay, Mr Coulson, I'll be on my way now."

He checked his watch, realising he felt hungry. He fancied a nice crayfish and rocket salad, topped with parmesan cheese and caesar dressing for his lunch. Taking one last moment to reflect on his decision, he wandered off to the kitchen in search of his chef when the phone rang. Pearson's number popped up on the screen.

"I've found something, boss. On Tuesday evening, I found around fifteen minutes of a blackout on the cameras. No uninvited visitors on the grounds, but the blackout seemed unusual. Has it ever happened before?" Pearson asked.

"Not that I'm aware of. I'll get on to the CCTV people tomorrow. Do you have any thoughts on it, Pearson?"

"Cameras going off suggests a malfunction in the master unit. As though it stopped communicating with all of them. Maybe your Wi-Fi went off or the signal strength dropped."

"Could have done Pearson, that's not ideal, it needs to be sorted, leave it with me."

Puzzled by the information, Coulson wandered off to the kitchen, hoping Ambrose could get a deal concluded.

Chapter 55

FULWOOD, SHEFFIELD

SUNDAY

E MILY LOOKED UP LIKELY locations in the Peak District for the next treasure hunt. Her research was based on the photo of the ancient map discovered yesterday. Her laptop laid open on the coffee table as she took a well-earned break from delving into articles, images, and Google maps. Euan had stopped at Sheffield Vaults on the way home from Whatstandwell yesterday. After the fracas with Bentley, she knew Reed was taking no chances. The civic regalia, fereter and fourth map were secure in his safe deposit box. No possibility of losing them if the goons broke into their house again. She felt comfortable with that arrangement, although she still felt concerned about Coulson's use of violence.

The morning drifted into the afternoon as she sipped her coffee. The doorbell rang. She jumped up, wondering who could be disturbing her peace. She opened the door and stood openmouthed, shocked for a few seconds. There stood the blonde woman, Ambrose.

"Hello Emily, sorry to bother you on Sunday, but I've something important to discuss with you and Reed. May I come in?"

"No way. Reed!" Emily screamed at the top of her voice, concerned she felt exposed on the doorstep of their home.

"Emily, no need to be alarmed. I'm confident what I'm about to say will please you."

"I don't care what you have to say. You've broken into my house. You've been tracking our campervan and recording our conversations. A complete invasion of our privacy. Oh, and you started a fight with my partner."

Emily heard the distinct sound of Reed's footsteps as he burst in through the back door, his energetic strides echoing through the lounge, looking for her.

"Out here Reed," she said.

"What the fuck are you doing here?" Reed spat at Ambrose as he spotted her standing on their doorstep.

"I was just telling Emily I have something important to discuss with you both. May I come in?"

"You are joking? No way. Whatever you want to talk about can be discussed outside on the doorstep."

"Okay, well the individual I'm working for would like to make you an offer for whatever you found yesterday," said Ambrose.

"Do you really think we'll be interested?" said Emily, fuming inside, her heart pounding with rage. The air felt heavy with tension. She looked at Reed for support.

"Just spit it out. We're very busy today," Reed said.

"First, what did you find yesterday? Another fereter? We know you found the crucifix before, so I'm going to assume you also found another piece of treasure."

"I'm surprised you don't know already. Using your sneaky tactics. We know you found Little John's quarterstaff," said Emily, anger still clouding her thoughts. Reed looked at her and she realised she had said too much.

"I'm not telling you anything. If you've an offer to make, just tell us and leave," said Reed.

"Okay, well subject to viewing any items we can offer eighty thousand pounds for another fereter and item of treasure."

"Hah, don't make me laugh. The museum will pay more than that." The atmosphere remained tense. Emily wanted to wrap this up quick, asking Ambrose to leave. Ambrose stood firm a few steps from their front door, causing Reed to bundle past Emily and push Ambrose away. Ambrose took up a fighting stance, so Reed followed suit. They both lunged forward, their legs slicing through the air with a whoosh, but their kicks sailed past each other. Emily's heart sank as she sensed the confrontation escalating, knowing things were about to turn ugly once more.

"Stop!" she shouted. "Reed, leave it. Get off our property or I'll call the police."

Emily pulled her phone from her pocket and held it up, ready to dial. Ambrose stepped back a few feet.

"Tell your boss he can sell what items I have for 10% commission," said Reed.

Emily stared at Ambrose and pretended to dial on her phone and held it up to her ear. She watched Ambrose turn and leave their property.

"I wasn't expecting that today, Reed. I'm still shaking with anger."

"Nor was I. Come and sit down and I'll get you a beer. That'll help."

"That was unexpected, and it's unnerved me. They just saunter up to our front door, bold as brass. How can we make our home more secure, Reed?"

"It's very difficult, even with brick walls and cameras criminals can get in," he chuckled.

"Oh sorry, I didn't mean to let that out of the bag."

"No problem, Em. I guess they already know. I think you need to take some self-defence classes like I've suggested before."

"Yes, you're right, I'll sort something out," said Emily, her heart rate now dropping back to normal. A surprise she didn't want today, further evidence of the greed from Coulson. Wasn't he happy with the wealth he already had?

Ambrose strode down the road to her car. Sitting in the black Audi, she sighed. That was difficult, she thought. She called Mr Coulson in case he wanted her to go back and ramp things up.

"Ambrose, how did it go?" asked Coulson.

"It didn't go well, boss. They downright refused the offer, kicking me off their property. It almost descended into another fight."

"What did you offer them?"

"I offered eighty thousand, subject to seeing the items."

"That's a fair offer, and they refused it?"

"Yes. Reed got aggressive and even said at the end to tell you he will give you ten per cent commission to sell anything he has!" Ambrose said, knowing this would inflame her boss.

"That guy needs to be taught a lesson. I can't believe he had the audacity to say that! I'm fuming, Ambrose. Come over Wednesday to discuss our next steps. I'm away for the next couple of days."

"Okay, will do Mr Coulson," Ambrose said. The conversation finished, she sat there for a moment, reflecting on what Mr Coulson's next steps could be. Maybe he wanted them roughed up again. If so, with Bentley injured, she may need other help.

Chapter 56

SCREWED SOFTWARE, SHEFFIELD

MONDAY

R EED MADE HIS WAY along the busy road to his office, lost in thought, still annoyed by Ambrose's visit yesterday. The sound of the traffic and the smell of exhaust fumes couldn't distract him as he walked on auto pilot. He paused outside the locked door, which led to the Screwed Software offices, to input the door entry code. He heard a weary voice behind him.

"Big Issue, Big Issue, buy your copy today."

Reed turned and spotted a young lad trying to sell copies of the weekly publication. He looked tired, and everyone ignored him. Reed felt a pang of guilt, remembering the encounter with the homeless man in Chesterfield the previous week. Reed had been one of those people, just walking past, focusing on himself and his bubble, not thinking about others. Emily was having a positive influence on him, he realised. We should all help others worse off than ourselves. The idea of people in unfortunate situations resonated with him as he remembered his childhood experience of being homeless. His struggle ended on a positive note as his mum and grandparents resolved the problem with hard work. He approached the young lad, noticing the rip in the arm of his jacket and the stains on his battered baseball cap.

"I'll take one please," Reed said.

"Thank you, sir."

Reed paid using his debit card. The young lad had a card reader, a further sign of the technology transition occurring in all areas of life. Everything used to be cash, not nowadays. Taking the magazine, he punched in the door code, bounding up the stairs to his office. A moment of realisation hit him. Besides selling the civic regalia to a museum, there must be another avenue available. The world appeared full of wealthy collectors who possessed sufficient funds for valuable treasures. If only he could find a solution. It would benefit himself and Emily, allowing them to pay off some of their mortgage. Maybe go on a delightful holiday and help his friends.

"Morning Reed," said Phil as he entered the office, his friend holding a steaming mug of cappuccino.

"Morning mate, how are you after Saturday?" asked Reed.

"All good. It was an interesting day. Nothing is boring with you around Reed."

"Thanks Phil. We had a visit from Ambrose yesterday. Coulson wants to buy the civic regalia and the fereter for eighty thousand. I told her to get lost."

"He sounds desperate to get hold of the treasures. They must be worth a lot of money to him. Her offer is less than we could expect from a museum for two artefacts," said Phil.

"Exactly my thoughts. This prompted me to consider if there's another route to selling the regalia for a higher price. With his big house and expansive gardens, Coulson must be making a lot of money selling artefacts. There must be an alternative to giving our artefacts to museums."

"How about we spend some time today exploring online for other selling channels?"

"Okay, let's catch up at lunchtime," said Reed.

Reed did some research during the morning whilst working. His manager was out on business today, giving him some spare time. He found many other auctioneers selling coins and pottery items, but nothing as elaborate as the civic regalia owned by the Sheriff of Nottingham. Their experts authenticated each item and followed the law. He felt damn sure Coulson didn't do that.

Time to check on Phil as it neared lunchtime. He wandered over to Phil's workstation and explained what he had discovered. "Have you found anything of interest?" asked Reed.

"Nothing different to you."

"I wonder how Coulson sells items, as he must have plenty to offer. He can't just have Little John's quarterstaff. We know he's an archaeologist by trade, so he must have contacts. Perhaps he has a website. Can we search for that?"

Reed watched Phil enter a few words into the Google search engine, then check out the results. They were all entries referring to his career as an archaeologist, nothing from recent years. Puzzled, the lads continued, but hit a dead end. Reed felt confident there was an alternative way to sell artefacts.

"Why don't I ask Jed if he can have a look for us?" suggested Phil.

"That's an excellent idea. Fire an email off to him now. I'm certain there must be another way to sell ancient artefacts, although taking it to the Finds Liaison Officer could get us more than Coulson is offering if we have two items."

Reed waited while Phil composed the email to Jed before they made their way downstairs to head off to the sandwich bar. Outside, Reed spotted the young lad still trying to sell the Big Issue as they joined the queue at the sandwich shop. Phil went for ham and cheese as always, whilst Reed ordered his favourite tuna mayo, with salad, but minus the cucumber. Then, on a whim, he ordered an extra sandwich of cheese and pickle. On their way back to the office, he gave the extra sandwich to the young lad selling the Big Issue.

"Oh thank you man, I appreciate your kindness," responded the young lad with a smile.

Reed felt the inner warmth that came with helping someone worse off than himself. Emily would be proud of him. Filled with satisfaction and a generous serving of optimism, he ascended the stairs. The sunlight spilled through the windows, casting a warm golden glow on the office surroundings. The air carried a faint hint of freshly brewed coffee, invigorating his senses. With a renewed sense of purpose, he began his work once more.

———————◄O►—————

Reed had finished his work for today when Phil rushed over to him with a massive grin on his face.

"Jed has just answered my email. Guess what, Coulson has a website on the Dark Web. You can't see anything because it has a login procedure which requires contact with him. Jed looked at the source code behind it and the keywords used mentioned archaeological items, relics and artefacts."

"So that's how he sells them, ingenious. How can we replicate that? Is anyone else doing the same thing?"

"I don't know. Shall we get Jed to carry out some work for us?" said Phil.

"Yes, let's do that. I'll go to the safe deposit box now and get photos of the civic regalia."

"Okay mate, I'll come with you as I want to see the fourth map."

Both lads closed down their computers, picked up their backpacks and headed off downstairs. Reed locked the door as they were last to leave and, turning, he got a wave from the young lad selling the Big Issue. He returned the wave. He sent Emily a message, using code for the location.

Reed: *'Hi Em, I'll be a bit late home tonight, just popping over to the SDB to check a couple of things with Phil, x x x'*
Emily: *'Okay, see you soon xx'*

They strode off to the safe deposit building and entered the vault. Onni had given Reed some specialist cleaning tools, so he spent a bit of time tidying up the civic regalia. It gleamed under the stark lights overhead as they marvelled at its magnificence. It had an aura about it and the centre piece depicting Nottingham Castle shone with brilliance. What an amazing piece of treasure. After getting dozens of photos of the civic regalia, they poured over the fourth map, Phil taking a photo so he could do some research that evening. It looked more simplistic than the previous ones. A cluster of rocks with a cave next to a wooded area and a rocky outcrop. They locked the items back away in the safe deposit box and headed off home, wondering what Jed may come up with.

Chapter 57

Fulwood, Sheffield

Monday

REED ARRIVED HOME FROM work just after seven o'clock and found Emily reading a book in the lounge.

"What're you reading, Em?" he asked.

"It's Robin Hood."

"That's interesting."

"Yes, I found it in the school library today and thought I'd familiarise myself with his story, especially since we've found two of his treasures," she said.

"It might give us some clues about the next location. I'm hoping we find his bow or sword."

"That'd be incredible, although what Onni said the other night about Little John's quarterstaff, it'd be a miracle if a wooden bow survived."

"Very true, you never know. I'm starving. Is tea ready?" asked Reed.

"Should be, just jacket potatoes with tuna."

"Super, thanks Em."

Reed grabbed a beer from the fridge as they sat down to eat. He updated Emily on everything that had happened during the day, including the interactions with the young lad selling the Big Issue. He spoke about the dark web and their request to Jed to help them. Reed knew Emily would express her discomfort with his idea, but she was coming around to it, especially after Ambrose's visit yesterday.

After tea, Reed popped into the back garden and sat on the wooden bench, looking at the trees and bushes lining their fence. He watched the bees buzzing around the flowers and smiled as a couple of white cabbage butterflies dive-bombed each other through the garden. His thoughts wandered back to lunchtime. He picked up the Big Issue he had brought out with him and glanced through the pages, reading the stories of people's misfortune. He felt compelled to help more, as he remembered his personal plight when his dad became imprisoned. Most people struggled to get out of their difficult situation, but he felt lucky. His mum was a dynamic person with a lot of fight in her, a character trait he had inherited. His thoughts tumbled around like a murmur of starlings, twisting, turning, swooping. Then the light-bulb moment hit him. If they sold the civic regalia for a significant sum of money, he could help homeless people improve their situation and share the rest with his family and friends.

There it was, he thought. The paradox of being a thief. If he broke the law, he could help other people worse-off than himself. He mulled it over for several minutes, considering the pros and cons, but couldn't find a genuine reason not to do it. He decided it was a risk worth taking.

His mind conjured up a plan to split the proceeds into ten lots, one lot for each of the six friends, and then four lots to help others. He remembered the homeless man's worn out sleeping bag and vowed to give some money to the homeless charity of Sheffield. The way he felt today giving the sandwich to the young lad was a feeling he wished to experience again. An inner warmth of genuine pride, having helped someone who couldn't always help themselves.

Reed hurried indoors to explain everything to Emily. She was still reading the Robin Hood book. The gold initials caught his eye. Then it hit him like a lightning bolt. His initials were the same: RH. Is this fate? Was it written in the stars? Should he relieve the wealthy of their cash and give it to the homeless?

Emily agreed the idea of sharing the wealth made his idea more palatable, so he organised a get together with everyone on Thursday evening. Reed wanted to share his plan with the team, so he booked a table at the Mediterranean Restaurant in Mansfield. It would be his treat. All he had to do was sell the civic regalia in the black market. And convince his friends of his plan.

Chapter 58

Screwed Software

Tuesday

P HIL HAD RECEIVED A detailed email from Jed early that morning. He raced to the office, wanting to go through it with Reed. He felt like he was adding real value to his friend's quest to sell the civic regalia and couldn't wait to share the news with him. Phil didn't have to wait long, as Reed arrived twenty minutes before their usual start time. Phil almost ran over to Reed when he entered the office.

"Hey Reed, I've got some news for you," Phil said, almost tripping over the waste bin.

"What've you got, Phil?"

"Jed did some deep diving on the dark web last night. There are many black market activities that'd attract attention from the authorities if they were on the legal internet. He found another couple of artefact traders in the UK, other than Coulson. One in Scotland and one in Cornwall."

"Excellent news. So how do we contact these people? What about doing it ourselves?" asked Reed.

"I asked him about setting up a site to sell the civic regalia. He thought it would take too long before potential buyers found us through searches. He's got hold of the names of both traders, their addresses and mobile numbers. Jed suggested trying the two artefact traders first and see if they were interested. What do you think?"

"I think it's the perfect solution. We should get more money than selling it to a museum," said Reed.

"I'll ping over their details so you can call them today. In the meantime, I'm setting up a website on the dark web so we can upload the photos and description," Phil said.

Phil was about to return to his workstation when Reed stopped him.

"I've decided, Phil. If we can sell the civic regalia for more money than following the lawful process, then I'm going to divide up the funds ten ways. One lot for each of the six of us. The remaining four lots would help people worse off than us, like the homeless charity in Sheffield. I chatted it through with Emily last night and she thinks it's a fantastic idea. That's assuming you all agree, of course," Reed said.

"Oh mate, of course I agree. I think that's a brilliant idea," said Phil.

"The idea struck me last night when I noticed Emily reading a book on Robin Hood and realised our initials were the same. Almost like its fate."

"Of course. You're taking from the wealthy and giving to the poor. Man, that's just awesome."

Phil sat down at his desk, thinking about Reed's decision. He felt honoured to be a part of this whole adventure, thrilled about the challenges ahead. He reminisced about the mad motorbike chase the other weekend, and now he rattled around the dark web like a pro. Plus, he stood to earn some extra cash out of it too and help homeless people. A win-win situation. Time for some work. I'll start on the dark website at lunchtime, Phil thought.

Phil beavered away for twenty minutes, setting up the website, when

Reed came over smiling away.

"I've spoken to both people you gave me and they're both interested in the civic regalia. They both wanted to see photos and full disclosure of where we discovered the civic regalia as soon as possible. They don't want any email exchanges, just somewhere they can look at it on the dark web," Reed said.

"I've started on the site. I'll get it finished today if you can let me have the photos you took. Bluetooth them over, don't send by WhatsApp. You can give them the website address over the phone."

"That's amazing Phil. Thanks for your help."

"Happy to help. I'll crack on and let you know when it's done."

Phil watched Reed wander back to his desk, a bounce in his step, and cracked on with setting up the site. He settled on a name, '*Peak Treasures*', uploaded the photos, and completed the description. He set about adding in security so no-one could view the artefact without a login. Phil generated logins for the traders wanting to view the civic regalia, passing the details to Reed. Everything was falling into place. Let's hope one of them puts an offer in, he thought.

Chapter 59

THE PEAKS UNIVERSITY, NOTTINGHAM

TUESDAY

O NNI STOOD BESIDE THE carbon-dating machine as it tested the sliver of leather he had found in the claws holding the emerald in the crucifix. Garcia had told him to carry out all the tests today. This was the penultimate one to complete. Everything was going to plan. The tests identified the crucifix as six to eight hundred years old. He had crossed referenced the inscription on the back, *'Tooke'*, to other research papers providing evidence of the medieval surname. Once the tests were complete, he would write everything up in a research paper and present it to Garcia.

Onni waited for the machine to complete the first testing process and spotted Garcia rushing down the main corridor of the department, exiting the building. He hoped his manager would return soon as the crucifix needed to go back to the safe tonight. He didn't want to wait for Garcia before going home. The machine beeped to show it had finished, so Onni took the crucifix for the remaining test. He calculated the weight of the gold and the size of the emerald, working out the estimated value of the artefact based on current market prices. It came to around thirty thousand pounds. He expected a museum to pay double that because of the historical importance of the crucifix.

Onni headed to the manager's office, hoping Garcia had returned.

After knocking twice with no reply, he tried the door handle. Locked. He checked his watch. Four thirty already. He was concerned, as he wanted to get home. What if Garcia wasn't returning today? Had Garcia forgotten Onni had the crucifix? Panic spread through his mind. He couldn't leave until it was secure in the safe. He searched for his team leader and found him at his workstation.

"Hello Larry, I'm looking for Mr Garcia so he can put the crucifix back in the safe, but his door's locked. Do you know where he is?" Onni asked.

"He rushed off, something about an emergency at home. Let me phone him."

Onni waited whilst his team leader tried three times to call Garcia, but each time it went straight to voicemail.

"Put it in the general storage cage for tonight," Larry advised.

"I can't do that. It's against the department rules."

"I don't see what option you have."

After a brief thought, Onni concluded he wouldn't proceed with that suggestion. He had an idea and strode off to his desk, picking up his phone and called Mike Miller, the Finds Liaison Officer. Only Garcia and Mike could access the safe. He explained the situation.

"Leave it with me Onni, I'll try to get over to you, but I can't guarantee it. You might have to follow your team leader's instruction if Garcia doesn't come back soon."

"Okay Mr Miller, thanks," Onni said.

Onni wasn't happy with this. He suspected Garcia worked with Coulson, and the cynical side of him wondered if it was a ploy so they could steal the crucifix from the general storage cage. He sat at his desk and waited, hoping Mike Miller would turn up.

Garcia sat in his kitchen at home and checked the time. Gone nine o'clock. Time for him to complete the last step of his plan, getting the crucifix. He popped his head around the lounge door.

"I've had a message to say the alarm is ringing in the department and security wants it reset," he said to his wife.

"Okay, love, take care," she replied.

He returned to the archaeology department, letting himself in, with a black baseball cap covering his face. He wasn't sure how to play the situation, as he needed his card to gain entry to the building. Perhaps he should 'lose' his access card later on tonight and go into work without it? He would mull it over some more.

Garcia had parked his car outside of the campus and took care to not encounter anyone on the walk to the archaeology department. He crept down the corridor, keeping to the darker side until he reached the main testing room with the general storage cage. With the bolt cutters gripped in his hand, he was ready to snap the lock. He used the torch on his phone to look inside the cage, peering into the dark corners. The crucifix wasn't there! A well of sickness started in the pit of his stomach, clouding his thoughts. Where was it? Had Onni taken it home? Mr Coulson would be furious. He thought about his house in Seville and wondered whether he should travel there tomorrow and jack all this in. He calmed himself and had a thought.

Garcia headed to the safe and punched in the code, opening the door. The crucifix sat there on the shelf. Damn that Scandinavian idiot. Onni must have spoken to Mike Miller to put the crucifix in the safe. His plan had been blown apart.

Chapter 60

COTGRAVE, NEAR NOTTINGHAM

WEDNESDAY

C OULSON HAD TWO IMPORTANT jobs to do today. First task was to call Garcia, to learn how his plan to recover the crucifix had played out. He needed some caffeine from the kitchen. A delicious caramel latte would do it. He sipped on the steaming coffee as he wandered back through the hallway to the library. Picking up his phone, he called Garcia.

"Alejandro, have you recovered the crucifix?" he asked, straight to the point.

"Not exactly, Mr Coulson. The plan didn't work out. The idiotic Scandinavian phoned Mike Miller, the Finds Liaison Officer, then waited until he came over to put the crucifix back in the safe. That made it impossible to steal it."

"Why does nothing work as you intend Garcia?"

"It wasn't my fault. He should've put it in the general storage cage," stuttered Garcia.

"Yes, you told me. But he's more capable than you gave him credit for. What's your next suggestion?"

"I haven't got one yet."

"When will you have one? I can't keep waiting for you to resolve this issue, Garcia. You messed it up to begin with. It's all too sloppy."

"I don't know. Let me think about it."

"I can't wait forever. You could organise for a couple of hitmen to break in when you are working late and they could force you to open the safe and steal the crucifix, then beat you up to make it look authentic. What about my plan?" asked Coulson.

"I don't like that plan," responded Garcia, his stomach doing somersaults at the thought of getting smashed by one of Coulson's hoodlums.

"Well, you had better think of another plan soon, otherwise it will happen, Garcia."

Coulson ended the call, frustration building inside him, which wasn't good for his blood pressure. He expected Ambrose and Bentley to arrive soon. The sky looked clear blue as he gazed out of the large library windows, the sun's rays penetrating the gloom of the far corner of the room. He finished his coffee and strode off into the sunshine, enjoying the warmth on his face and the perfume smell of summer flowers in the air. He walked around the grounds, catching up with the gardener, asking him to clean the fishpond after the quarterstaff had laid in it for several days.

Half an hour later, he returned to the library as Ambrose arrived, bringing Bentley with her.

"Bentley, how's the leg?" Coulson asked.

"Much better thanks," he replied, showing his uncle the stitches on his calf.

"Good, can you walk okay now?"

"I'm fine walking. Running is painful, but the doctor suggested it will be fine in another week," said Bentley.

"Good, good. Let's focus on our top priority for today. I want the two of you to kidnap Emily Barrington."

The other two looked at him open-mouthed, causing him a wry smile, the response he expected. Ambrose spoke.

"I wasn't expecting that, Mr Coulson. What action should we take? Where are we going to hold her? When? Sorry, that's a lot of questions," Ambrose said.

"I've thought this through. Reed Hascombe pissed me off with his comment to you. He must have an artefact and stored it in a safe location, so I can't see the point of breaking into their house. We found nothing before. So I thought, let's hit him hard where it would hurt the most. He can't go to the police as we know he has some illegal treasures he wants to keep, albeit they would still be within the fourteen day rule."

"True, but what if he involves the police?"

"I've already considered that and one of my clients is the Chief Constable of the local police force, so a quiet word in their ear would make any problems go away. Also, I'm hoping it will shake him up, making him realise he is in over his head and accept my last offer of one hundred grand."

"I assume you have a plan, boss?"

"I do Ambrose, you know me too well. I suggest you take her Friday after she's left school, maybe in the car park or on the way back to her house. Bring her here. She can stay in one of the spare bedrooms upstairs, one with a lock on it. It means you'll have to take shifts in guarding her. The chef can prepare her food. We can use the spare room with the en-suite. That way, you won't get any extra hassle from her as it's a fully contained room. What do you think?"

"That sounds like an excellent plan. I'll need to get some chloroform and scope out her journey home the next two afternoons to fully understand her route," said Ambrose.

"Marvellous. Will you be okay with this Bentley?"

"Yes, of course, I'm pleased it's not the other girl, as she can run like a greyhound," replied Bentley.

Pleased with the outcome of the conversation, Coulson said, "Check with me on Friday before you take any action."

"Will do, boss. We better get going so we can start today's surveillance. Ready Bentley?" asked Ambrose.

"Yes, let's go."

Coulson watched them head off down the driveway, pleased with himself. An excellent plan. This should move things forward. He spoke to the maid and told her to prepare the spare bedroom, also advising the chef he needed to add a head to his catering requirements for a few days. He placed a call to his client, the Chief Constable, just to touch base in case they needed help to smooth things over. A little sub-conscious reminder for them. They might uphold the law, but only when it suited.

Chapter 61

CENTRAL MANSFIELD

THURSDAY

W HILST REED LOOKED FORWARD to tonight, he also had slight trepidation, hoping the discussions with his friends would go the way he wanted. He and Emily arrived in Mansfield earlier than planned, eager to explore the market square. They walked along, studying the historical buildings in the area. The sounds of their footsteps blending with the hum of cars passing by. As they arrived, the sun set behind the town hall and The Court House, which became a pub a few years ago. It gave a glow to the sandstone built buildings, giving off an ethereal feel if you squinted. The bustling market place had stood the test of time, its origins dating back to the thirteenth century.

They strolled to the Mediterranean restaurant, a bit out of town, but enjoyed the bustle of the early evening trade. They arrived just as the others were entering the restaurant. The waitress ushered them to their table. Despite the early hour, there appeared a decent crowd inside, and the restaurant exuded an authentic Turkish ambiance with its tasteful green and light brown decor. The gentle hum of soft Turkish music played in the background as aromatic spices wafted from the kitchen. Reed thought the menu looked interesting, deciding to treat his friends, even though it would cost the best part of three hundred pounds.

"Here we are again," Reed started off. "You all deserve a treat for your past week's efforts. I have an unusual idea to share with everyone. Based on what has happened so far with the crucifix, I've been thinking about alternative ways to sell the civic regalia. Before I start, is there any update on the crucifix testing, Onni?"

"Yes, I've examined the crucifix and proved it's authentic. I've also referenced the word '*Tooke*' against other research which backs up the data. In terms of current precious metal and gemstone valuations, I've estimated it to be worth around thirty thousand pounds. It depends on how much a museum will pay for the extra historical significance. I just need to mention what happened on Tuesday. Garcia left me with the crucifix and before I'd finished testing it, he rushed off home in an emergency. Unable to reach him, I had to call Mike Miller to put it back in the safe. It all felt strange to me, like he hoped I would slip up, opening an opportunity for it to be stolen."

"You outfoxed him, Onni, well done."

The waitress appeared with their drinks and to take their food order. They opted for the large tapas option, which gave them twelve unique dishes to try, ranging from grilled prawns to wild boar mini sausages to roasted red peppers and goat's cheese humus. Once she had left their table, Reed carried on.

"Phil has done some work digging into how to sell the civic regalia ourselves, similar to how we believe Coulson does. With Jed's help, we've found a couple of other artefact dealers in the UK. Phil has built a website on the dark web, so we can offer it for sale to interested buyers. I realise some of you are uneasy with this idea and to be fair; I have concerns, but on Tuesday evening it came to me. It's like a paradox. If we break the law, then we could have funds available to not only benefit ourselves but help others like the homeless. Another thing I realised, my initials are the same as Robin Hood. It feels right to follow in his footsteps, by giving some money to the poor. I know it sounds cliche but Emily has made me realise we are fortunate in our lifestyle whilst others struggle."

"That's pretty deep, mate," said Euan.

"I know, but maybe it's fate? So my suggestion is we sell the civic regalia on the dark web and split the funds into ten lots. We'd each get one lot and then earmark four lots to help others. I'd like to start with the homeless shelter place in Sheffield. What do you all think?"

"I think it's an excellent idea, Reed, even with the risk of getting caught. How does the dark website work?" asked Lynsey.

Phil interjected, "I've built it with sign-in security, which is accessed once Reed or myself have spoken to an individual. If someone comes across the website, they have to email requesting access. We can then trace the IP address to ensure it's not the police or other authorities. Jed has helped me as he operates sites like this for some of his clients."

"That sounds very secure and I agree with it, as long as I'm not involved with selling it because of the risk to my job," said Onni.

"Yes, I agree with Onni," confirmed Lynsey.

"Same for me, Reed, but you knew that anyway," said Emily.

"Sounds spot on, count me in too," said Euan.

Before Reed could continue, the waitress brought over the steaming plates and bowls of food. A multitude of smells, reminding each of them of their growling stomachs. Everyone grabbed pieces from the twelve assorted dishes, tucking in to the Mediterranean feast. While busy eating their food, Reed remembered the next important part of the conversation he needed to discuss with them.

"Phil, do you want to update everyone on our two new friends?"

"Yes, okay. The two artefact traders I mentioned earlier have lodged offers for the civic regalia. The highest bid is three hundred and fifty thousand pounds!" Phil exclaimed.

"Oh wow, that's an enormous amount," said Euan.

Everyone buzzed with the news. They couldn't believe the item was worth that much money. Reed could see the calculations whirring in their heads. Calculating this would give each of them ten times the value the crucifix would yield. Besides that, there would be one hundred and forty thousand pounds to help charities and others worse off than themselves. Lynsey chipped in.

"But how'd we explain the money coming to us if we got asked by our banks?"

"Brilliant question Lynsey," Euan said, winking at her. Reed couldn't help but grin. His mate still trying to impress Lynsey, but so far, it had yielded no results.

"I've got that covered. I'm going to say I had some artefacts handed down to me as family heirlooms and sold them. Then split my inheritance with friends and made a charitable donation," said Reed.

Lynsey nodded in approval. "I'm pleased with your answer. It works for all of us."

The conversation continued around the crucifix, coupled with finishing their food. The waitress came to clear the plates. Reed ordered a bottle of champagne to celebrate, the loud pop of the cork attracting attention from other diners, but he didn't care. Life felt good. Clinking their glasses, the friends were all smiles.

"Reed, did you find another map in the fereter?" asked Euan.

"Oh shit, I forgot about that in the euphoria."

Reed pulled out six photos of the map from the fourth fereter. He laid them on the table, each picked up a copy to look at. It had a cluster of rocks, a cave next to a wooded area, and a rocky outcrop.

"Does anyone have any thoughts? Phil, have you looked for potential locations?"

"Yes, mate, I checked all places with Robin Hood in the name and got a hit early on. It looks like Robin Hood's Stride to me. There's a place called Hermits Cave, and a rocky outcrop called Cratcliffe Rocks. Look at Google maps and see if you agree?"

They all scrambled for their phones, comparing the map to Google's digital version, all nodding in agreement.

"It seems a close match," suggested Emily.

"Yes, I agree. Shall we aim to have a look on Saturday?" asked

Reed.

Everyone agreed. They planned to arrive by eight o'clock at Robin Hood's Stride before too many people were around. It always worked better that way. Reed felt relaxed, the alcohol and euphoria of his plan combining. The conversation continued about the map and artefacts, but Reed drifted into his own world, considering how to help the homeless shelter. Just give them a lump sum or send them a smaller amount each month? Would he get involved in helping there? What other charities could he help?

Chapter 62

SHEFFIELD HIGH SCHOOL

FRIDAY

A MBROSE STOOD UNDERNEATH THE large willow tree, covered by the drooping branches and bright green leaves next to Sheffield High School. She could see Bentley on the opposite side of the car park, sitting on a wooden bench pretending to read a newspaper. The chain link fencing made it easy to observe the movements of staff. They had seen several teachers leave the school and were waiting for Emily Barrington to appear. Mr Coulson had invested in a two-way radio to assist their efforts, so Ambrose checked in with Bentley.

"Bentley, anything from your side?" she asked.

"Nothing yet."

"Keep awake."

"Of course Ambrose, I'm not stupid."

He wasn't, she thought, but could drift off thinking about his boxing career and how he would be the next Muhammd Ali. Three more teachers left via the main entrance of the grey concrete building that passed as a high school. Quite nondescript, Ambrose thought. She spotted Emily amongst the three people and alerted Bentley.

"Heads up Bentley."

"On it."

Ambrose checked her pocket for the ready prepared cloth with chloroform. The chemical emitted a faint metallic scent from her jacket. She waited and watched the group, hoping Emily would get to her car alone. One other teacher stopped and got into her car whilst Emily and the other teacher continued towards Emily's car. Damn. They had parked next to each other. That made it impossible to kidnap her here. Ambrose made a quick decision.

"Bentley, not here. We need to follow her. Head back to the car."

"Okay, will do," he responded.

They both darted back to their car, jumping in and entering the stream of traffic, following Emily's car several vehicles ahead. Ambrose considered her two options. Try to intercept her during the journey home or kidnap her afterwards. She kept an open mind whilst pursuing Emily's car. They came to a set of traffic lights which turned red, causing them to get stuck behind several slower cars, losing sight of her as she turned left towards Fulwood. This is going to be difficult to intercept her with that level of traffic, Ambrose said, "Let's leave it until Emily reaches home." They never caught up with Emily's car until they watched her pull into the drive at her house.

Ambrose parked down the road and discussed her plan with Bentley, so he was crystal clear on how to proceed. After they had ironed out the finer details, Ambrose pulled into the driveway of Reed and Emily's house. They needed to get her into the back of Ambrose's vehicle. This seemed like the simplest solution. Bentley positioned himself round the corner of the house, out of sight from the front door, while Ambrose pressed the doorbell. After a couple of moments, Emily answered the door, her mouth wide open as she recognised her.

Ambrose put the cloth with the chloroform over Emily's mouth and nose in one swift motion, pushing her into the house. Bentley rushed into the house behind her and closed the door. Ambrose held the cloth to Emily's face as she struggled, hitting out at Ambrose's arm with her brown hair flapping around. Bentley jumped behind Emily and held her arms by the wrist as instructed.

Emily's efforts to get away were waning, the chloroform taking effect, and another minute later, her body went limp. Ambrose struggled to hold her upright, so they laid her on the teal corner sofa whilst they prepared the next step.

"Well done Bentley, that's perfect. Now the difficult bit, getting her in the car with no one seeing."

"Shall I open the back door first?" he asked.

"Yes, but move the car closer if you can."

Ambrose watched Bentley disappear out of the lounge and return a couple of minutes later. She put a coat over Emily's head and tried to walk her out of the house upright. It worked until they got to the car door. They reverted to a horizontal hold as Bentley slid into the car and pulled Emily inwards. It became difficult manoeuvring her limp body as they knocked her head on the car door and grazed the back of her right leg. Ambrose looked at Emily laying across the leather seat and checked the coat obscured her face. They were ready to leave.

Fortunately, they had seen no one passing the house whilst they carried out their manoeuvres. Ambrose reversed out of the driveway and headed back to Cotgrave, aware the chloroform would wear off soon.

Chapter 63

Fulwood, Sheffield

Friday

R EED RETURNED HOME FROM work, eager for their adventures tomorrow, hoping it would lead to another piece of treasure. It felt like they were getting close to the end of the treasure trail after finding the Sheriff's civic regalia. He entered the house through the kitchen door. He didn't see Emily in the dining room, so shouted, "Hi Em, I'm home."

No answer. The house felt hushed. It's usual to hear Emily rustling her students' homework or listening to some music. He dropped his bag on the floor beside the dining room table and wandered into the lounge. She wasn't there. He shouted upstairs, "Hi Em, I'm home."

Still no answer. Strange, he thought, she's normally here when I arrive home from work. He strode up the creaky staircase, checked in their bedroom, the bathroom and the spare bedroom. Emily wasn't there. An awful feeling arose in the pit of his stomach. He rushed downstairs and spotted her handbag on the coffee table. Checking inside, he found her phone, purse, and keys. But her coat was missing. She must have gone for a walk. Satisfied with that reasoning, he grabbed a shower, thinking Emily would be back once he had finished.

As he dried himself Reed thought, hang on a minute, if she hasn't taken her keys how did she plan to get back in the house? Maybe she took the spare front door key off the key hook. He got dressed and checked, but the spare key hung where it always did. He opened the front door and checked if she had locked her car. She had. Everything inside the car seemed normal. He returned to the house and called Euan.

"I think Emily's gone missing Euan," Reed blurted out, his anxiety building.

"What do you mean, Reed? She can't just disappear?" asked Euan.

"She isn't at home. She has locked her car and both house doors. Her handbag with her phone, purse and keys is in the lounge, but her coat is missing."

"Maybe she's gone for a walk?" asked Euan, sensing his mate's rising panic.

"That's what I thought. She rarely goes for a walk without me and the spare key's on the hook. How did she intend to enter the house?"

"Don't know, mate, it doesn't seem right. Call some of her friends and I'll be over soon."

"Thanks Euan," Reed said.

Reed sat for a moment racking his brains for any other reasons for her absence? Maybe she planned to go to the shops and forgot her handbag, locking herself out and is round a neighbour. Time to be practical, Reed, he told himself. He picked up Emily's phone and called a couple of her teacher friends. Both said she appeared fine and left the high school at the normal time, nothing untoward. Okay, so that just leaves checking with a neighbour. The likely option was the elderly lady next door. Emily would sometimes pop round hers with some leftovers from meals to help her out.

Reed knocked on the door. The elderly lady greeted him with a friendly hello. He asked her if she had seen Emily today. She hadn't, but did mention Emily had a visitor earlier in a black car. The elderly lady didn't get out often, entertaining herself by watching the comings and goings on the street. She identified a blonde woman and a young lad. Reed panicked. The bloody goons have taken her.

He thanked the old lady and rushed back to the house. He was about to phone the police when a message pinged on his phone from an unknown number.

'We have Emily. Do not contact the police, we have friends there. You need to accept my offer to get her back. I'll be in touch about a meeting soon.'

Reed fumed. The arrogant man. How dare he do this? No wonder he has so much money. He just wipes the floor with normal people. He had kidnapped Emily. But Reed held an ace. Coulson wasn't aware they knew where he lived. He would wait for Euan and together, they would generate a plan to get Emily back.

Chapter 64

COTGRAVE, NEAR NOTTINGHAM

FRIDAY

EMILY OPENED HER EYES and surveyed the unfamiliar surroundings. She felt tired and groggy, feeling a bump on her head and a cut on her right calf. The room wasn't her bedroom; it was much larger with a high ceiling and an ornate picture rail. Through two large windows, she could see patchy clouds as the sun disappeared behind a looming dark cloud. Where the hell was she? Her mind raced to unscramble the situation and make sense of the strange bedroom. As the blanket of fog cleared in her brain, she recalled the last thing her eyes had seen.

That bloody blonde woman on my doorstep, she thought. She drugged me. They kidnapped me. The realisation hit home, and she panicked. How would she get out of here? Would Reed come and get her? What did they want her for?

Sitting up on the bed, she took in the full extent of her surroundings. The bedroom felt unused, a stale smell lingering in the air. The king size bed with a bright leaf patterned quilt coupled with the dark wood wardrobe and dressing table gave the bedroom an almost bed-and-breakfast vibe. She checked her watch and realised over two hours had elapsed since she arrived home, Reed would be home from work by now. He would be worried sick about her. She stood up, but the effect of the drugs forced her to sit back down as she felt unsteady on her feet.

Emily started feeling better after a few more minutes. Shuffling over to the window, she gazed at the enormous expanse of gardens. She observed the walled perimeter in the distance with the sweeping driveway exiting the property in the east. She felt sure this was Coulson's house, as it matched Reed's description when he clambered over the wall last week. Emily spotted the fishpond close to the house, with its brick wall sides and large koi swimming around in it. This confirmed where she was. She sat back on the bed and noticed the en-suite door. Despite the bathroom having simple fitments, it had fresh towels. The kidnapping felt pre-planned.

A loud knock came at the door as she heard a key turning in the lock, her heart rate jumping. An unfamiliar face appeared at the door.

"Hi, I'm Rosa the maid. Mr Coulson wants you to join him for dinner in an hour. I'll come back to collect you."

"Wait, Rosa, why am I here?" Emily asked.

"You're Mr Coulson's guest," replied the maid as she closed the door and relocked it.

Emily sat down on the bed. What should she do? She tried the handle of the bedroom door several times. The door didn't open. She called out.

"Rosa, can I speak to you, please?"

No answer, so she tried again. Then she heard footsteps approaching the door and a voice she recognised answered.

"I suggest you get some rest, Emily. Mr Coulson wants to discuss a few things with you later," said Ambrose.

"You bitch, how dare you kidnap me," spat Emily, her venom towards Ambrose, having now risen to untold levels.

"Get some rest."

"What do you want with me?"

The footsteps disappeared into the silence. Emily realised she wouldn't get an answer, so listened to the advice and laid on the bed. She couldn't relax as her mind raced with crazy thoughts.

Without warning, a loud knock at the bedroom door and Rosa's face reappeared.

"It's dinnertime. Please follow me," the maid said, leaving the door open for Emily.

Emily dismissed any thoughts of running as she would struggle to climb the wall, even if she could escape the house. She walked onto the landing, spotting Ambrose sitting on a chair a few metres away from her. She sent a glance of daggers at her.

"Don't think about escaping. We'll be outside monitoring you," Ambrose said as a warning. Emily ignored her and followed Rosa downstairs to the dining room.

The house was immense, with a curved grand staircase, its steps leading down to the ground floor, into a vast hallway. Dark wooden bannister rails shined in the slivers of sunshine streaming through the tall windows, crystals in the chandelier glistened in the ceiling centre piece. The opulence made her feel sick, knowing how Coulson had gained his wealth. Tricking people, stealing from others and now kidnapping. She wondered if he had killed anyone to get what he wanted?

She entered the dining room and stared at the gigantic table with seating for twenty people. It would dwarf her dining table at home. The thought of her house and Reed worrying brought a pang of sickness to her stomach. Rosa ushered her to a seat at the end of the table, which had two places set at opposite ends. She waited and observed everything she could. The fireplace glowed with a fire crackling away. The large windows giving a view over the rear of the property, a cluster of trees in the distance beyond the wall. She sensed a thunderstorm coming as dark clouds gathered to the north.

Coulson entered the dining room and smiled at her. Emily didn't return it. He sat down and introduced himself.

"I know who you are," Emily responded.

"Very well, my dear. I won't apologise for you being here as you will receive my normal hospitality, so think of it as a weekend break," Coulson said, laughing at his own ironic comment.

"What do you want from me?"

"Some information to start with. Second, for your boyfriend to accept my offer. He knows you're visiting me. I've messaged him. I'll meet him tomorrow so we can get this resolved and you can go home."

"What'd he say?"

"He hasn't responded, but I'm sure he'll see sense and accept my offer."

"Reed will call the police, then you'll be in trouble."

"He won't. I've some very high-ranking friends in the local police force. I'm sure they'll agree it's all just a minor misunderstanding. Also, he has some undeclared treasure, which they could arrest him for possessing them. Which leads me on to my first question. What did you find last weekend?"

"I'm telling you nothing," Emily said, with defiance in her words.

Rosa entered the dining room with a trolley. She had two plates on it with silver cloches covering the food. She gave them each one and removed the cloches. Emily looked at the prepared game bird spatchcocked across the plate decorated with potatoes and vegetables. She wasn't a lover of game and ate little meat, but it smelled amazing. She felt conflicted about eating such expensive food while her stomach growled, but her desire to get out of this place made her realise she needed to eat, so she tucked in.

"I'm hoping we could do this without antagonisation," Coulson said.

"I think kidnapping me was antagonistic!"

"Maybe, but as your boyfriend is intent on infuriating me, I had to take drastic action. So tell me what you found?"

"I told you. I'm not telling you."

"We must then pursue an alternative approach. I hope you can handle pain well?"

Emily didn't answer straightaway, she wasn't keen on being beat up or having a finger cut off or whatever else this evil bloke had in mind. Her thoughts were to negotiate with Coulson.

"What's your offer?" she asked.

"Ambrose offered him eighty thousand pounds, but I'll go to one hundred thousand pounds."

Emily laughed, knowing full well the civic regalia itself was worth at least £350,000. She upped the stakes.

"We've had an offer way above your hundred grand for just one item. You'd need to offer a million pounds," she said with derision. She watched Coulson's face scowl with anger. His reaction showed her she had hit a nerve.

"You think you're clever trying to bluff me? You're as bad as your boyfriend. I can send my team to your house and find what I want. So you've got more than one artefact. That's interesting. Are there more maps?" Coulson asked.

"That's all I'm telling you. Think what you like. We have the artefacts under lock and key, so you can break into our house as many times as you like," Emily sneered, feeling she had the upper hand now.

Emily watched Coulson take this in. He wasn't happy, and it became obvious he hadn't planned on her answers. She had rattled him and hoped this situation wouldn't take a turn for the worse. They sat in silence as she finished her food. This suited her. The less she spoke to this horrible vulgar man, the better.

"I can see we aren't getting anywhere this evening. You can return to the bedroom and I'll consider what to do with you tomorrow," Coulson said to her in a matter-of-fact manner. Coulson rose from his chair, striding out of the dining room, leaving Emily to her own devices. She glanced around the room, disappointed by the lack of furniture to rummage through. Determined, she opened the door to the hallway, eager to explore the house. Ambrose appeared like magic from around the corner and grabbed her wrist, cutting short her attempt to investigate the property.

"Time for you to return to the bedroom," Ambrose said, pulling Emily towards the staircase. Emily didn't resist. It would be pointless. The blonde woman could catch her in a flash.

Locked back in the bedroom, Emily's eyes darted around the room, her gaze sweeping the furniture. She opened the wardrobe, the musty smell inside escaped, filling her nostrils, only to find it devoid of anything, as were the other pieces of furniture. She wandered over to one window and opened the side panel to get a bit of fresh air. As Emily peered out of the window, she noticed it overlooked a flat roof canopy above the main entrance to the property. It must be at least twelve feet down, too far to jump. She resigned herself to staying in this room for the night, trying to sleep, which became difficult, thinking about Reed and hoping he was okay.

Chapter 65

COTGRAVE, NEAR NOTTINGHAM
SATURDAY

E UAN DREAMED ABOUT AN over-sized badger stealing chips off his plate in a large cafe painted yellow, when a buzzing noise came from the building across the road. His mind raced, trying to grasp the situation. As the fuzziness cleared from his head, he realised his watch alarm had caused the noise. The badger and chips faded away to be replaced by the breaking dawn. Reed stirred, so Euan jumped out of bed to stretch.

When Euan had arrived in Fulwood yesterday evening, Reed wanted to go to Coulson's house and challenge him. Euan had persuaded Reed there was a better way and after some discussion they went there in Reed's campervan, parked in Cotgrave village overnight, ready to make a dawn raid on Coulson's house. Euan had spoken to Lynsey to let her know the change of plans whilst Reed had advised Phil. They had come prepared with the drone, UGV, and a couple of baseball bats. Euan knew his mate was still fuming, but he had to keep him focussed.

Euan whipped up two coffees whilst Reed found a cereal bar for each of them. They were soon ready to begin their assault on Coulson's house and rescue Emily. They left the campervan in the village and jogged up the lane towards the massive property. Back packs on, black balaclavas covered their faces and baseball bats in hand. They looked formidable. Fortunately, it was early morning as the sun edged over the horizon, with nobody wandering around. As they neared the front gates, the cacophony of bird song grew as the number of trees increased. A light drizzle in the air coated them in a fine film of rainwater.

"Last week you climbed over the wall here, Reed. We need to be closer to a cluster of trees to anchor the rope. Down there, about fifty yards, looks ideal," said Euan.

"I agree, I just want to get started," said Reed, pushing ahead towards the trees.

Euan tied two ropes to the trees for safety whilst Reed climbed up to the top of the wall and surveyed the camera positions.

"How close are we to the nearest camera?"

"Nearest one is about thirty yards to my left. Are you ready to send the drone up?"

"Almost. I've put on the large battery which has a maximum of thirty-five minutes charge. Let's set our watches for thirty minutes, to be sure."

Euan passed the drone to Reed, climbed the wall, and they set their watches for half an hour. He started up the drone, sending it up, hovering over the house, scanning for any sign of movement. They couldn't see anything, but Euan spotted a window open over the front entrance canopy.

"Look Reed, perhaps we could get in that window?"

"We don't know where she's being held. She could be downstairs. I'm thinking we should break in the rear door. The front door looks too secure."

"Okay, let's check it," Euan said, moving the drone around to the rear of the house. The kitchen door appeared as sturdy as the double fronted main door. He didn't spot any other open windows on the ground floor or the second floor. As Euan scanned the building, Reed jumped down and ran towards the clump of trees near the rear corner of the building. Shit, thought Euan, he will go blundering in if I don't catch up with him. He pressed the jamming button on the drone, causing the cameras to disconnect from the master CCTV unit. Euan jumped down and scampered across the open lawn, desperate to catch up with Reed before he smashed a window or something.

"Hold on Reed," Euan gasped as he tried to get his breath.

"We need to crack on, lets look around the ground floor. If there's no easy entry, we'll go in the top window," Reed said.

They scurried along the wall, checking the lounge and the library. Neither room had curtains in the windows so they could see inside. At the corner to the front of the house, they turned round and retraced their steps, accessing the rear of the property. No obvious entry point there either, unless they broke a window. They passed the dining room, kitchen and back door, reaching the far corner. Euan checked the drone screen as he had positioned it over the front of the house, arrowing in on the open window. He watched the curtains move. Then a girl's face appeared.

"Look Reed, it's Emily in that window," he said, nudging his friend.

"Brilliant, let's get round there now."

They made their way past the kitchen wall, pausing by the window of the gym. There was an impressive assortment of exercise equipment in the room comprising a treadmill, rowing machine, cross-trainer, and multiple weight training machines. A reminder of this man's wealth and perhaps his fitness if they encountered him. They crept along the ivy-covered front wall to some bushes beside the front door. They paused for Euan to get the UGV ready from its carry case, manoeuvring it to the front of the property beside the front door.

"Reed, you go up the pillar. I'll boost you up. There don't appear to be any anchor points. Tie the rope off using the window and leave it there. Don't make any noise."

Reed stood on Euan's shoulders as he got on to the flat roof of the canopy above the grand entrance to the house. Euan watched Reed create a large knot at one end of the rope and threw it at the window.

PARADOX OF THE THIEF

He noticed Emily's face appear. She looked tearful and relieved to see Reed. They anchored the rope, with Emily easing down a couple of minutes later. The rope was long enough for Reed and Emily to drop beside Euan.

"So pleased to see you, Em," said Euan.

"I'm so happy to see you both. Thanks for rescuing me. We need to get a move on. The young lad Bentley is guarding the room and may hear us."

Euan checked his watch. "We still have nine minutes left. Can you take the UGV remote control?" he asked Reed, passing him the unit. Reed snatched it from Euan and caught his finger on the fire button, which shot out a bolt. Fortunately, it faced away from them but it hit a large pot with a bush in it, making an unearthly noise which seemed to echo across the landscape in the early morning silence. The pot smashed into pieces, earth exploding everywhere, and the bush crumpled on the floor, looking quite forlorn.

"Oh shit Reed, you have to be careful," said Euan.

"Stop!" came a shout from above.

This grabbed their attention, and they spotted Bentley hanging out of the upstairs window. Now they had to run. Euan manoeuvred the drone to above the property wall and grabbed the UGV control unit back off Reed. He would need this. They hurtled past the front door, rounded the corner of the library, heading towards the clump of trees. Euan noticed Emily struggled, limping on her right leg.

"You okay, Em?" he asked her.

"I've got a cut on my leg, which hurts. They must've done that when they kidnapped me."

"I'm still angry with Coulson. We'll get our revenge," said Reed.

"Let's focus on getting out of here," said Euan, leading the way across the immaculate lawn as they headed towards the ropes hanging over the wall a hundred yards from the main gate.

273

———◄O►———

Bentley raced down the grand staircase as fast as his injured leg would let him, unlocking the front door and looking for the fugitives. He spotted them running across the lawn towards the wall and realised if he went for the front gate, he might cut them off. He nipped back in the house, punched the code in, unlocking the front gate, and sprinted as fast as he could down the driveway. His leg hurt still, from the mini-bolt injury he had sustained last weekend. He reached the front gate just as it closed, but squeezed through. He had beaten them to it; they were heading straight towards him. Bentley pressed the buzzer on the front gate to alert his uncle in case he needed backup.

Bentley spotted the bloody vehicle that shoots bolts as it crept towards him. He searched around for something to protect himself with, but couldn't spot anything other than a broken branch, so he grabbed it, intending to hit the metal monstrosity. Bentley advanced towards the vehicle, brandishing the branch when it spat out a bolt, but he was ready this time and jumped aside as it whistled past his leg.

The machine spurted out smoke so he couldn't track its movements. He heard the engine hum and the crunch of the wheels on the ground. If it shoots another bolt out, I'm done for, he thought. He backed up towards the front gate and shouted out instead.

"You won't get away with this!"

No reply. He couldn't see anything because of the cloud of smoke billowing around him. Damn this machine. Without that, he could have stopped them. He waited by the gate for the smoke to clear. The group had disappeared.

Chapter 66

Cotgrave, near Nottingham.
Saturday

R EED CHECKED TO ENSURE Bentley wasn't following them, as Euan put all their gear back in the campervan. He hoped Bentley would be too scared of getting injured again. Reed had comforted Emily as she broke down in tears, recalling her kidnapping. He was still fuming with Coulson. The drizzle had continued unabated, so they sheltered under the propped up boot of the campervan. Reed sat next to Emily on the edge of the vehicle, his arm around her, pleased to have her back.

"What made you open the window, Em?" he asked.

"The room smelled musty."

"How come you were awake?"

"I couldn't sleep. It was horrible being there. I felt worried about you and have been tossing and turning throughout the night. The light came through the curtains as they were so ridiculously thin."

The discussion turned to the conversation Emily had with Coulson the previous evening, and how she had informed him only a million pounds would cut it.

"That's brilliant, Em. What was his reaction?" asked Reed.

"His face turned to thunder. He wasn't happy," Emily said with a smirk on her face now.

"That's given me an idea for revenge. Let's set it up," Reed said, sending a message to Coulson.

Reed: *'You have crossed the line by kidnapping my girlfriend. One million pounds is the only offer we will accept. Your decision.'*

"Time to head home," said Reed.

"Yes, I'm whacked," said Euan.

"I'm thinking we should rest up today and get ready to find the next lot of treasure first thing tomorrow. What do you think, Euan?"

"We should do it soon, then we can sell both artefacts. I've enjoyed the adventure, but it's getting more dangerous."

"What about you, Em?"

"I don't know at the moment Reed, I'm exhausted. I might sit this one out. You should do it tomorrow, otherwise it will be another week before we can attempt it."

"That's fair enough, I understand. Let's see how you feel tomorrow morning. I'll ring Phil. Can you ring Lynsey, please?"

They made the phone calls and arranged the meeting for tomorrow at eight o'clock in the layby near Robin Hood's Stride. As the village woke up, they watched the postman on his rounds and a couple of people out walking their dog. It had been an eventful early morning jaunt. Reed started the engine, and they headed off back to Sheffield, pleased with their successful rescue.

Coulson stirred, hearing the gate buzzer, wondering who was visiting at this time of the morning. Bentley will take care of it, he thought. Then it buzzed again. He got out of bed, wandering onto the landing in his M&S striped pyjamas. Bentley wasn't there; the spare room door swung open. He rushed in, seeing the open window and the knotted rope. Shit, they have rescued her.

He could feel his anger rising. Bentley must have gone after them. He heard the buzzer again. Damn this, he needed to get dressed quick. He rushed back into his bedroom, grabbing his clothes, as his phone buzzed. A message from Reed Hascombe. His anger exploded, and he restrained himself from throwing the phone through the window. How dare this insignificant man have the audacity to enter his premises and give him an ultimatum? He should be the one giving out ultimatums. He fired a message back.

Coulson: *'No deal. The treasures will be mine.'*

He hurried down the staircase to see what was happening at the front gate. Bentley stood there, looking quite forlorn. He let him in. He needed some time to calm his temper and make another plan.

Chapter 67

Robin Hood's Stride, Peak District

Sunday

E
UAN GRABBED HIS BACKPACK from the boot of the car, ensuring the drone sat inside. He passed the UGV to Phil to carry. After yesterday's intense and successful rescue of Emily, Euan had taken the rest of the day to relax and chill out, watching re-runs of his favourite comedies on Netflix. Yesterday's drizzle had developed into heavier rain this morning, but with a promise of sunshine in the afternoon. Euan had brought his waterproof jacket, as he expected this to take a few hours, assuming the location was the right one. He wandered over to Reed's campervan parked next to his car in the layby.

"Hi Em, how're you feeling today?"

"Much better thanks, Euan. I couldn't face staying at home worrying about the goons turning up whilst you were all out enjoying yourselves. I feel safer being here," she said.

"That makes sense. You're safe with Ugly here," Euan said, watching Emily's face take on a puzzled look.

"Who's Ugly?"

Euan laughed. "I've named the UGV Ugly, just for shits and giggles."

"Oh, Euan."

"Everyone ready?" Euan asked the group.

The other five confirmed they were. The group crossed the road to join the Limestone Way and head up to Robin Hood's Stride. Euan's eyes spotted the breathtaking Cratcliffe Rocks, their full grandeur hidden by the nearby house and the green foliage of the surrounding trees. It looked formidable, especially with all the cracks in the rocky sections. He wondered why they had never climbed it before. They reached Robin Hood's Stride within minutes. It also appeared impressive. Another collection of rocks with vast cracks and a double-pointed peak, resembling an alien's helmet that would spark between the peaks, Euan thought.

He found a secluded spot, setting the drone up, ready to provide its aerial picture of the landscape once again. The motors whirred into action and the grey machine burst into the sky with a blast of wet air enveloping the group. Euan manoeuvred the drone over the Stride and Cratcliffe Rocks, but not spotting any potential caves.

"I'm not getting anything Reed. whereabouts is this cave?" he asked

"According to the map, it should be between the Stride and the rocks."

"We need to look on foot. This isn't giving me anything. Let's check the Stride first. Then head over to the rocks."

The group wandered around Robin Hood's Stride, not finding anything. Phil brought up Google maps as they entered the wooded area, looking for Hermits Cave. It took a while to find it. Nestled underneath the jagged rocks, the shallow spot could only accommodate a solitary person. The authorities had erected a railing fence in front with a carving of Jesus, or someone on a cross gracing the rear cave wall. It looked a different colour, not quite matching the surrounding rock. As though someone had added something to block an opening, Euan thought.

"What do you think, Reed? It doesn't match," Euan said.

"Just what I'm thinking. Perhaps the entrance is now blocked off. We can't get through there?"

"Could there be an alternative entrance?" suggested Onni.

His comment gave Euan a lightbulb moment, unpacking the drone again.

"What're you thinking, Euan?" asked Lynsey.

"If there's another entrance, I'll bet it's near the bottom of the rocks over there. Where we can't see because the house is blocking it."

Murmurs of agreement convinced Euan he was right and sent the drone up, navigating it above Cratcliffe Rocks. Then he dropped the drone down, monitoring the cliff face as he went. The drone disappeared out of sight, hidden by the overgrown trees. Everyone crowded round him, trying to get an eye on the screen. He loved this moment, everyone waiting on him as the centre of attention, the smell of Lynsey's perfume embracing his nostrils as she leant in close. This caught him off guard for a brief second, almost crashing the drone into a fir tree branch, pulling it away, just in time. Focus, Euan, he said to himself. He planned to ask her out, perhaps later when the day drew to a close.

The drone hovered close to the ground when he spotted it. A three foot wide teepee-sized crack in the rock. That must be the entrance to the cave, about fifty yards from Hermits Cave. Maybe this entrance leads to it?

"Can you see that?" he asked.

"It's an entrance. How will you lads get to it?" asked Lynsey.

"I'm thinking we'll need to climb down from the top. It's blocked on two sides by the fence. It looks impossible to get down this path, too dangerous. What do you think, Reed?"

"The same Euan. We should assess the summit and descend from the top. Are you coming with us, Onni?" asked Reed.

"Not this time, Reed. It must be a hundred feet down," said Onni, his voice shaking.

Euan brought the drone back and packed it up as the group retraced their steps, ascending the hill to the rock summit. They examined the surroundings, looking for any potential hazards, and concluded it was indeed a secure spot to fasten the rope. As they assessed the descent, a sense of challenge hung over them. The height they were about to drop seemed daunting, surpassing their typical climbing endeavours. The rock's rough surface promising ample handholds for their ascent, but the sheer scale of the rock-face sent a tingling sensation down Euan's spine. He put on his harness, pulled together all his other gear and picked up the metal detector from Onni, securing it on his front.

"Lynsey, can you take control of the drone, please?"

"Yeah sure Euan. Do I need to use it?"

"It might be useful for you guys to monitor us descending and climbing back up."

"Okay, I'll try."

"Thanks. Em, you use the other two-way radio. Phil, can you and Onni take sentry duty please?" he asked.

They all nodded their agreement. Everyone was ready for the action to begin. Euan and Reed did their pre-climb ritual, gaining laughs from the two girls. Euan winked at Lynsey. She returned the gesture with a smile and a wave of her hand. Spot on, he thought. Euan watched Reed disappear over the edge and gazed at the clouds now breaking, with patches of blue sky appearing. The rocks, weathered and aged, adorned with a thick layer of grey and white lichen, formed over centuries. The air carried a subtle earthy scent, as if the rocks were exhaling the essence of time itself. Running a hand over their textured surface, he could almost feel the stories they held within. Two men against nature. Euan hoped they would prevail. The radio squawked.

"There's a cave entrance," said Reed. Euan heard the tinge of excitement in his friend's voice.

"Oh awesome Reed, shall I send Euan down?" Emily asked.

"Yes, go ahead."

Euan took the cue, smiling at Lynsey again, and walked towards the summit. He became so engrossed in impressing Lynsey; he caught his foot in a rabbit hole. His face ended up in a pile of soil. When he stood up, it had covered every inch of his face, making him look like a ginger bigfoot. Lynsey laughed at him but came to his rescue, brushing the soil from his face. He enjoyed the feel of her fingers against his skin, almost asking her out on a date right there, when the radio crackled with Reed's voice.

"Are you coming Euan?"

"He fell over Reed. He'll be on his way now," replied Emily.

Euan thanked Lynsey, turned around and edged backwards until he was horizontal over the rock edge. He walked down the rock face, taking one step at a time, letting the rope out as he descended. The cracks in the rock-face were more pronounced than he had seen whilst climbing rocks in the Peak District. The rock face wasn't vertical either. It curved inwards, making the walk down more difficult. He came to a section where water dripped, enhanced by the recent rain. It sprayed the ends of his trousers. He could see the cams Reed had positioned in cracks on his way down. Ascending would be much easier, he thought. A few seconds later, Euan stood on the ground next to Reed. They peered in the teepee-sized crack with their head torches; the light cutting through the darkness. The damp, musty air drifting out of the rocks. Time to investigate.

Chapter 68

SHEFFIELD

SUNDAY

A MBROSE SAT IN THE plush leather seat of her sleek black Audi car, the sun's rays glinting off its polished exterior. With her aviator sunglasses shielding her eyes from the glare, she glanced at her reflection in the rearview mirror, adjusting the brim of her blue bucket hat to conceal her flowing blonde hair. She watched Reed and Emily's house, her mind still whirring from her recent conversation with Mr Coulson. She had reported the campervan wasn't there and no-one at home. He asked her to sneak into their house, snoop around, searching for any useful information. The road looked busy at the moment. A pair of energetic children played on skateboards and a couple walked past with their barking dogs as she waited for her window of opportunity.

The opportunity appeared several minutes later when the children disappeared back into their home. Ambrose scooted over to the house, slipping around the back, coming to a halt. Her eyes scanned the surroundings before reaching into her bag to retrieve her trusty lock-picking kit. She inserted a lock pick into the keyhole of the kitchen door and, with a faint click, accompanied by the soft creak of the door, it swung open. She entered. It felt familiar. This was now her fourth time inside the house, including the previous break-in. Nothing had changed, she thought. She searched in the kitchen cupboards, moving pans, shuffling cutlery and looking inside coffee mugs. She finished the sweep of the downstairs, finding nothing, before heading up the creaky staircase. Then she spotted something.

Propped up against the desk in the spare bedroom, she noticed a laptop bag. Ambrose pulled out the laptop with a Screwed Software label affixed to the lid. She didn't bother trying to fire it up, as it was improbable it would contain any information regarding treasure or a fereter. She rummaged around the inside of the bag, finding nothing, then spotted a zip pocket with a bulge in it. A safe deposit box key for Sheffield Vaults with the number seventeen on the label. An idea formed in her head.

Ambrose pocketed the key, replaced the bag and rushed back to her car, eager to speak to Mr Coulson.

"I've found a key for a safe deposit box at Sheffield Vault's boss, and they're open today. Should I try to get in?"

"Excellent Ambrose. I had a safe deposit box many years ago before I built *The Safe.* You'll need an access code. It became part of the security procedure. Let me speak to Pearson and get him to hack the number for you. I'll get him to call you back," said Coulson.

"Yes, Mr Coulson, I'll head over there now," she said.

Ambrose started the engine and steered her vehicle towards central Sheffield.

Ambrose found a space in the busy central multi-storey car park and made her way to Sheffield Vaults. With no phone call from Pearson yet, she took out her phone and dialled his number, positioning herself on the opposite side of the road from the Vaults.

"Pearson. Have you sorted the code for me?" asked Ambrose.

"Almost there. They have a high level of security. I'm in the third layer. Give me another twenty minutes."

"Okay, message the code over to me."

"Will do," said Pearson.

As Ambrose waited, her gaze swept across the Vaults, capturing every detail of the security guard's movements. She stored each observation in her memory, preparing herself for what lay ahead. He didn't stand still for long, moving every five minutes to one of four places he positioned himself at. One position was at the block of CCTV screens in the reception corner area. She spotted a holster with a gun hanging around his waist, creating a partition between the gold shirt and grey trousers of his uniform. Two customers came and went while she waited for Pearson's message to appear. Then her phone pinged. The secure message app they used showed a new message. Now she had the code, perfect.

Ambrose ambled through the front door, confident she could now gain access to the safe deposit box. She gave the code and box number to the receptionist. The woman didn't respond. Something felt wrong. Next thing, the security guard stood beside her, grabbing her arm.

"Madam, can I have the key, please? You aren't the owner of the box according to the identification we have on record," he said.

Ambrose didn't answer and considered her options. Bluff her way out? Grab the vault door keys from the receptionist's desk? Punch the guard and run off? She took another option.

"I'm coming on behalf of my boyfriend, Reed Hascombe. He asked me to collect something from his box. Can you let me through, please?"

"Sorry madam, only owners of boxes may gain access to their boxes. They can, of course, bring one person in with them."

"It's taken me half an hour and a car park ticket to get here."

"The rules are quite clear madam, Mr Hascombe was aware of them when he took out the contract. I also need to ask you to give me the key."

Ambrose wasn't ready to give up the key just yet, brushing the guard's hand off her arm and striding towards the front door without a word.

"Stop!" shouted the guard, pulling his gun out of the holster. Ambrose froze. She wasn't expecting that. With no other option, she pivoted while a wave of disappointment washed over her. She reached into her pocket, her fingers trembling, before surrendering the key to the guard. A sense of despondency washed over her as she reflected on how everything had gone wrong.

Chapter 69

ROBIN HOOD'S STRIDE

SUNDAY

R EED GAZED AROUND THE interior of the cave, taking in the dark granite rock with scattered moss coverings. Inside, the air smelt damp and earthy, with a faint breeze coming from the back of the cave. The space felt like a narrow passageway rather than a cave, making him feel a little claustrophobic. The lads couldn't stand beside one another, so Reed advanced in front. He inched forward through the dark passageway, his head torch illuminating the path ahead. With each step, he scanned the surroundings, wary of any lurking danger. The uneven ground beneath his feet kept him alert, avoiding any potential stumbling hazards. As they advanced, a sense of unfamiliarity washed over him. This differs from their previous cave exploration.

Anticipation coursed through his veins as they came to a corner, which turned left. It headed further under Cratcliffe Rocks, back towards Hermit's Cave. It opened out further, more like a tunnel, allowing Euan to join Reed, hearing running water in the distance. Reed stopped as he heard a rustling noise. A bat on the roof, adjusting its position.

"This is scary Euan, do you think we should carry on?" asked Reed.

"I'm up for it if you are, mate."

"Okay, have you got any chalk with you? We should mark the

route just in case."

"Hang on. Yes, I have some in my bag. I'll do it as we go. Let's take our time," said Euan.

They walked a further fifty steps, clambering over some fallen rocks, and came to a junction. Reed felt a sense of trepidation within the confines of the narrow tunnel, glad he wasn't alone. He wondered how many humans had walked through this tunnel over the centuries. He felt a faint breeze again, coming from the smaller tunnel that joined the one they had walked down. In front of him, a rustling noise, as he felt something run over his foot. Rats. He spotted a pair scurry up the smaller tunnel as he considered which way to go.

"What do you think, Euan? Up that way or straight on?" Reed asked.

"I'm thinking straight on. That route looks like it heads to Hermit's Cave, coming up behind the rock piece with the carving on it," responded Euan.

"The direction would be about right. This main tunnel is heading towards Robin Hood's Stride. Let's carry on. Glad we have our helmet's otherwise my head would be black and blue with bruises."

"Yes, let's go."

Reed continued leading Euan deeper underground, their head torches creating shadows in their peripheral vision. He stopped to scrutinise the map on his phone and noticed for the first time the wavy line looked beneath the level of the cave marking, rather than inside it, like the other maps showed. He shared this with Euan and carried on, the tunnel twisting and turning as the water sound became much louder. As they rounded the next corner, the unmistakable sound of rushing water grew. A gushing stream cascading down from the rocks above. The icy cold water sprayed the lads as it bounced off rocks before disappearing down a crevice. They sidestepped the running water, jumped over the crevice, and surveyed the ground as it changed to small segments of rock, making walking easier.

Further twists in the tunnel led to an open area, bringing their journey to a close within a cavern. The rock overhead extended up several feet, tiny droplets of water dripped creating a gentle pitter-patter on the ground. Reed studied the rock faces, taking his time searching for anything interesting, spotting something over in the far corner. The feather symbol again. His face lit up with a smile, knowing they were in the correct location. The air had a foul odour to it, akin to the smell of death, he thought.

"Get out the metal detector, Euan," he said.

"Okay, hang on while I turn it on," replied Euan, fiddling with buttons as Onni had instructed.

Then came the reassuring beeping sound, low key where they stood. The red light pulsed. They had to scan the whole cavern, around fifty feet by thirty feet, so it would take time. Reed watched Euan begin the scan near the cavern entrance, then crept across to a mound on the far side. The foul stench increased as he approached it. Then he discovered why. Several decomposing rat bodies laid beside an earthy mound as though there had been a mass vermin fight. Prodding the mound with his foot, he noticed a sliver of white in amongst the earth, almost like a finger clawing to get out. He knelt down and brushed the earth away, leaping back when he realised it looked like a finger bone. Oh shit, it's a dead body. He panicked and shouted Euan over. The metal detector's volume rose and the red light flashing intensified. Between them, they cleared some of the earth using the trowel.

"Oh my god Reed, it's a fucking skeleton!" exclaimed Euan.

"This is someone's grave," Reed said, his level of fear increasing a notch.

"I wonder who's it is?"

"I don't know. Let's leave the bones alone and scan around. That machine is doing my head in."

Euan scanned the mound, finding an area behind it which gave a higher reading, so they left the body hidden in the mound and excavated the other area. It didn't take long using the pickaxe to hit something hard. The detector went mad, beeping, and flashing. Reed used the brush Onni had given him and, after several minutes, the partial outline of a sword appeared. It didn't take long before they had uncovered the entire sword, Reed lifting it out of the ground with care.

The blade, tinged with patches of rust, appeared to be crafted from either steel or iron. The cross-plate and hilt caught Reed's eyes as they shimmered with a gold hue in the light of his head torch. Both lads traced their fingers along the hilt's contours and the sharp blade. Reed turned over the sword and spotted a letter on the cross-plate, a distinct 'R'.

"Look Euan, see this. It could be Robin Hood's sword," said Reed.

"Oh wow, that would be incredible. We should double-check the hole, just in case there's another fereter."

Reed held the sword as Euan checked the hole, the metal detector continuing to beep and flash. As they pressed on with their excavation, Euan found metal arrowheads, remnants of a forgotten era. The wooden shafts, long decayed, had vanished into the earth. Reed put them in a pocket on his harness as Euan metal detected the hole for a third time. Nothing. Just the low level beep and flash.

Reed took a couple of pictures of the half covered skeleton, fingers poking out and the stare of a skull almost mocking him. Satisfied they had everything, they filled in the hole, as Onni had taught them to do. They had almost finished when they heard a deafening crash behind them. Reed turned and watched rocks falling from above.

"Oh shit Euan, it's caving in. Quick, we need to go!"

Reed grabbed the sword while Euan picked up the metal detector as they sped towards the cavern entrance, dashing between the rocks that continued to fall. Reed's level of fear rocketed, his heart near to bursting, concerned they could get buried alive. Back in the tunnel they raced as fast as they could along it, their helmet's bumping the tunnel ceiling at every step. The sound of the rocks falling diminished as they reached the stream, jumping over the crevice as they continued the ascent to the exit.

Reed's heart rate decreased as they came to the junction, knowing they were only a few minutes away from getting out of the underground prison. He felt desperate for fresh air. Without stopping, he reached the last corner, twisted round it and squeezed through the hole they had entered almost an hour before. He drank in the fresh air, trying to get rid of the cloying foul stench from his nostrils. The radio squawked for the first time since entering the cave. The signal disrupted by the thickness of the rock whilst in the tunnel.

"Reed, are you there? I'm getting quite worried now. Please answer me," Emily said, her voice wavering as she spoke.

"I'm here, Em. We're in an underground tunnel and lost the signal. We've found a sword. And a skeleton."

"Oh my god, please hurry and tell me all about it once you're back up at the summit."

"Yes, will do."

Reed secured the sword and started the arduous climb up the sheer rock face. He took his time, letting his heart rate drop back to normal levels. He felt glad he had positioned some cams on the way down. Ascending became much easier. It wasn't long before the pair were back with their friends, showing them the sword, the arrowheads, and recounting the story of the tunnel adventure. The sword transfixed everyone. An artefact of true significance, glistening as the sun's rays burst through the leafy cover. As he showed the others the photo of the mound and skeleton, he realised it must have been the legendary Robin Hood's sacred burial place.

Chapter 70

PEAK DISTRICT

*T*HE FIRST SHOOTS OF *spring cluttered the landscape in 1403AD,
providing an intensity of green across the landscape.*

The fight continued as the heavens opened, throwing huge droplets of water at the men that fought on the bridge across the river Bradford close to Youlgreave. Robin had used most of his arrows as the Sheriff's men advanced to his position, drawing his sword ready to take on the horde of men opposing them. They were just a band of five outlaws battling against the strength of the Sheriff's army. After being pursued for countless miles, their horses now gasping for breath, they positioned themselves at the weathered bridge. With sheer determination, they whittled down the overwhelming horde to a mere twenty men.

Robin could see his men were waning. They needed to finish this soon. A flash of lightning crackled across the skyline, reflecting a spark of light from his gold handle. Wielding the sword, he cut down the next soldier to oppose him, dispatching him onto the bridge. He caught sight of his minstrel being overwhelmed by three other soldiers, so jumped over the fallen soldier to assist. He drove his sword into the side of the nearest foe as a strike from another soldier surprised the minstrel. Robin watched him drop, as the soldier showed no mercy.

The deafening roar of thunder reverberated in the sky as the crimson hue of men's blood splattered the bridge. Only three outlaws remained: young Much the Miller's son, Will Scarlett, and Robin himself. How were they supposed to overcome the remaining fifteen soldiers? Out of nowhere, an arrow struck Robin in the shoulder. Will Scarlett stood at his side right away, trying to remove the offending arrow. They exchanged glances. Despite their years of friendship, this fight was their most challenging. Robin watched young Much battling against four soldiers, but he could not help him as another four focussed their attention on him and Will.

"This is difficult Will, stay strong, my friend," Robin said.

"We must battle hard, Robin."

The sound of swords clanged as the rain continued to pour, making their undergarments wet and heavy, reducing their ability to make any swift moves. Robin faced off with two soldiers, defending himself the best he could. His shoulder hurt and restricted his movement. One soldier caught him across the leg. Blood oozed from the wound, dripping onto the wooden bridge, adding to the crimson stains.

"Will, we need to get away. Let's get the boy now," Robin shouted.

"Yes, master."

Robin watched Will turn towards Much, but too late. He had fallen. The soldiers were on him, trussing him up like a Christmas turkey. Robin felt a massive pain as a soldier thrust his sword into his side. Time to leave, he thought. He hobbled to his horse with Will hot on his heels. They jumped onto their steeds and made haste. This caught the soldiers unawares, as their horses were fifty yards away.

"We should travel to the hermit's cave. We can hide out there," said Robin.

"I'm with you Robin."

They raced up the hill, reaching the summit before galloping over and on towards the nine stones worship circle. The rain continued to fall like a river from the clouds, both riders drenched. Robin felt weak. He knew the injuries were severe and hoped the hermit could help him. He spotted the distinct mound of the cluster of rocks in the distance. They were close now and the Sheriff's men had lost their trail. They followed the track to the east, stopped and tied the horses to some trees. Robin's blood had covered his undergarments. The wound on his side was open and painful.

They entered the cave through the lower entrance and made their way inside. Robin shouted.

"Hermit, it is Robin and Will. We need your help."

No answer. Just the eerie silence of the cave. Robin laboured, his strength disappearing as he struggled to walk. They slogged through the tunnel, using candles to light their way, flickering shadows following them. The hermit's cave was empty when they reached it. Robin sat on the floor whilst Will did the best he could, patching him up with some of the hermit's herbs. They both understood its futility, as the injuries were too severe. Robin laid down on the wolf-skin the hermit used as his bed. The blood wasn't stopping, his vision became blurred.

"Will, you must carry out my dying wish," he said.

"What is it, master?"

"You must hide the Sheriff's regalia, Little John's quarterstaff and Tuck's crucifix. Our secret places, known only to us. Give Marian clues to find them. She deserves to get out of the clutches of her evil step-father, who supports the Sheriff. She'll make sure my legend lives on."

"I'll do my best Robin, I need to lay a trail. I'll find a smithy to help, one I can trust. We always knew our time would end at some point," Will said.

"We did Will, that time is now. I feel weak. Bury my sword with me. This place is safe."

"Yes, master."

Then, with one last breath, he was gone. The archer had died. His life extinguished. But the poor would remember Robin Hood, the legend.

Chapter 71

COTGRAVE, NEAR NOTTINGHAM

SUNDAY

THE DAY HAD STARTED with optimism for Coulson, but since Ambrose's second phone call, he could not shake off his annoyance. A walk around the gardens would help. It always helped. The reminder of his achievements, the smell of flowers, the picking of herbs and watching the koi move around the fishpond. They all helped. He exited the kitchen door with a mug of his favourite coffee, a vanilla latte macchiato, and wandered around to the front of the house. He sat on the brick wall surrounding the fishpond, gazing at the multi-coloured fish, swimming around without a care in the world. Didn't they only have a few seconds' memory? He thought.

The sound of the ride-on lawnmower interrupted his thoughts. He glanced over to the workshop in the distance, spotting the gardener starting his Sunday grass cut. That reminded him. He wanted to have a word about the tree branches overhanging the east wall. Coulson disliked untidiness. He finished his coffee, leaving the mug on the fishpond wall, and strode over to the workshop, motioning the gardener to stop mowing the lawn.

"Bill, can you sort out the branches that are hanging over the east wall?" he asked

"Yes, Mr Coulson. It's on my list of jobs for this week, but I'll do it now," responded the gardener.

"Can you also tidy up the leaves under the clump of trees near the corner of the house? They just keep blowing round and round. It can be quite distracting when I'm looking out of the library window."

"Yes, Mr Coulson."

"Thanks Bill."

Coulson felt in need of some exercise so began his fifteen-minute walk around the perimeter of his property, noticing the cluster of fluffy clouds appearing overhead. He stopped at the south wall to admire his house, a reminder of his status in the world. His thoughts turned to the lost treasures of Robin Hood, making him annoyed again. He walked further to the wooden bench, pulled out his phone, settling down to make a phone call.

"Pearson, tell me what ANPR data you have on Reed Hascombe's campervan and the other vehicles this morning?" he asked.

He waited whilst Pearson tapped away on his keyboard, the sound of him slurping his tea in the background always annoyed Coulson.

"The campervan, Euan Spencer's car and Lynsey Dewhurst's car are all out, heading towards the Peak District from where they started in Sheffield and Nottingham," said Pearson.

"Mmmm, just what I thought. Seems like they have been out treasure hunting again. Any messages or social media activity?"

"No, nothing Mr Coulson. I've been monitoring them."

"Okay, let me know when you get anything further on vehicle movements. Let me know when they are home."

"Yes, Mr Coulson."

Coulson sat mulling everything over. The kidnapping, his conversation with Emily, their rescue, and the message from Reed yesterday morning. He felt sure they now had at least two items of treasure. It was challenging to get the artefacts. But what were they? If one item was Robin Hood's bow or sword that could fetch a million pounds on its own, he thought. Perhaps he could negotiate with Hascombe, get two items for half a million, depending on what they were. Even though that galled him having to accept paying a much higher price, it seemed the only way. His plan of action became clear. He fired over a message.

Coulson: *'I'm prepared to discuss what items you have and agree to a fair price. Come to the house with them. I can then assess the value.'*

He had opened the door, hoping Reed would walk through it and negotiate. He could, of course, take the artefacts off them by force. A smile broke across his face. That would be the perfect solution.

Chapter 72

SHEFFIELD

SUNDAY

REED SAT IN THE lounge, relaxing with a beer after the exertions of the previous two days, contemplating their next steps. He checked his emails, not having read them for the last 48 hours, and discovered one from the Sheffield Vaults earlier that day. He had intended to take the sword there later in the afternoon. They came home first after their adventure at Robin Hood's Stride earlier. Emily felt exhausted and needed to chill out. The email stated there was a breach of his security and the Sheffield Vaults had his key for safekeeping. He rushed to his laptop bag, discovering his key was missing. Had he dropped it? Or didn't close the zip correctly from last Monday? He looked for Emily, finding her in the garden, listening to some music through her earphones.

"Em, the Vaults have emailed to say my safe deposit box key is there. I think someone handed it in earlier today," he said.

"Oh, maybe you dropped it?"

"I'm very careful about putting it back in the zip pocket. The email said there was a clear security breach and I should appear in person today. I intended taking the sword anyway, so I'll pop there now. Did you want to come?"

"No, that's fine Reed. I need to chill out. It's been a stressful few days."

"Sure, I understand."

Reed headed off to get the sword, admiring its beauty and craftmanship. It looked resplendent after Onni had cleaned it up yesterday. He held it in his right hand, swirling it around, pretending to be Robin Hood. "Take that," he voiced out loud to an imaginary audience. Then his phone buzzed. A message from Coulson, offering to meet to discuss a fair price for the items. He nipped out to the garden again and relayed the message to Emily.

"You can't go to his house with the items, Reed. He'll just take them off you," she said.

"I wasn't intending to. He's taken the bait, and I've got a plan for revenge. I'll meet him in a public place and take some photos. Let's see how greedy he is."

"Be careful Reed. Where will you meet him?"

"I'm thinking about the Winter Gardens in the city. I'll get Euan to come with me," said Reed, happy with the revenge he had planned, striding inside to message Coulson.

Reed: *'I told you before it's a million pounds, nothing less. I won't be coming to your house. Meet me at the cafe in Winter Gardens, Sheffield, 6pm tomorrow. I'll have photos.'*

He took some photos of the sword, printed them off, as well as photos of the civic regalia, plus some of Robin Hood's grave. Reed felt prepared for tomorrow's meeting if it takes place. He wrapped up the sword and grabbed the keys to Emily's car to drive into town.

Reed felt conspicuous carrying the well-wrapped sword through the centre of Sheffield as he approached the Sheffield Vaults. His phone pinged with a message.

Coulson: *'I agree to meet at the Winter Gardens tomorrow, but I need to see the items before we can agree on a price. Bring them with you.'*

Reed: *'I don't trust you. It will be photos only. If you agree to my price, then you get to see the items.'*

He waited for a quick answer, which didn't arrive. Reed entered the Sheffield Vaults building, keen to put away the sword in his safe deposit box. First, he had to sort out the lost key. Reed approached the receptionist, explaining who he was. She called over the security guard to explain what had happened. This puzzled Reed. He assumed he lost the key.

The security guard outlined the events of this morning. "Hello sir. Earlier today, a woman tried to enter the vault by pretending to be you. She had the correct access code and your safe deposit box key, but she failed in the visual identification. She claimed to be your girlfriend."

Reed felt dumb-struck for a few seconds when the realisation dawned on him. It must have been Ambrose.

"Can you describe the woman please?" he asked the security guard.

"She looked medium height, had blonde hair, wore trousers and a smart jacket, almost like a business suit."

"I know her. She's stolen my key," said Reed.

"That's what we assumed. How did she get the access code?" the security guard asked.

"She has ways of hacking messages, so it doesn't surprise me. Can we change my access code?"

"Come to the desk sir, we'll do it straightaway."

Reed and the security guard walked over to the receptionist's desk and sorted out the new access code, allowing him to enter the vault. He placed the sword inside the safe deposit box. The box looked quite full now, two items of treasure, a couple of fereter's and maps. His level of anger towards Coulson had risen another notch, knowing Ambrose had broken into their house again, and then attempted to get into his safe deposit box. He mulled over his plan and, satisfied with his course of action, he closed the box. As he left the vault to make his way back to Emily's car in the car park, his phone pinged again.

Coulson: *'Fine, I agree.'*
Reed: *'Tomorrow 6pm, come alone.'*

Reed needed to phone Euan to ensure he could make tomorrow, so he called his mate. Reed explained his idea to him. Euan agreed with it. Perfect, now to set up the last part of his plan, he thought, dialling his Jeet Kune Do instructor.

Chapter 73

CENTRAL SHEFFIELD

MONDAY

R EED CHECKED HIS WATCH. He had another twelve minutes until his meeting with Coulson. He felt prepared. His Jeet Kune Do instructor had organised for the guys in the class to help him out. The normal session started at 7pm, but as he had missed some sessions during the past few weeks, he wondered if the guys would be reluctant to assist. He didn't need to worry. They were well up for it. Four of them, including the instructor, had turned up at five thirty to go through Reed's plan. Positioned around Winter Gardens, they were ready to observe and intervene if Coulson showed up with his goons.

The pedestrianised area around the building lacked activity during the period between lunchtime and the evening hustle. Although to be fair, Monday evenings weren't busy in Sheffield, most of the students would still have hangovers from their boozy weekends. Most people moving through the area were on their commute home. Reed surveyed the area, spotting one of his Jeet Kune Do guys sitting on a bench about fifty yards away, holding a newspaper with two holes cut in it! He laughed to himself. One stood by the entrance to the enormous glass fronted building playing on his phone, whilst the instructor sat talking at a table in the cafe section inside with the fourth member of the martial arts group. He waited for Euan, who would arrive soon, delayed by traffic. Reed had a hidden microphone attached to his t-shirt, with the instructor and one guy outside having an earpiece. They were ready.

Reed watched Euan striding over the concrete pedestrianised area, ready to join him. They headed inside Winter Gardens and sat at a cafe table where they could see the entrance door and gaze through the impressive glass fronted building into the pedestrianised area. The building felt comfortable to sit in, warm and alive with abundant plants and flowers. Sounds of mini waterfalls cascading through the foliage mingled with the hum from the chatter of the cafe's customers. He glanced at his watch again. Two minutes to go. He spotted the grey hair and confident body language of Coulson heading to the entrance. Neither Ambrose nor Bentley were with him. He felt sure they would appear at some point. Reed waved at Coulson to join them.

"Reed, pleased to meet you in person at last," said Coulson.

"Can't say the same after you kidnapped my girlfriend. This is Euan," Reed responded, trying to keep calm.

"Pleased to meet you too, Euan. I gather you are the one with the gadgets from what my team has told me."

"I am," said Euan.

"Show me the pictures, Reed."

Reed laid out the photos of the civic regalia, explaining it belonged to the Sheriff of Nottingham. He mentioned Whatstandwell with a smile. Coulson scrutinised the photos for several minutes with no conversation. Reed glanced around. Still no sign of Ambrose and Bentley.

"I'd be interested in buying this. How does one hundred thousand sound?" asked Coulson.

"We already have an offer of three hundred and fifty thousand pounds on this item. I told you it's a million pounds for everything, nothing less."

"Come now Reed, you can't expect me to just accept that. We need to negotiate. What else do you have?"

Reed laid the photos of Robin Hood's sword on the table and watched Coulson's eyes light up, even though he kept a poker face. He brought out two photos of Robin Hood's grave to help endorse the authenticity of the sword.

"Fascinating Reed. Where did you find this?" asked Coulson.

"I'm not prepared to divulge the location at the moment."

"Very well. Do you have anything else?"

"Some arrowheads," Reed said, laying the last photos on the table.

"Where are you storing the artefacts?"

"You know full well where they are. You sent Ambrose to steal then yesterday."

"Oh yes. She got into a bit of bother. Which reminds me, I think Bentley owes you both for the injuries he has sustained," said Coulson, lifting his arm and giving a little wave.

Reed couldn't see anyone in the cafe or outside that resembled Ambrose. He felt a hand on his shoulder. They had appeared from behind him. Reed jumped up, knocking over his chair and brushing the hand off his shoulder. He took a fighting stance as he faced Ambrose. She stood there ready to attack with Bentley readied in a boxing pose. Audible gasps escaped the mouths of the other patrons of the cafe. The counter servers looked concerned.

Reed's intense dislike of Coulson had wound him up tight, causing him to kick out at Ambrose. She avoided it, knocking into another table, clattering cups and plates onto the floor. The individuals seated at the table stood up and darted away.

"You didn't think I would let you walk out of here without me getting my hands on the artefacts, did you, Reed?" said Coulson, laughing.

"The goons have landed," said Reed into the microphone, using the planned code words. His two friends sitting close by stood up and appeared behind Ambrose and Bentley, locking their arms.

"I'm ready for your little games, Coulson."

"I thought you would be," said Coulson, waving his hand for a second time.

Oh shit, Reed thought, this could get ugly as two heavies appeared from outside the building. Coulson had come prepared to frogmarch him to the vaults. The heavies approached the scene of conflict whilst Reed's friends held on to Ambrose and Bentley.

"Need a bit more help, boys," Reed said into the microphone.

Reed's final two friends joined the congregation at the table, now stacked six five in Reed's favour. They opposed the two heavies ready to get involved if required. Reed wondered if Coulson had any more rabbits to pull out of the hat. If so, they were dead and buried. He watched Coulson shift in his seat. Reed had out-manoeuvred him.

"Let's all calm down. Seems we are even Reed. You surprise me with your forethought," said Coulson.

"I wouldn't call it even. We're one up on you."

"Well, I guess if you are being picky, then perhaps so."

"Well, what is to be Coulson? One million for all the items. You'll still profit from the treasures, just not as much as you expected."

"I must see the items before deciding. One million is excessive. Bring them to my house this evening and we'll agree on a price," Coulson said.

"No. If you want them, come with myself and Euan to the Vaults. No goons. You get to look at them there. I'll lock 'em back in until you pay the million. Then you'll get them. I've other artefact collectors lined up to take them if you don't want them or don't pay."

Reed waited whilst Coulson tried to stare him down without saying a word. He stood firm, matching icy stare with icy stare. The room hushed as the remaining patrons of the cafe sensed the tense atmosphere at table number nine. Coulson's left eyebrow twitched. Then he stood up.

"Vault, let's go. Everyone stand down," he said. Reed nodded to everyone to follow suit as he followed Coulson out of the door with Euan hot on his heels. Reed's friends helped the cafe owner sort out the mess before departing the scene.

———◆○◆———

The sun settled down below the skyline of the Sheffield city centre buildings, a dusky low light hanging over the place. As they approached the Sheffield Vaults, Reed turned to Coulson.

"We're going in the rear entrance. I'm only allowed one person at a time in the vault. I've agreed it with the security guard."

"Okay, very well," Coulson responded, his greed clouding his judgement.

The group of three reached the rear of the building, turning into the narrow alleyway running behind it. Litter flapped around the floor as the lid of a wheelie bin bounced open in the gusting wind, channelling through the alleyway. The impending night brought ever-increasing darkness as they approached the end of the alleyway, having already passed the rear door for the vaults. Backed by commercial properties, there were no prying eyes or hidden cameras to record what happened next. Euan had slipped behind Coulson as Reed advanced to the end of the alleyway, blocked off by a stack of broken pallets. Reed stopped and turned, watching Coulson's look of surprise as Euan grabbed his wrists from behind.

Reed didn't need a second invitation and kicked Coulson between his legs, causing the older man to double over. He followed it up with a swift kick to his face, launching Coulson backwards as Euan let go of his wrists. Reed laughed.

"Did you think I would sell our hard-earned items to you?"

Euan took his turn, punching the older man on the temple, his head lolling back as a tooth dislodged. Coulson tried to run, but Reed put paid to his attempt at freedom with a leg sweep, taking him to the floor.

"You had the audacity to kidnap Emily and your goons broke into my house several times. This is my revenge, you fucking horrible greedy snob," Reed spat at Coulson, real venom in his voice. Reed and Euan both kicked Coulson on the floor, blood now seeping from his face, causing a crimson stain on his expensive shirt. Reed poised, ready to go in for another kick, when Euan stopped him.

"That's enough mate, I think we've made our point. Let's go."

Reed paused and let his adrenaline drain from his body as he surveyed the scene. Coulson lay prone on the floor, coughing, covered in blood and looking dazed. That will do, Reed thought. He leant down close to Coulson's ear, "The artefacts will be gone tomorrow, never cross my path again, otherwise I won't stop next time," he said, with spittle landing in Coulson's ear. The lads hustled from the alleyway, glancing back at the mess they had made of their arch-enemy.

Chapter 74

Homeless Shelter, Sheffield

Saturday

R EED AND HIS FRIENDS received an invitation to visit the homeless shelter to discuss with the manager how they were going to utilise the two hundred thousand pounds they had gifted to the charity. The local newspaper had a journalist and photographer present to capture the event. They planned to portray Reed as a modern day Robin Hood, although the source of the funds would be undisclosed. Reed sold the artefacts to the dealer from Scotland on Tuesday. The man had no qualms about parting with the money, explaining they would sell quick, generating a profit. Coulson lost out because of his greed. A successful conclusion, Reed thought.

Reed observed the shelter, taking in the sight of its walls stained with shades of brown, the flooring marred by cracks, and tables and chairs seeming on the verge of collapsing. The air in the cramped dining area felt heavy and suffocating, crowded with an overwhelming number of people. Several of the regulars showed up for the event, keen to meet the person who would improve their lives. The manager led Reed into the kitchen area, and the range cookers, donated three years ago, caught Reed's eye. The sight of them in such fine condition was a pleasant surprise. However, as they approached the fridge and freezer, the loud hum of their aging motors was noticeable. Reed couldn't help but notice these appliances had seen better days. The storage area looked tiny, crammed with huge catering tins of food, massive sacks of potatoes and packets of every dried food you could imagine, coupled with a strong smell of spices. The manager led Reed through the back door, stepping out into the empty rear garden as traffic noise provided the backdrop to the bare area. A few picnic benches and sand buckets full of cigarette ends dotted the lawn.

"My primary plan is to take half of the garden as an extension, turning it into the kitchen and storage area," she explained, waving her arms in an imaginary architectural way.

"That would be perfect. You'll need an electrician. Euan is your man."

"Excellent, thank you. We just need a capable builder."

"What's your plan for the current kitchen?" asked Reed.

"I want to encompass around half of it into the dining room. The rest will become part of the sleeping quarters. Come, I'll show you," she said.

Making their way back into the building, they ambled into the sleeping area. The manager, once again, explained her plan with waves of her arms. The dormitory comprised fifteen worn-out single beds, each with a distinct creaking sound whenever someone shifted their weight on them. A slight musty smell lingered in the air, hinting at years of use.

"I can double this area with part of the old dining room. We just need to move the partitioning wall. Then I'm also hoping we can stretch to new beds. We should be able to squeeze thirty beds in if we add a few bunk beds."

"I'd love to pop in sometimes and see how you're doing with the changes," he expressed.

He didn't want to intrude, but felt compelled to ensure effective use of the money. With Euan involved, this would help.

"Of course, we'd love to see you," said the manager.

They headed back into the dining area for photos and an interview for the newspaper amid the sound of cameras clicking.

With that wrapped up, the manager had organised a simple lunch for everyone. There was a buzz around the place, giving Reed a warm feeling inside. This felt incredible to help homeless people. As lunch finished, he noticed Euan and Lynsey talking and laughing together. He smiled and nudged his mate when she walked off with Emily.

"Getting on well, mate?"

"I've just asked her out. She said yes!" Euan enthused.

"About bloody time, mate. Have fun."

"I intend to Reed."

Reed picked up his cup of coffee and wandered outside into the garden, sitting on a picnic bench at the end. He took a moment to reflect on the activities of the past four weeks. Amid the sound of city centre traffic and the fumes of vehicles wafting over the walled garden, he recollected that first Saturday morning discovering the first fereter. This outcome was beyond his comprehension. His thoughts drifted off to his mum, pledging to buy her a holiday for instilling in him a strong work ethic and positivity from his teenage years. He thought about his dad, who he hadn't seen since twelve years old. He couldn't ever reconcile his dad's actions, unable to forgive him for the situation he put his children in. Besides the donation, Emily suggested they move house with their extra money, which he agreed to. He had two hundred thousand left to aid others in need later. He had aligned his thinking with the paradox of being a thief.

ABOUT THE AUTHOR

I hope you enjoyed Paradox of The Thief and if you could, please leave a review. Head over to the website you purchased the book from, as it helps other people to decide to buy the book.

This is my first foray into writing and chose self-publishing as the best option for me. There's always been a creative element to my character, but until Paradox of The Thief, I hadn't found a suitable vehicle for the flair. Hopefully, this is it. Please let me know your thoughts via email – nigel@unearthedquill.com.

I have written a short story that sits alongside Paradox of The Thief, with Reed and Euan having a day's adventure in the Peak District. It's called Downfall and is available for free on my website. Head over to **www.unearthedquill.com/free**.

I've planned the idea for the second book of the Reed Hascombe series and it will be available in Spring 2025. If you sign up for my newsletter, you will get information when it's published. I promise not to bombard you with loads of emails, maybe one a month. You can join at **www.unearthedquill.com/newsletter**.

Don't forget to tell your family and friends if you enjoyed my book, maybe they will too.

Thanks Nigel

Printed in Great Britain
by Amazon

44038625R00179

INSPIRED MAGIC

YOUR GUIDE TO
TRANSFORMING YOUR LIFE
WITH THE POWER OF THE MIND

Michelle Hillier

DEDICATION

———— ◆ ————

For my husband, Chris,
for your unwavering love, support
and sense of adventure.
And for my mother, Bic, my father, Joe,
my sister, Jenny, and my nieces,
Mila and Josie.